Grand Opening 2:
A Family Business Novel

Grand Opening 2:
A Family Business Novel

Carl Weber

with

La Jill Hunt

www.urbanbooks.net

Urban Books, LLC
300 Farmingdale Road, NY-Route 109
Farmingdale, NY 11735

Grand Opening 2: A Family Business Novel
Copyright © 2017 Carl Weber
Copyright © 2017 La Jill Hunt

ISBN 13: 978-1-62286-604-5
ISBN 10: 1-62286-604-5

First Hardcover Printing September 2017
Printed in the United States of America

10 9 8 7 6 5 4 3 2 1

This is a work of fiction. Any references or similarities to actual events, real people, living or dead, or to real locales are intended to give the novel a sense of reality. Any similarity in other names, characters, places, and incidents is entirely coincidental.

Distributed by Kensington Publishing Corp.
Submit Orders to:
Customer Service
400 Hahn Road
Westminster, MD 21157-4627
Phone: 1-800-733-3000
Fax: 1-800-659-2436

*Each book is dedicated to all the Urban Books fans
who have supported us over the years.*

Prologue

1978

It was almost three in the afternoon when the dusty Greyhound bus turned the corner into the Waycross, Georgia bus terminal. As it pulled into a spot, four impeccably dressed Negro men stepped out of a brand new baby blue Fleetwood Cadillac. Their imposing presence was noticed by all, and they were given a wide berth until they stopped six or seven feet in front of the bus. The men waited patiently for the bus doors to open as a mixed-race crowd filled in behind them, for the most part keeping their distance.

"Afternoon, gentlemen." Mickie Carter, a black porter in his late fifties, pushed a metal cart between the men and the bus, stopping in front of the luggage compartment, which he opened. Like most black folks in Waycross, he didn't know the men well, other than to trade pleasantries, but he did know their reputation. The Duncan brothers were no joke, and to see all of them together garnered even more notice. People rarely ever saw all four of them as a group in public, unless there was going to be some type of trouble or, as in this case, a very special occasion.

"Today's the big day, huh?" Mickie said.

"Sure is, Deacon Carter." The handsome, six-foot-two Lou Duncan grinned, chomping down on his signature torpedo-sized cigar. Lou, the oldest of the four brothers, was considered a ladies' man, but he was not to be taken lightly, because he could be as deadly as they came if provoked. He was standing to the far left of his brothers Levi, Larry, and LC, who could all be equally lethal, if not worse. "You and your wife should come on down to Big Shirley's about seven, eight o'clock tonight. We gonna have one hell of a celebration."

"Count us in. We'll be there." Mickie nodded his head then turned back to the luggage compartment as the bus doors opened, but Lou knew he wouldn't be seeing him. Mickie and his wife were church folks, and church folks didn't frequent Big Shirley's, a place formerly known as Big Sam's whorehouse before the Duncans took it over five years earlier.

"Waycross, Georgia. Last stop, transfer to Macon, Savannah, Valdosta, and Jacksonville inside the station." A portly white driver stepped out and stood by the bus door as passenger after passenger began to file out. Finally, there was a break in the steady stream of departing passengers, and a minute or two passed during which no one else exited. The Duncan brothers were still standing there, waiting, passing nervous and confused glances amongst each other as the clock ticked.

"Where is she?" Larry, the only light-skinned Duncan brother, took an angry step toward the bus. He was a former Army Ranger and Vietnam veteran who'd come back from the war mad at the world. He was by far the most unpredictable Duncan and had a tendency to react first and ask questions later—something the driver was about to find out when he made the decision to block him from entering the bus.

"Where is who?" the bus driver snapped back.

The man had no idea it was his lucky day when, just as Larry was about to put him on his ass, an aged black woman appeared at the top step of the bus. There was no question that she was related to the four men, but the years hadn't been kind to her.

"M–M–M–M–Ma!" Levi Duncan stuttered, grabbing the woman and lifting her over his head like a sack of potatoes before she could reach the bottom step. At six-foot-eight and four hundred pounds of muscle, Levi was by far the largest and most physically intimidating Duncan. He was also the kindest of heart. However, where he was blessed by God in size, he'd been cursed with stuttering and a very low IQ. He was considered by most people outside the Duncan circle to be a simpleton, though most weren't bold enough to say it to the brothers' faces. "M–M–M–Ma, you're home!"

"Boy, if you don't put me down!" The woman swung her bag at him to no avail as he continued to plant wet kisses all over her face. "Put me down. I gotta pee."

"Levi, please put Momma down," LC Duncan, the youngest and closest thing the Duncan brothers had to a leader, asked politely. Levi kissed her one more time then did as he was told. LC stepped up to his mother, placing his hand on her mahogany brown cheek.

"I missed you, boy," she whispered, holding back tears. Bettie Jean Duncan loved all of her boys, but she had a special place in her heart when it came to LC. Maybe it was because of the difficult pregnancy she had with him, or perhaps their shared love for learning and books, but most likely it was because he was the spitting image of his father.

"I missed you too, Ma," LC said, unable to hold back tears as he pulled his mother in for a hug. It had been more than three years since he'd visited her in prison, and in that time, he'd gotten married, had a child, and grown a small gas station into the biggest used car lot in town. He'd also killed a man for the very first time and helped establish his family as the leading underworld figures in southern Georgia and northern Florida.

LC released his mother from their embrace, and she went to Larry and Lou and then back to Levi. When the ceremonial greeting was done, she turned to the boys and said, "How did you do it? How in the world did you get them white folks to release me?"

All eyes turned to LC.

"That, Momma, was all the college boy's doing," Lou replied.

"You said he was the smartest one of us all." Larry laughed with a nod. "Well, he proved it."

"But how?" Bettie Jean looked happy but confused. She'd spent the last twelve years of her life in a federal prison for killing a white man who had just shot and murdered her husband. She had expected to spend the rest of her life in there, until yesterday, when a guard gave her the new set of clothes she was wearing, a bus ticket home, and five dollars for food, then sent her on her way out the front gate. Up until a few hours ago, she'd thought she was dreaming. She still wasn't sure this wasn't some big mistake and the police weren't on their way to take her back.

"You always said I could do anything I put my mind to, Momma," LC finally responded. "Well, I wanted you home, so I put my mind to it and put the effort into soliciting people to see things my way. If dealing with Donna and her family taught me anything, it's that this is a who-you-know world that's dictated by color."

"And that color is green. Your freedom cost us a small fortune." Lou grinned, chomping down on his cigar. "Way more than the average ten black folks could afford in this lifetime."

"But it was worth every penny to get you from behind those bars, Momma," LC finished.

"Amen to that." Larry laughed, wrapping an arm around Bettie Jean's shoulders. He was smiling for the first time since he'd stepped out of the car. "We finally beat those crackers at their own game."

LC

1

I'd just finished toasting the bride and groom as their best man, and I was now happily watching Maria and Juan Rodriguez dance for the very first time as husband and wife. Juan was a good man and the closet thing I had to a friend, aside from my wife and my brothers.

Things had been rough between us in the beginning, when he first came into Waycross with a broken-down station wagon, looking to get it fixed. He pretended to be a traveling salesman named John, but what I didn't know was that the car was filled with marijuana in hidden compartments. He was delivering them for a boss who had threatened the lives of his family members.

The auto parts had to be shipped to Waycross, so Juan stayed at the gas station, making himself useful for a few weeks while we waited. I thought he was a decent guy, until I found the drugs in the car's undercarriage and he pulled a gun on me. Needless to say, things got pretty tense between me and him, but when all was said and done, he'd proven himself to be a true friend, placing his life in jeopardy for my family on more than one occasion.

My thoughts were thrown off when my own bride, Chippy, slid in behind me, grabbing my waist and rubbing her belly behind me to get my attention. She'd been pretty frisky these past few weeks despite being eight months pregnant with our second child. Unfortunately, that wasn't the reason she wanted my attention.

"Are you sure your momma can handle those boys?" she asked with the concern of an overprotective mother written all over her face. We'd left our son, Junior, along with my brother Larry's boy, Curtis, with my mother so we could attend the wedding. Usually, Chippy wouldn't let Junior out of her sight for anyone but me.

I chuckled, pulling her into my arms. "My mother raised four truly hardheaded boys, so I'm sure she can handle those two just fine. Stop worrying and enjoy yourself."

"But that Curtis is a terror. Do you remember the lump he left on Junior's head last time we left him at Nee Nee's?" she said, referring to the only other time we had left him with someone else.

I tried to reassure her with a kiss, but she was right about my nephew. Curtis had a bit of the devil in him—but then again, so did my mother.

A voice with a deep Southern accent came from behind us. "Excuse me, are you LC Duncan?"

Chippy and I turned around to see a well-dressed, light-skinned man in his forties with a twelve-inch scar running from the top of his face on one side to the bottom of his face on the other. If it weren't for the scar, the man would have been considered very handsome.

"I am. How can I help you?"

"Name's James." He pointed across the room at an elderly man. "Mr. Mahogany would like to have a word with you."

"Mr. Mahogany," I repeated, glancing at Chippy. Juan had already warned me that there would be a lot of so-called underworld figures at the wedding. Some of them I knew, like the Fernandez brothers, Alejandro Zuniga, and Sal and Tony Dash from New York, to name a few. I'd never met Mr. Mahogany, although I'd heard of him.

Mr. Mahogany was not unlike me and my brothers. He ran a lucrative area north of us, which included Atlanta and parts of North and South Carolina. He'd run his operation for damn near twenty years, and he was not a man to be taken lightly. Still, he did have a reputation for being a fair man. With his proximity to Waycross and our territory in southern Georgia, it was inevitable that we would one day cross paths, and evidently, that day was today. So, I kissed my wife, who I was sure would alert my brothers, and confidently headed over to see the man.

"Excuse me, are you Mr. Mahogany?" I said politely when I approached his table. Now that I was standing in front of him, I felt a little less confident because of the way he was staring at me. Suddenly it occurred to me that maybe he wasn't called Mr. Mahogany because it was his name, but because of the hue of his skin. I swear he had to be the darkest man I'd ever met, and I'd lived in Georgia my entire life. "Your man James said you wanted to see me."

To my relief, he stood and offered his hand with a smile, showing off teeth that were remarkably white for a man at least seventy years old. "Pleasure to meet you, young man."

"Pleasure to meet you, Mr. Mahogany." I took his leathery hand with a firm grip.

"Have a seat, LC." He released my hand, gesturing to an empty chair. We sat down, and he pointed to the man in the seat next to him. "LC, this my son, EJ."

"Nice to meet you." I offered my hand, but EJ hesitated, only relenting after a glance from his father. EJ's expression was somewhere between a grimace and a weak smile, revealing a row of gold teeth that gleamed against skin not quite as dark as his father's.

"LC, I have to apologize for staring, but looking across the table at you is a little spooky," Mr. Mahogany said.

"Pardon?" I replied.

"Looking at you is like being in a time warp, because I'll be damned if you don't look just like your father." His words had respect in them.

"You knew my father?" This was news to me.

"One of the most loyal men I've ever known. I knew him and your mother." His face became serious. "I'm sure she's proud of all the hard work and effort you put into bringing her home from prison. How is Bettie?"

"Good." I was surprised that he knew about that. "She's at my brother Larry's, playing grandma to our two boys."

His smile widened, and he chuckled, glancing over at his son. "Good for her. Grandchildren are what this world is all about when you reach our age. Please give her my best."

"I will, but I'm sure you didn't call me over just to give my mother your best wishes." Men like Mr. Mahogany weren't usually interested in small talk, and neither was I. We might as well get right down to business—whatever that was. "So, to what do I owe the pleasure?"

"We just wanted to meet the man who took out our old friend Big Sam," EJ interjected, his gold teeth sparkling.

I really wasn't sure where this was going, but I sure as hell was glad that Larry, Lou, and Levi had just shown up and were standing behind me. EJ and Mr. Mahogany glanced up at them, but I figured introductions were unnecessary at this point. "Well, in all honesty, EJ, the only reason Sam isn't with us here today is because he forgot who his friends were." I glanced over at my kin. "My brothers Larry and Lou here used to work for Sam. Hell, Lou even considered himself Sam's best friend."

"That still doesn't explain why Sam is dead," EJ snapped, making it clear how he felt about the way we'd handled Sam.

"Sam is dead because Sam was greedy. He wanted to take over shit we'd grown from the ground up," Larry interjected, a little louder than I would have liked.

"It was his territory," Mr. Mahogany replied calmly. "You would deny him a taste? I'm sure you wouldn't put up with that in your present position."

"A taste would have been fine, but Sam wanted the whole thing," I explained, keeping my tone respectful. I didn't want anything escalating at Juan's wedding reception. I could see in his eyes as he nodded at me that Mr. Mahogany understood our dilemma. His son, on the other hand, did not.

"Bullshit!" EJ exploded. "I was told this all started because you were in love with one of his whores and stuck your nose where it didn't belong." He leaned his chair back on two legs and glared at Chippy, who was lingering at a nearby table, watching us all closely.

My first instinct was to jump up and smack the taste out the man's mouth for insulting my wife, but when I glanced at Chippy, she shook her head and gave me a look that told me to stay calm. Unfortunately, she didn't give my hotheaded brother Larry that same look.

"Who the fuck you calling a whore? You calling my sister-in-law a whore?" Larry slipped past me and kicked the bottom of the chair EJ was sitting in, making him fall on his ass.

"Motherfucker, obviously you don't like living." EJ jumped up, along with every man on their side of the table—except for Mr. Mahogany, who remained remarkably calm. They may have jumped up in defense of EJ, but it was obvious that his men would not make another move without his approval.

I tried to mimic his demeanor, but I could not say it would have the same effect, because Larry was such a loose cannon that no one could predict his actions.

"I'm not sure what this is all about, Mr. Mahogany, but Big Sam Bradford was a piece of shit whose death should be celebrated, not fought over. Now, I'm sorry if you lost a friend, but we had to deal with him, and it was either him or us. We chose him."

Mr. Mahogany snapped his fingers, and all of his men sat down. "I respect what you're saying, LC, and Sam was more of an associate than a friend"—He looked toward EJ, who was breathing heavy and glaring at Larry—"although he and my son had some dealings that they did not know I was aware of." I could tell from Mr. Mahogany's voice that whatever he was talking about was deeply personal. EJ's expression softened, and he too his seat as nonchalantly as possible.

Mr. Mahogany's eyes went from EJ to each of my brothers as he continued to speak. "Look, we don't want no trouble with you boys. I've been watching you from afar, and I'm impressed. You've earned my respect. Matter of fact, that's why I wanted to talk to you, LC. I've come to offer you the opportunity of a lifetime."

Larry

2

"I still can't get over how beautiful that wedding was." Nee Nee placed a well-positioned hand on my thigh, letting me know that I was going to get some that night. We'd just pulled up the driveway to the farm, and I was glad to be home, mostly because for the past twenty minutes, I'd been trying my best to listen but not listen to Nee ramble on and on about how spectacular Juan and Maria's wedding had been. I loved that woman to death, but I hated how she tried to manipulate me, because what she was really trying to say was that she wanted to get married and have a wedding too. Nee was good for using reverse psychology on folks, me especially, but this was a little too obvious.

"Come on now, Nee, you knew Juan was gonna go all out," I replied, placing the car in park. "That flashy Puerto Rican thinks he's a white boy for real sometimes. Do you know how much money they pissed away?"

"Yeah, but that wedding was extra special. I ain't never seen nobody have fireworks at their wedding. Even the white folks who ran the country club couldn't believe that. It was like something out of a movie. Did you see the fireworks and the all-white horses pulling that Cinderella carriage?"

"Yeah, of course I saw it. Everyone saw it." The truth of the matter was that I spent more time watching that blue-black Mr. Mahogany and his snaggletooth son EJ talking my brother LC's ears off more than I did anything else at that wedding. Something about those slick motherfuckers from Atlanta just didn't sit well with me, especially that son of a bitch EJ. I probably should have just killed his ass when I had the chance, instead of just knocking over his chair. I was particularly concerned now that LC and Chippy were on their way up to Atlanta for some big, top secret meeting without me and Lou. I sure hoped Mr. Smarty-Pants knew what he was doing.

"I swear that wedding was so beautiful, it was like something out of Disney World." Nee shook her head, looking starry-eyed as she sighed. "I don't even have the words."

"Or the money," I said with a laugh. "I can think of far better things to do with that kinda money than piss it away on a wedding. He must have spent thirty or forty grand on that wedding, and in a day or two, folks won't even remember that shit. It'll be back to reality for the citizens of Waycross, Georgia."

"Maybe. Maybe not." Nee shrugged. "But it's something the two of them will remember the rest of their lives, and that's all that matters."

"I hear you. Good for them." I reached for the door handle. "I'd still rather have the cash."

"You're such a romantic." Nee sucked her teeth and rolled her eyes, opening her door with a hard shove. I knew at that moment the chances of me getting any were slim and none, so I might as well keep playing my part.

"Thank you," I replied. I knew I was just pissing her off even more, but why pretend? I wasn't planning on marrying her anytime soon. I didn't need any white man's piece of paper to prove my commitment to her. We had a son together, and that was commitment enough.

"Hey, you think the boy is up?" The thought of seeing our son brought a smile to my face. I loved Nee and the rest of my family, but my son Curtis was my reason for living.

Nee Nee glanced at her watch. "He better not be. But then again, you know your momma. She spoils those boys to death."

"She's just being a grandma. We'll see how you act when you're in her position." She laughed right along with me, because we both knew she would spoil her grandkids ten times worse than my momma ever could.

By the time I got out of the car, Nee Nee was already walking on the porch. She opened the screen door and asked me over her shoulder, "You got your key?"

I reached into my pocket for the house key, but when she put her hand on the door knob, the door opened up right away.

"Got dammit!" I cursed, stepping up behind her. "How many times I gotta tell Momma about leaving that door unlocked?" It was one thing when Levi had his dogs there, but now that he'd moved into Big Shirley's and taken the dogs with him, that door should have been locked at all times.

"Relax. You know she ain't used to locking no doors," Nee said, stepping inside. She switched on the light and screamed.

I rushed in and saw what had her so upset. The house was tore up from the floor up, like a cyclone had run through there, and sitting right in the middle of the mess were Curtis and Junior.

"What the hell?" I thought it was cute the way my mother spoiled the kids, but even I thought this was going too far.

"I'm sorry, but I am not gonna be *this* bad," Nee joked, but I didn't find a damn thing funny.

I had to step over a couple of pillows and pick up a potato chip bag as I walked into the room. "Momma!" I called out.

The boys were sitting over by the television. There was an empty tub of ice cream and two spoons on the ground. A couple of bottles of Nehi soda sat on the coffee table, along with a few empties on the floor. As Curtis picked one up and started chugging away, neither he nor Junior took their eyes off the cartoons they were watching.

"Momma!" Getting no response, I headed toward the kitchen. "Ma—" My words halted when I saw that she wasn't in there either.

"She's probably in her room drunk," Nee said, shaking her head. "Mr. Byrd came by with some of that corn liquor he be making the other day. I bet she mixed it with some of that Nehi orange that she likes so much. She's probably passed out on the bed."

I spun around and headed for Momma's bedroom.

"Jesus, Larry! Knock me down why don't you?" Nee said when I smashed right into her.

"Sorry, but something ain't right." I apologized but didn't wait for a response as I made a beeline toward the bedroom. I was starting to get a bad feeling about this.

"Momma!" She wasn't in her room, so I continued to call out as I went from one room to the next in search of my mother. I finally stopped searching and walked into the living room where Nee had started picking up some of the mess.

"She's in there drunk, ain't she?" Nee asked.

I shook my head. "I couldn't find her. I don't think she's here."

"What do you mean? She has to be here." Nee Nee's face finally revealed the same panic I felt. We looked over at the boys. "I know your mother. No way would she leave them here alone."

"I know," I replied, "but where the fuck is she?"

I stepped in front of the TV, staring down the boys, who looked annoyed when I turned off their Betamax tape. "Hey," Curtis whined. "We was watching that."

"Where's Grandma Bettie?" I asked sternly.

"She's not here," Junior replied.

"What do you mean she's not here? Where is she?"

"She gone," Curtis answered, still trying to look past me at the static TV screen.

"Yeah, she went with the men," Junior said, clearly hoping it would be enough information for me to let them get back to their show.

A wave of heat ran through my body. "Men! What men?" I was not about to believe Momma left these boys alone while she went out with some men.

Junior scratched his head as if he was thinking real hard. "Umm, one of them had a toy gun."

Curtis chimed in, "He let me play with it, and I was gonna shoot it, just like you, Daddy." Nee and I glanced at each other, neither of us able to speak.

"No, you wasn't," Junior snapped at Curtis. "He didn't even let you play with his gun."

"Yes he did," Curtis shot back, smacking Junior in the head. Junior started crying.

"Curtis!" Nee yelled. Under normal circumstances, she would have whipped Curtis's behind for hitting his cousin, but this shit was anything but normal. If what the boys were saying was true, someone with a gun was in my house, and now my momma was missing.

Nee grabbed my arm, and I could feel her trembling. I'm not sure if she could see the terror in my eyes, but I sure as hell saw it in hers.

"You think someone took her?" Nee asked as we stepped away from the boys to talk.

"Sure as hell looks like it." I felt about ready to break something in half.

"Oh my God, Larry, what we gonna do?"

"First I'm gonna get out of this piece-of-shit tuxedo. Then I'm gonna call my brothers." I started walking toward my bedroom, already taking off my tuxedo shirt. "Then we're gonna hunt down the motherfuckers who took my momma and kill they asses."

Bettie

3

Three hours earlier

I'd been invited to Juan and Maria's fancy wedding, but I chose to stay home with my grandbabies. I said it was to give their mothers a break, but mostly it was because I just loved those two boys to death and wanted to spend as much time with them as I could. Besides, I felt a little uneasy going to a wedding for two people I barely knew. I'd met Juan a few times since I'd been home, and he appeared to be a nice enough fella—hell, everyone seemed to like him, including Larry, who didn't like nobody—but after being in jail so long, I didn't do well in crowds. So I told them to wish Juan luck as I did everything I could to get them out the door.

But that Chippy still resisted.

"You know what? Maybe I'll stay home with you, Miss Bettie," Chippy said, taking off her shawl. "These boys are gonna be a handful for you to handle."

"No, they're not! Now, you take your wiry behind with your husband to that wedding and have a good time. Grandma Bettie got this. Me and my grandsons have some ice cream and cake to eat, and mommies and daddies aren't invited, so carry your asses." I picked up her shawl and handed it to her.

"But—"

"Git!" I pointed at the door.

Chippy looked at LC for backup, but he just shook his head before taking her arm and leading her out the door. She didn't look happy, but I didn't really give two shits if she got mad.

She'd get over it. Besides, a woman is supposed to get mad at her mother-in-law at least one time in her life. I had to admit, though, that I liked the women LC, Larry, and Levi had chosen for themselves. Now, if I could only get Lou to settle down before I closed my eyes, I'd be all right.

I glanced over at Nee Nee, who raised her hands in surrender and followed them out the door.

"Bye, Momma." Larry leaned over and kissed my cheek. "Lock the door behind us."

"Okay, baby. Bye-bye." I closed the door, leaning up against it as I chuckled to myself. "Damn, I thought they'd never leave."

"What's so funny, Grandma Bettie?" Junior, a pudgy little mound of joy, asked as he looked up from the Hot Wheels cars and tracks that he and Curtis were playing with. Junior was four months younger but almost twice Curtis's size.

"Your momma, that's what's so funny." I was still laughing—until I realized what was about to happen. "Boy, if you don't put that down, I'm gonna whip you with it until your momma and daddy come home."

"I didn't do nothing," Curtis whined, dropping the Hot Wheels track he had been holding. His slick ass was about to slam that track up against Junior's head. It would have left a serious mark, which was the last thing I needed, considering Chippy was the most overprotective momma I'd met in my life.

"You was about to." I shook my head, and Curtis tried to play innocent, showing off his momma's dimples as crocodile tears ran down his face. Bad as he was, that boy couldn't help but melt your heart. He was so cute. "Who's ready for a bubble bath and then some ice cream?" I shouted, and his tears instantly dried up.

"And cake!" Junior added as both boys jumped up and ran toward the bathroom. All I could do was smile and thank God for giving me the chance to know them.

Twenty minutes later, they were clean, but getting those boys cleaned up 'bout laid me out flat. Chippy wasn't lying when she said they were a lot of work. But then again, I'd never been against hard work.

"Grandma Bettie, you said we could have ice cream and cake, remember?" Junior announced no sooner than I'd slipped his pajama top over his head. He was one of the happiest and bubbliest kids I'd ever met. His sweet, gentle spirit reminded me of my son Levi. Levi was still a big ol' kid to this day, trapped in a big ol' man's body. But that Curtis, on the other hand. He was wild and rambunctious, just like Larry. I mean, if that boy didn't remind me of his father when he was a child, he didn't remind me of anyone.

"Yeah, we gonna have ice cream and cookies, right?" Curtis chimed in.

"Son, there is one thing you gon' learn." I turned and spoke to Curtis, who was already in his PJs, sitting on the toilet seat, waiting for me to finish up with Junior. "And that's that your Grandma Bettie is a woman of her word. If I say something, I mean it. Now, let's go get some ice cream and cake."

"Yay!" the boys shouted in unison then darted out of the bathroom.

"You boys sit down and watch TV. I'm coming, I just gotta clean out this filthy tub first," I said as I grabbed a rag and some Comet. I swear there was so much dirt left in that tub, those boys must have had half the dirt in Waycross on their bodies. It took me a little longer than I expected, but once I'd finished straightening up, I headed down the hall and into the living room.

It was quiet, and the boys were nowhere to be seen. I figured they must have been in the kitchen. Still, that silence didn't sit well with me.

"Curtis? Junior? Where y'all at?"

"In the kitchen, Grandma Bettie," Junior hollered.

"So, are you boys ready for some ice cre—" I entered the kitchen but froze dead in my tracks at the sight before me. I honestly could not believe my eyes. Junior was sitting at the table, eating ice cream directly from the carton. Meanwhile, Curtis was sitting on the lap of a man I'd never seen before, holding a huge hunk of uncut cake.

"As you can see, they've started without you." A piss-yellow man smiled at me, showing a mouth full of rotten teeth.

"I don't know who you are, but you have ten—I mean five seconds to get the fuck out of this house."

"Why such a party pooper?" the man said, leaning over to take a bite of Curtis's cake. "Look at 'em. They're all happy and shit. It would be a shame to disturb their moment. So why don't we spare traumatizing these kids by you taking a little drive with me?"

"I ain't going nowhere with you." I whipped a pearl-handled .38 from my apron. Lou had given it to me as a homecoming present. "Now, get the fuck out my house."

He sat there, staring at me like I had two heads at first; then he busted out laughing. "Whoo-wee, Granny is gangster! Now I see where your fathers get it from," he said to the boys, who were so wrapped up in eating their sweets they seemed oblivious to what was happening in the room.

"Yeah, she's gangster all right," I heard a voice say from behind me. The next thing I heard was the unmistakable click of a gun being cocked. Then I felt something pressing against my spine and hot breath against my ear. "Heard she took out two white men without even giving it a second thought, but if you don't put that goddamn gun down, I'm gonna take you and those little brats out without giving it a thought myself." He pressed the gun harder against my back.

I looked at Junior and Curtis, who weren't the least bit scared, as they were having a pretend sword fight with their spoons over the tub of ice cream.

The man at the table nodded toward the man who was holding the gun at my back.

"Think about it, Granny," the man with the gun said. "Would you rather put that gun down and come with us, or get your brains blown out in front of your grandchildren?"

I couldn't even answer before he was making an even worse threat.

"Or better yet, watch your grandsons' brains get blown out? Doesn't matter to me. I get paid either way."

He made his way from around the back of me to stand near Junior. I had to admit that after the life I'd lived, I didn't give a shit about getting shot, but those babies were another story. They still had a long life ahead of them. It was because of me my own boys didn't get to live the childhood they should have. I could not be the reason why my grandchildren didn't get to live at all.

"What is this about? Why are you doing this?" I asked.

"I bet if you think long and hard, you'll figure it out, Miss Duncan." There was something about the way he spoke that seemed awfully familiar. He wasn't like his rotten-tooth friend. This man had some polish to him, and there was no doubt he was in charge.

"Well, kiss my ass. You're his son, aren't you?" I said when it came to me.

"Can you see the family resemblance?" He grinned as he aimed his gun in the direction of Junior's temple. "Now, drop the gun and let's go. You have a date with destiny, and I'd hate for one of your sons to show up and ruin it."

I dropped my gun to the floor.

"Junior, Curtis." They both looked up with ice cream–covered faces, and I wanted to cry. "Grandma Bettie's gonna step outside with these men for a minute. You boys finish your ice cream and cake and watch some TV, okay? I love you."

"Okay, love you too," they said in unison.

I was escorted out of the house and into a black sedan, leaving my grandbabies alone to fend for themselves . . . but alive.

Lou

4

"*Hijo de puta! Con cuidado, papi! Eres enormo!*"

I don't know what was turning me on more—the way this chick was moaning in Spanish, or her watermelon-size ass bouncing around as I fucked her doggy style. There was nothing like some Latina pussy. This mamacita could take some dick, and trust me, I was packing a monster. I yanked her hair with one hand and smacked her ass with the other.

"*Nadie me lo da como tú!*" Rosa, who happened to be Juan's new sister-in-law, continued what I assumed was dirty talk, turning me on even more. I couldn't translate what she was saying, but I really didn't care, because her accent was making me rock hard. I tightened my hands around her waist and slammed into her, forcing her to cry out in a mixture of pleasure and pain. I closed my eyes just as I felt myself about to erupt. I swear, if this wasn't some of the best pussy I'd ever had, it was damn close to it.

"Yeah, that's it! Take all of this, mami!" I said.

BAM! BAM! BAM!

The sound of banging on the hotel room made me lose my rhythm for a second, but I was determined to nut, so I kept my eyes on Rosa's massive ass and continued what I was doing.

Rosa turned and looked at me from the corner of her eye, "*Que, papi?*"

BAM! BAM! BAM!

"Lou!" Someone shouted my name.

"Turn the fuck around. Don't worry about that," I said, enjoying the feeling of her wetness and still set on reaching my goal.

"Lou, open the fucking door!"

"Fuck!" This time I recognized the voice as Larry's. I knew that he wouldn't stop until I let him in. Knowing him, he was probably drunk and Nee Nee had kicked his ass out for the night.

I slipped out of Rosa, grabbed my tuxedo pants, and covered myself as I walked over to the door and snatched it open just wide enough to peek through.

"What the fuck do you want? I know you could hear this bitch in here screaming all the way down in the lobby, so you know I was busy," I said.

He pushed his way past me and stepped inside the room. "Get dressed. We gotta go. Now!"

"I ain't going nowhere. I'm in the middle of something." I turned to look at Rosa, still in the bed. She had pulled the rumpled sheets over her fine-ass body, trying to shield herself from my brother's view. "You do see I got a naked woman in here, don't you?"

"I don't give a fuck! Get dressed! Now!" Normally, Larry wasn't the type to get in the way of me getting some pussy, so I knew that something must be very wrong. I took another look at him and realized he was covered in sweat and his eyes were full of terror. I instantly sobered up. There weren't many things in this world that could scare my brother Larry.

"What is it, Larry?"

"She's gone!" He sounded out of breath.

"Who? Nee Nee?" I shook my head. Those two were forever fighting over dumb shit. "Please, she ain't going nowhere. But you do need to start treating her better."

"No, not Nee Nee," Larry said, sounding panicked. "Momma! Someone's got Momma. She's gone."

"What the fuck do you mean she's gone? Someone grabbed her?" I was already snatching up the rest of my clothes and putting them on.

"When Nee and I got to the house, she was gone. Kids was there, but Momma was gone. Curtis and Junior said she left with some men with play guns. But I don't think they were so play, if you know what I mean."

I balled my fists and pressed them on the sides of my head, understanding now why Larry was in such a panic. "Fuck! Who would do this shit?"

"I was thinking it could be Norman Tilman. You know that nigga is crazy enough to do something like this, and he hates you. Larry was pacing back and forth.

"Why you trying to pin this shit on my shoulders, man?" The fucked up part was that he was probably right. Norman had been promising for almost a year to get my ass back for fucking his wife. The damn pussy wasn't even that good.

"Don't act stupid, Lou. More of our problems come from you fucking these bitches than anything else, and you know it," Larry said.

No way was I owning up to that one, even if there was some truth to it. "What about LC and Levi?" I asked to move the subject away from me.

"I got Levi in the car. LC's halfway to Atlanta by now, following behind that black motherfucker Mr. Mahogany. By the time word gets to him, Momma should be 'sleep in her bed."

I nodded. "Either that or half of Waycross is gonna be on its way to Fluker's Funeral home, 'cause I will tear this town apart if anything happen to Momma." I leaned over and kissed Rosa's cheek as I removed my gun from the nightstand.

"Where you going?" she asked in her thick, sexy accent. I tried not to stare at her nipples which were showing through the thin sheet.

"Sorry, mami. Family always comes first."

My Benz screeched to a halt in Norman's driveway, and Larry and Levi pulled in right behind me in Larry's blue Caddie. We got out of our cars and headed for the house. I was carrying my new Dirty Harry .44 Magnum, while Larry carried his signature sawed-off shotgun. Levi wasn't carrying a gun, but then again, when you're six foot eight and four hundred pounds, you don't need a gun. I pointed at the front door, and Levi went barreling toward it like a runaway train. He hit it full speed with his right shoulder, and we heard the sound of splintering wood as the door came off its hinges and fell sideways into the house.

"D–d–did I do good, L–L–Lou?" he asked as Larry and I stepped past him into Norman's living room.

"You sure did, big guy. Now, go back to the car. We don't want you getting all shot up. Larry and I will handle it from here." My stuttering brother might have been as big as an ox, but that just made him a bigger target for bullets, so whenever I could, I liked to remove him from the action.

Levi quickly did as he was told, which was a good thing, because just as he stepped out of the house, Norman came running out of a back bedroom with his gun drawn. His wife was not too far behind him.

Boom!

Before I could blink, Larry's sawed-off exploded, and Norman fell to the ground.

"Oh my God! You killed him! You killed him!" His wife started screaming.

"Shut up, bitch!" Larry yelled, kicking Norman in the ribs. "He ain't dead. I just shot him in the leg. But he will be dead if he don't tell me where my momma is." Larry grabbed Norman by his Jheri curl, keeping the shotgun raised in his other hand. "Where is my momma?"

"I don't know what you talking about." Norman looked more scared than I'd ever seen a man. "I been here all day painting. Ask Debbie."

"You're a liar!" Larry spat, raising the gun higher, as if he was about to smash it into Norman's face.

I turned to Debbie, who was crying.

"He's telling the truth. Go look for yourself. Please, Lou," she begged.

I gestured for her to lead the way. She reluctantly started moving but didn't take her eyes off Larry. She definitely didn't trust him alone with her husband. Neither did I.

"Lou, why are you doing this?" she asked me as we entered the hallway.

"Because that piece of shit husband of yours took my momma, that's—" The familiar sound of fists pounding on flesh, followed by Norman's screams, stopped me mid-sentence.

"Jesus Christ, he's going to kill him!" Debbie yelled at me. "He didn't do anything. He's been here with me all day. Look for yourself. He's been painting the baby's room all day."

The room she was referring to definitely did smell like fresh paint, and the can and paintbrush were still in the corner on a small tarp. Another corner held a crib.

"He didn't take your mother, Lou. He's been here with me all day. I swear to God. We are having a baby."

In spite of the fact that I'd fucked her a few times, I didn't really know Debbie all that well. Still, when I looked in her eyes, I knew she was telling me the truth.

"Shit. Larry! Larry!" I ran back to the living, grabbing my brother's arm just as he was about land another blow to Norman's already bloody face. "Stop, Larry. Stop!" I had to wrestle with him for a few moments, but he finally calmed down enough for me to get through. "He didn't do it! He didn't do it!"

"Then who did?" Larry asked, panting hard from the exertion of beating the shit out of Norman.

"I don't know, but we gotta find out. Let's go down to Melvin's. I'm sure someone knows something down there."

"They fucking better, or I'll crack every skull in the place," Larry said, and I had no doubt he meant every word.

I nodded silently at Debbie, which was as close to an apology as they were going to get, and then I led Larry out of the house and back to our cars.

"Wh-what happened?" Levi asked.

"You don't wanna know," I told him. "You drive. Larry needs to calm down for a minute. Follow me to Melvin's."

I was going so fast that I almost missed the driveway of the hit house sitting behind the trees. The tires screeched as I swerved into the makeshift parking lot out front, which was full. There were old beaters, newer model sedans, and even a shiny new Corvette. Any other time, I would've taken the time to check it out, but I was on a mission and didn't even give it a second look.

I jumped out and popped open the trunk to get my baseball bat. Larry was right by my side, grabbing a tire iron. Wasting no time, we hopped the porch steps, and Larry snatched the screen door so hard that it came off its hinges. In that same instant, I burst in the front door with such force that everyone inside froze.

"Where the fuck is she?" I exploded, my eyes scanning the room for any signs of my mother. My heart was pounding, and the anger had me seeing red.

"Lou, man, what the—" A guy jumped up, and before he could finish, I punched the shit out of him. He fell backward and hit the floor hard. Two other guys jumped up to his defense, but Larry punched one and then kicked the other one in the stomach. That was enough to deter anyone else who might have been thinking of stepping in. I flipped over tables; cards and money flew in the air. There was an old radio blasting music in the corner of the room, and I smashed it with the bat.

"Somebody better tell me something in this muthafucka!" I roared.

No one moved, even though the room was filled with some of the most hardcore, deviant characters in Waycross. Everyone from dope dealers to bank robbers frequented this house that we secretly owned. All eyes were on me as I circled the room, waiting for someone to tell me something.

I reached over and grabbed Vernon, a guy who had been talking shit about me around town for the past few days because, like Norman, he found out I'd been fucking his wife. He stood six foot six and was built like an NFL linebacker, but I wasn't intimidated.

"I know yo' bitch ass did this!" I held the bat up near his face, preparing to strike him. "Where the fuck is she?"

Beads of sweat began forming on his forehead, and a vein popped out of his neck. "I don't know what the fuck you're talking about! I swear!"

"Lou! Larry!"

I turned around to see Melvin running over to me. He was a friend of Larry's, which was probably the only reason he was brave enough—or stupid enough—to approach me when I was in this state.

"Bro, you need to calm the fuck down! What's wrong?" he whispered in my ear.

I stared at him, breathing hard. "Get the fuck back, Mel. We handling business."

"Naw, bro. You fucking shit up, and nobody knows why." Melvin frowned. "At least tell him that before you smash him."

I tightened my grip and stared into Vernon's terrified eyes. "Somebody went into Larry's house and took something that belongs to us. Something very important."

"I . . . I ain't take shit. I swear. I been here since this afternoon." Vernon choked the words out.

"He ain't lying! He been here!" someone yelled. Larry found the owner of the voice and grabbed him.

"Shut the fuck up," he hissed.

Melvin tried again to be the voice of reason. "Whatever it is they took, y'all know we gon' get it back. But these muthafuckas in here been here all damn day. Ain't nobody leave except for me, and that was to go over to Big Shirley's to get some change."

My eyes turned to Larry's, who was staring at Mel. If it had been anybody else, things probably would have gone a different way, but Mel and Larry had been boys for a long time, and we trusted him. I let Vernon's big ass go.

"I want my shit back! If none of you muthafuckas took it, chances are you know who did, and I'm gonna fuck shit up until it's returned. I mean that shit. So, y'all better help me get back what's mine!" I announced before storming out the door, stepping on broken card tables on the way.

Larry was right on my heels. As we made our way back to the car, we took turns using our weapons and striking whatever we could reach. Headlights, hoods, windshields, and windows of vehicles were destroyed.

"Yo!" Mel came running out of the house just as I opened the door to get into the car.

I paused long enough for him to reach us. "Not now, Mel."

"What the fuck is going on?" he asked. He was just as ready for action as we were. Mel always was. "What the fuck did they take?"

I stared at Larry and waited for him to answer.

Larry looked over at Mel and finally said, "My mother."

"Shit! What the fuck you gonna do now?" Mel asked.

I looked at Larry and told him, "We gonna go find the college boy, and then we can fuck up the rest of this town."

5

"You sure about this?" Chippy asked as she slipped on her sunglasses. We'd just stepped out of the Omni Hotel in Atlanta, where we were staying compliments of Mr. Mahogany. We had driven up directly after the wedding so that the two of us could talk business in a more suitable setting.

"We don't know anything about this man other than he was supposedly friends with your father, and now we're going to his house like we're old friends. Maybe you should have made Lou come with us, or stopped by and talked to your mother first."

"I probably should have talked Ma, but its too late now. Besides, Lou was drunk, and there was no way we were dragging him away from Maria's sister. You know how he gets when he thinks he's gonna get some new—" I stopped myself from saying what I was thinking, but Chippy finished my sentence.

"Pussy, LC. The word is *pussy*. You don't have to act like I have virgin ears all the time. I used to work in a whorehouse, remember?"

I shot her a look. "*Used to* being the operative words," I told her. It was true that when I met her, my wife was working at Big Sam's, but she'd been tricked into that life, and as far as I was concerned, it was ancient history. She was a queen, and there was no reason to dredge up a past that no longer mattered.

"I love you. You know that?" She leaned over and kissed me, her big, pregnant belly rubbing up against my thigh. "You're going to protect my honor until the day you die, aren't you?"

"Yes, and from the grave, if I have to."

She took hold of my arm and squeezed it affectionately. As we waited for the valet to bring my 1957 Corvette Roadster, she let out an exasperated sigh.

"Shit. I can't believe I forgot to call the farm and check in on Junior. My poor baby. He must think I'm the worst mother in the world."

I could feel her pulling away from me like she was about to go back inside the hotel and make that phone call.

"Relax, baby," I said, holding on to her so she couldn't go anywhere. "I'm supposed to check in with Larry and Lou at noon. I'll check on him then."

She was still agitated. "We didn't even tell your mother or Nee Nee what hotel we were staying at. What if something happens?"

"Like what?" I asked skeptically. "We haven't even been gone half a day. What could possibly happen?" The valet pulled up, and I led her toward the car, helping her in to the passenger's side.

"You're right," she said as she settled in. "I just miss my son."

"I miss him too, but we'll see him tonight. For now, let's just enjoy ourselves in the big city. How about I take you shopping after my meeting?"

"I'm going to hold you to it." She gave me a big grin and leaned back in the seat.

The beaming sun was inviting as we drove down the busy streets of Atlanta. Maybe it was the anticipation of my meeting, but to me, even the air was better in this city. I looked over at Chippy, who was finally smiling as she took in the sights. Her hands were tenderly placed on top of her swollen belly. There was something so damn sexy about her being pregnant that turned me on tremendously. Her breasts were fuller, her hips wider, and I swear, when she smiled, she had the glow of an angel.

"This place is so nice. One day I'd like to live in a big city," Chippy said as she gazed out the window.

"I was just thinking the same thing."

"Hmmmmm, I guess it's true what they say, huh?"

"What's that?" I asked.

"Great minds think alike." We laughed together.

I was following the directions to the location Mr. Mahogany had given me for our nine o'clock meeting. The sounds of the Doobie Brothers on the radio drifted through the speakers as we traveled on Peachtree through Five Points, then downtown, finally arriving at our destination on a busy highway right outside midtown. I double checked the address to make sure I was at the right place.

"I though you said we were going to his house," Chippy said.

"That's what he said."

"That don't look like no house."

"No, it sure doesn't." I blinked and stared at what seemed to be a commercial building located on a barren lot.

In my rearview mirror, I saw a long, black Oldsmobile Toronado pull up behind me. I leaned over to the glove compartment and retrieved my .45, but by the time I sat up, I saw it was Mr. Mahogany stepping out of the other car. I watched him walk around the car and help an attractive woman, who appeared to be about his age, as she got out of the car. Her presence eased my anxiety a little. I slipped the gun under my seat and got out of the car.

"LC, Chippy!" Mr. Mahogany called out to us as I was helping my wife from her seat. "Welcome to my city!"

"Good to be here, I think." I shook his extended hand when he approached. He leaned over and gave Chippy a kiss on the cheek.

"Nice to see you again, Mr. Mahogany." Chippy smiled at him. "So, do you live here? I thought we were supposed to be going to your house for breakfast."

"We will go there eventually," was his cryptic answer.

Mr. Mahogany and I locked eyes for a moment. I wanted him to know without saying it that I didn't like whatever game he was playing. He broke the tension by doing introductions.

"By the way, this is my wife, Belinda." Mr. Mahogany grabbed the hand of the woman who stood nearby.

She smiled at us like a debutante. "Welcome to Atlanta."

"Well, enough with the pleasantries. Come on in," Mr. Mahogany said like a king inviting people into his castle.

We followed Mr. Mahogany and his wife inside the building, which was devoid of any furnishings except a long conference table surrounded by high-back chairs.

"Is there a restroom I can use?" Chippy asked.

"Certainly, young lady. Follow me." Belinda took Chippy by the hand and led her through another door, chatting all the way. "I know exactly how you must be feeling. When I was pregnant with EJ, that boy stayed sitting on my bladder. I was running to the bathroom every five minutes."

When we were alone, Mr. Mahogany said, "Your wife is lovely. I think she'd love Atlanta. You ever thought about moving up here?"

I hoped the look on my face didn't show how I felt about the boldness of Mr. Mahogany's question. This man had more confidence than anyone I had ever met, including my brother Lou, and that was saying a lot.

"Of course. I live in a one horse town. Everyone in Waycross dreams of moving to the big city one day, but for me, that's all it is. A dream."

"And why is that?" he pressed. "You're a smart young man. You can do anything you put your mind to."

I laughed. "That's what my momma always says."

"Your momma's a smart woman. Always has been." He smiled and gestured toward the large front lot. "This property spans over two and a half acres. More than enough space for you to build a first class dealership, don't you think?"

"Yeah, right." I guffawed. "I wish."

"No need to wish, son. It's already done. We've got financing and investors all lined up. I hope you don't consider this presumptuous, but I've already taken the liberty of getting this fast tracked with the planning and zoning boards. You could break ground in a week if you'd like."

"You're joking, right? What, do you have me on *Candid Camera* or something?" I was only half joking as I began to look around for the hidden cameras.

"This is not a joke. This is our gift to you if you're ready to take your place on the Black Council." He looked serious, but this dude was confusing the hell out of me. He barely knew me, and here he was offering me everything I needed to get into the Atlanta market.

"You mentioned them last night. What exactly is the Black Council?" I asked, trying not to get too excited about the offer before I had some concrete details. "I've never heard of them before."

"Few have." Mr. Mahogany put his hand on my shoulder. "Come over here and sit."

We walked to the table and sat across from one another. Mr. Mahogany inhaled deeply and somehow, I knew that what he was about to say was important.

"The Black Council is one of the most powerful black organizations in the South," he said, his eyes never leaving mine. "We settle disputes the law can't or won't handle, make loans to people who would never go to a traditional bank when they need a loan. You name it, we're in it, legal and illegal. Oh, and most importantly, we protect one another and our allies. Sam Bradford, or Big Sam as you knew him, was a member. I'm offering you his seat."

"No disrespect, I'm no Big Sam, and neither are my brothers. He was a low-down snake who would eat his own young if it made him a few more dollars. Me and my brothers may not be totally on the up and up, but we have honor. I don't think your council is the right fit for my family. We're just small time hustlers."

"Really?" Mr. Mahogany said with a hint of a smirk on his face. "That surprises me, considering your father was one of our founding members."

I sat up straight in my chair and opened my mouth to speak, but nothing came out. "When he was killed and your mother went to jail, that seat was filled by Sam, and now that he is gone, the seat is empty, and we feel that the time has come for a Duncan to fill it again. And that would be you," Mr. Mahogany explained.

I chuckled, because the whole damn thing was so off the wall it didn't seem real. A few years ago, I was a college kid getting ready to marry a girl from the other side of the tracks, and now I was sitting here, being asked to take my family's criminal organization to a whole new level. "So let me get this straight," I said. "You mean to tell me there is a secret illuminati organization that nobody knows about, that controls and finances the black underworld . . . and they want *me* to be a member."

He folded his hands in front of him. "Yes, that about sums it up, although we're not quite as big as you make it sound. Our reach only extends through the Southeast."

"This is bullshit, right? You're messing with my head. This council stuff is BS, isn't it?" I looked around for the cameras again.

"Nope. Ask your mother when you get back. I'm surprised she hadn't told you boys already."

"Okay then, why me? Why not Larry or Lou?" I attempted to explain my reasoning. "They're the oldest, and I've only been in the business a few years. Larry's been sharking since Daddy—"

Mr. Mahogany shook his head. "Your brothers have done a good job with what they do, but this requires some skills and talents that we feel they don't possess."

I was starting to feel like this man knew a little too much about my family and how we ran our organization. It put me at a distinct disadvantage, because I knew very little about him. I also felt my anger beginning to rise. I was not about to sit here and let this man disrespect my brothers. They might not have been the most educated brothas, but they each had their own talents that made them valuable to what we did.

"I don't appreciate you talking about my brothers that way," I said.

"One seat, one man. It's no disrespect to you or your family. It's just that we've been watching you for a while, and we prefer the way that you operate. Like I said, we can appreciate the way that Lou and Larry have continued handling the Duncan businesses," he said, attempting to lower the heat between us. "They don't have a problem taking care of the dirty work that comes along with it, but we also know that you were instrumental in the release of your mother. Your intellect and education are going to take you farther than you ever dreamed. You, son, have the mind and the potential to become one of the richest black men in America, and I am here to help you achieve that goal."

Hell, I can't lie. I had imagined having the finer things in life: opening a larger car lot, purchasing a nice home for Chippy and me, buying a couple of cars, money in the bank, and an education fund for my children, but I had never dared to dream about one day becoming the richest black man in America.

I let that fantasy settle in for a minute then said, "What are you asking me to do?"

"Just take your rightful seat at the table, use the resources at your disposal, and make yourself and your partners a lot of money. It's just that simple," he said with a shrug.

"What about your sons? Why not allow them to fill the empty seat?"

Mr. Mahogany laughed, which took me completely by surprise. "Absolutely not. I love them dearly, but my sons are not equipped to handle all that comes with that position. My sons, for lack of a better term, are closed minded. I'll be lucky if one of them ends up with my seat."

I tried to comprehend everything he was telling me, but I still didn't completely understand. "So, let's say I accept your invitation and take this so-called seat. Then what happens?"

"Well, for starters, we assist you in opening this place."

"My car lot?"

"No, son, not your car lot. Your dealership. Think luxury cars, GM, Ford, Cadillacs, maybe even Porsche. I need for you to have the mindset of a billionaire, boy."

"Okay, I open a dealership. Then what?" I said, still waiting on the bait and switch that I was sure was about to happen.

"Not *a* dealership. *Your* dealership."

"*My* dealership," I emphasized, playing along. "Then what?"

"Then you assist us in finding those creative financial opportunities I mentioned." He leaned in closer with a serious expression on his face as he finally got to his point. "Young man, there is going to be an explosion of illegal drugs in this country in the next ten years, and our associates are going to a have a lot of cash that is going to need to be washed. Your job is going to be to wash it."

Mr. Mahogany continued explaining the various ways that my seat on the Black Council would be beneficial to everyone involved. The more he talked, the more intrigued I became. I was still surprised that I had no knowledge of this organization, especially after realizing how much control and power they had. I wondered if Lou and Larry knew of the Black Council's existence. They sure had never mentioned it before. I also realized that if what Mr. Mahogany was saying was true, I now knew how Big Sam was able to finance a lot of his business transactions.

"Well, are you ready?" Mr. Mahogany asked after allowing me some time to sit silently with my thoughts.

"I have to discuss this with my wife and brothers." As tempting as his offer was, I was not the type to make a decision without first weighing all the angles.

"I understand having to discuss matters with your wife. I'm sure Belinda has already enlightened her a bit. However, your brothers can have no knowledge of the Council or your position. As far as they are concerned, you're just branching out."

"What do you mean? My brothers and I always discuss business. I can't do this without talking it over with them." There was no way I could agree to do any of this without informing Lou and Larry, and even Levi. My brothers were the reason I had achieved anything in life. They financed my education and my first business. I damn near owed them my life.

"I understand your feeling this way; however, this is for your protection and theirs. LC, this thing is bigger and deeper than you probably understand, but if you trust me, I promise you will learn the reasoning behind a lot of what we do. Your father was a good man, and like you, he was a brilliant businessman. His life was taken way too soon. I owe it to him to mentor you and make you into the man he was destined to become, had he been given the chance to live. And you owe it to him to continue the legacy that he started."

I stood up slowly and looked out of the picture window. Mr. Mahogany was right about one thing: my father had been a brilliant businessman. It was from him that not only did I inherit my love of cars, but also my love of numbers. He taught me how to count money, and often talked to me about the power that came with it. I had no doubt that had he lived, our lives would have been completely different, and he would have achieved everything Mr. Mahogany suggested. But how could I do this without the consent of my brothers? Was it worth risking the bond of our bloodline?

As I stared out the window, a car pulled up, and EJ stepped out. He had a worried look on his face as he headed toward the building. A few seconds later, he was standing in front of me and Mr. Mahogany, looking grim. Mr. Mahogany picked up on his son's mood too. He glanced at me and then pulled his son closer to whisper something in his ear.

EJ leaned in close and said something I couldn't hear.

"Shit." That was Mahogany's response. I hadn't known the man long, but his curse seemed out of character. "Are you sure?"

"Positive," EJ replied. They were no longer whispering.

"Put our best people on this. I want to know who did this right away."

"I'm on it, Pop." EJ nodded then left abruptly.

Mr. Mahogany approached me with a dismal expression. Whatever his son had told him, it had to have been some bad, bad news. "LC, I think we are going to have to cut this meeting a little short."

"I take it something has come up," I said, trying not to sound alarmed. After all, it was none of my business—or so I thought.

"Yes, you could say that, but unfortunately, it has more to do with you than me."

"I don't understand."

"LC, we just got a call from your brother Lou. You're going to need to get home as quickly as possible."

I did not like the sound of that. Immediately, I thought of Junior. *Please tell me nothing happened to my son,* was the quick prayer I sent up.

Mr. Mahogany then delivered news that was almost as bad.

"Someone has taken your mother."

Lou

6

Larry was still going around town busting heads when LC returned to Waycross, so I was the one who had to explain to our little brother what had happened to our momma. Of course, he didn't take it well and wanted to bust some heads of his own, but once he calmed down, he went back to being the logical one. He took control by bringing the cops in, spreading money amongst the state and local departments.

I didn't like or trust cops, so after answering their questions and listening to their bullshit, I had to get some air. In my opinion, those greedy-ass pigs didn't give a shit about bringing my momma home safely. All they wanted was LC's money. Well, experience had shown me that cops weren't the only ones who knew how to come up with information, and they damn sure weren't the only ones who loved money, so I made a few calls then headed down Georgia Highway 13 toward Brunswick.

I stopped at a Waffle House I frequented right outside of town, taking a moment to stretch before I walked in. I was immediately greeted by Izzy, a short, thick redbone who had easily become my favorite waitress after pleasuring me with her mouth in my car one night after her shift. I'd been meaning to try out that thing between her legs, but her husband, a truck driver, always seemed to be in town when I came around.

"Well, hey there, stranger!" she damn near shouted as soon as she spotted me.

"Sounds like you missed me," I said with a grin.

"A little bit." She led me to a table in the back, handing me a greasy menu. "I'll be back with your coffee. You want the usual?"

"Yeah." I swatted her ass as she sashayed away, causing her to giggle.

Izzy brought back my coffee just as a skinny, light-skinned man about ten years older than me sat down in the chair across from. He looked very nervous.

"I'm leaving for the night, Lou. Why don't you stop by the house when you finish your business? We ain't never really finished what we started, and my husband's on the road for the next few days," she stated boldly, not even trying to hide her cheating ways from the guy across from me. Grinning from ear to ear, she handed me a folded up piece of paper.

I glanced at the paper then back at her, smiling. "I'll see you in a few." She walked away, and I turned my attention to the man sitting across from me.

"You know those bitches is gonna be your downfall," Eddie Monroe said in his creepy-ass voice, looking around suspiciously, like he was in witness protection.

Eddie was one weird fuck, but I tolerated him because he was also the best source for any type of information. Don't ask me how he did it, but this scary-acting motherfucker was probably the most informed black man in South Georgia. If you lived within a fifty-mile radius of him, he could probably tell you what color drawers you were wearing yesterday.

"Yeah, well, at least I'll die happy." I snapped my fingers to get his attention. "Hey, Eddie, face front. I'm over here."

It took a second, but he finally turned his head and concentrated on me.

"Why the fuck do you keep looking around?"

"Man, the walls have ears. Always remember that," he whispered.

"I hear you, man. So, listen. You hear about my momma?"

He sat back in his chair with a grimace, his eyes once again darting around the diner, searching for God knows what. "Shit, the way you and Larry busted heads last night, everyone within a hundred miles of here heard about your momma." He shook his head. "Was all that necessary?"

"That was just the beginning. This is my momma we're talking about." I leaned in, all serious and shit. "You hear anything else about my momma? Like maybe where she's at?"

"No, just that you guys got a lot of people shook up, but information on that level doesn't come cheap."

Shit never did come cheap with Eddie. I didn't care, though; I would pay whatever it took to find my momma. I reached in my pocket and peeled off ten fifty-dollar bills, placing them on the table in front of me. He scratched his head then reached for the money. Before he could touch it, I smacked his hand, and he pulled it back.

"Not so damn fast. I want to know who's got my momma and where I can find them, Eddie, and I want to know yesterday."

Once again he looked around, paranoid, like the CIA or FBI might be watching. "No problem, Lou. I'll give you a call as soon as I hear something." He scooped up the money and moved like he was about to leave, but I grabbed him by the collar.

"Don't fuck me on this, Eddie. The minute you know something, pick up the damn phone." He nodded his head, and I released him just as someone walked up behind me. Despite his paranoia, a broad smile came to Eddie's face.

"Here's your two eggs and bacon. Izzy had to go, so I'll be your server."

The waitress's voice was familiar, but it couldn't possibly be who I thought it was. Slim fingers placed a platter of eggs and bacon in front of me. My eyes traveled from the hand up to the face, and our eyes locked. The look on her face was a mixture of shock, horror, and utter surprise. I was certain my face wore the same expression, because I was definitely feeling the same way.

"Lou." She shook her head at me.

I turned to Eddie, who was staring at her as if he'd just been shot by Cupid himself.

"Who's your friend, Lou?" Eddie asked, still grinning. All of a sudden, this motherfucker wasn't paranoid at all.

"She's not my friend," I said, turning back to her. I couldn't help but chuckle at the sight of Donna, my brother LC's former fiancée, dressed in the same uniform that Izzy wore. A few years ago, she would not have been caught dead in a joint like this to eat, let alone to work.

"What the hell is so funny?" Donna snapped. "And what are you doing here?"

"Flying a damn plane. I'm an airline pilot. What does it look like I'm doing? I'm having something to eat. Now, can I get a refill on this coffee?" I lifted my cup, smirking as she snatched it from me. "Oh, how the mighty have fallen. You, the fancy, uppity, bourgeois broad who—"

"Shut the fuck up, Lou." Donna talked tough, but it was obvious she would rather be anywhere in the world at that moment than to be standing there in front of me. "Now, I'm not looking for trouble, because I need this job, but I'm not going to put up with your shit, either."

"I ain't here for no trouble, sweetheart. I'm just here to eat, that's all. Now, can I get that refill?" I laughed.

Donna rolled her eyes at me and walked away without saying anything else.

"That's one sexy woman." Eddie was still standing there, gawking at her ass as she walked away.

"That's one stuck-up bitch," I replied then pointed at the door. "And you need to get the hell outta here and find out who's got my momma. What am I paying you for?"

"I'm on it," he said, walking toward the door. Before he exited, he hesitated, trying to steal a final glance at Donna.

I had to laugh. For someone usually so well informed, that poor guy had no idea what he was looking to get himself into.

I dug into my food, and although I tried not to, I couldn't help but check Donna out as she served other customers in the diner. I couldn't wait to tell LC how far his first love had fallen. She had always been a pretty girl with her smooth, light skin and long hair. Now, she was a little thicker than I remembered, but Eddie was right. Donna was sexy. Truth be told, it was her uppity attitude that had always made her ugly in my eyes. And it was that attitude that had given LC fits while they were dating. Nothing he ever did or had was good enough, until her father, the big-time doctor, got caught up in Medicaid fraud and fled the country to avoid being prosecuted. He left Donna and her mother high and dry. LC was her saving grace, until my brother came to his senses and realized it wasn't Donna he was in love with, it was Chippy. He actually left Donna standing at the altar.

She glanced up and caught me staring at her, so I just shrugged, lifting my fingers to my lips as if I held an imaginary coffee cup. She once again rolled her eyes, but a few seconds later, she placed a fresh cup of coffee and a check on the table. I finished eating, placed cash on the table, and then left.

I was about to get into my car when I heard my name being called.

"Lou! Lou! Wait!"

"What now?" I mumbled to myself. It was Donna, running out of the diner like I hadn't paid my check. "Can I help you?"

"I . . . uh . . . this is hard for me to say, but thank you." She actually sounded humble.

"For what?"

"For the tip you left me." She held up a twenty-dollar bill.

"It was just a damn tip, Donna."

"It was four times more than the bill. I appreciate it." She actually looked sincere.

"It's no big deal. You look like you could use it." I stared at her face and saw exhaustion, and for some reason, I felt sorry for her. Despite her arrogance, this was not the life for her.

"I can use it, and it was a big deal to me." Her voice was barely above a whisper as she added, "Lou, how is he?"

Her eyes met mine, waiting in anticipation. I knew I shouldn't even comment. I should have just left it alone, but like an imbecile, I told her, "He's fine, Donna."

"He is?" She half smiled. "For real?"

"Yeah, he's good. But Donna, you need to leave it alone. Let it go."

"I know, but . . . I can't. Lou, despite everything, I love him. I need to know that he's okay." She had fat tears brimming in her eyes at this point.

"I told you, he's fine." I sighed, wishing I had just gotten in my car and left when I'd had the chance. Now the tears started spilling down her cheeks, and I felt stuck.

"I believe you, but take my number just in case." She reached in her pocket and took out a pad and pen. After scribbling some numbers, she folded the paper and tried to pass it to me. I resisted at first, until she said, "Please, Lou. Just take it. One day it might come in handy."

I took the paper from her trembling hand and put it into my back pocket then got into my car before she could say anything else. As I backed out of the parking space and pulled out of the lot, I looked into the rearview mirror and saw that she was still standing there, looking sad and defeated—but still sexy as hell, if I do say so myself.

Chippy

7

"I ain't never had my dick sucked by a pregnant woman before. How much that cost?" a drunk old fool asked as I walked through the crowded bar area of Big Shirley's whorehouse, which was filled with scantily dressed women and half-drunken men. Every time I walked through those doors, the horrible memories of working for Big Sam made me cringe. Despite the new name and change of ownership, it would always be Big Sam's to me, the place where I lost my soul and met my soulmate.

I stared at the man with a devilish grin. "Same thing it cost to have your dick bitten off by a pregnant woman," I snapped.

He took a huge step back, giving me all the room I needed to pass by. Wobbling my swollen body to the back of the building to what used to be Sam's office, I opened the door and was greeted by Lou, Larry, Levi, and Shirley, along with my girl Nee Nee. All were seated around a large table that took up almost the entire room. Everyone looked worn out, except for Levi. Miss Bettie's abduction was putting the whole family through hell, and it was more than starting to show.

"Where's LC?" Lou asked as I walked in.

"He's outside waiting for someone," I replied. Nee Nee patted the empty chair beside her, and I headed directly for it.

"Who the fuck is he waiting for?" Larry barked in his typical nasty tone.

"I don't know," I answered with a shrug. Larry had a way of talking at you instead of to you, but I never let that bother me, because he did it to everyone, not just me. "He said he'd be here in a minute. If you want him so bad, go on out there and get him."

Nee Nee waved her hand as she rolled her eyes at Larry. "Girl, please don't pay him no mind. How you feeling?"

"Tired as hell," I replied, settling into the chair as well as my big belly would let me. "It's been a good pregnancy, but I'm about ready to drop this load. I probably should have just stayed home."

"We all got shit we'd rather be doing, but your husband called this meeting, so your ass is gonna sit right here with the rest of us and suffer," Larry grumbled. I swear I'd never met anyone else so ornery. I didn't know how Nee Nee put up with him.

"Don't worry, Larry. I ain't going nowhere unless I go into labor. Then I'm gonna make you deliver my baby. You ready?" I sat back in my chair and opened my legs wide, making everyone but Larry fall out of their seats with laughter.

It was good to hear the family laugh again. Before Miss Bettie was taken, we used to laugh and play practical jokes on each other all the time.

"You ain't got enough money for me to be up between your nasty-ass legs, Chippy," Larry countered, making it clear I'd definitely touched a nerve.

"What the fuck did you just say to my wife?" LC's voice came out of nowhere, and he wasn't laughing. My husband had a way of always arriving just in the nick of time to come to my defense, although this time, I didn't need it.

"Mind your business, little brother. Your wife started this shit." Larry's voice boomed with irritation.

"Well, I'm ending it." LC stepped toward his older brother, and Larry did the same toward him. They stared at one another, each one waiting to see who would make the next move. The tension in the room thickened. A few weeks ago, this would have never happened, but lately it seemed like we were always sitting on a powder keg.

"You can do that shit to Nee Nee and Shirley, but you're not doing it to my wife. You need to learn some respect," LC said, inches away from Larry's face.

"And you're gonna teach it to me?" Larry damn near laughed, lifting his hand and pointing a finger, a telltale sign that things were about to escalate.

"Doesn't seem like anyone else is willing to."

"Do something!" Shirley gave Lou a shove, prompting him to jump in between his brothers, separating them with his hands.

"Hey, hey, we ain't come here for all this. Calm down, and everybody take a seat." He turned toward LC. "Larry was just having some fun with Chippy, is all. We was all just having a few laughs. Isn't that right, Chippy?"

"Yes, that's right. We was just playing, LC," I said.

But he didn't budge, and neither did Larry.

"I don't see a damn thing funny, and I'm sick of him disrespecting you." LC continued to stare Larry down until I gently reached out and touched his arm. Then his eyes met mine.

"Please, sit down. You're getting yourself all worked up for nothing." I patted my belly, reminding him of everyting he had to lose, and his body softened a bit.

"Okay, but nobody talks to my wife that way, not even my brother." He glared at Larry as he stepped back and reached for an empty chair. Pulling it beside me, LC took a seat.

Larry was being guided to his seat by Lou and Nee Nee. To my surprise, the look he gave me was somewhat apologetic—well, as apologetic as someone with his evil temperament could muster.

Just as things seemed to have calmed down, there was a knock on the door. Little Momma, a friend and one of the house whores, poked her head in. "LC, there's a man out here waiting on you."

LC snapped his fingers. "Damn, I completely forgot about him. Send him in."

Little Momma nodded, pulled her head back through the door, and a few seconds later, a tall white man wearing a suit and tie walked in. Something about the way he carried himself made me think he was ex-military.

"Who is this?" Larry asked, "and why does everything about him scream cop?"

"Maybe 'cause he is a cop. This is Captain Walker of the Georgia State Po—"

"State Police! What the fuck!" Lou hollered before LC could finish his sentence. None of us were too big on police, so you could imagine the look of disapproval and concern on everyone's faces. Sure, we interacted with them on a limited basis and paid them when we absolutely needed to, but we sure as hell didn't make a habit of inviting them up in our midst.

"You brought a cop here?" Shirley looked like she was about to shit her pants. "Why don't you just haul me and my girls down to the city jail right now?"

"Please. You think the cops don't know what you do in here, Shirley? They don't raid you because me and my brothers pay them not to," LC replied. I could tell from his response that he didn't give a shit how she felt. Shirley's name may have been above the door, but it was really LC, Larry, and Lou who owned the place. "Now, Captain Walker came all the way down here with some information about Momma he thinks we should know, so let's hear what the man has to say,"

Of course you know that piqued everyone's interest.

"What kind of information?" Larry asked skeptically, his eyes not leaving the captain. "You know I don't like or trust police, LC, and neither does Lou."

"I know, but he said it's about Momma and it's important, so would you shut up and listen?" LC turned to the captain and gestured for him to speak. "Go ahead, Captain Walker."

"Well, as you know, we've been investigating Mrs. Duncan's disappearance for the past few weeks."

"Yeah, and for what we're paying you, your ass should have found her by now," Larry snapped at him.

There was a slight twitch in his left eyebrow, but other than that, Walker maintained his composure and let Larry's insult roll off his back. "You're right. We haven't found much, but today we found this and wanted to know if you could identify it."

The room fell completely silent as the captain emptied the contents of a paper bag onto the table. It looked like jumbled up, mud-soaked clothes.

"What's that?" I asked, dreading his answer.

"That's what remains of a dress we found out in Okefenokee Swamp," the captain replied.

"Looks like the gators got to it?" Larry asked, his voice more hesitant than I'd ever heard it.

"You trying to say the gators got my momma?" LC's question had a hint of fear in it.

"Unfortunately, that's what I came here to find out, Mr. Duncan."

He was full of shit. I could tell by the way he was shifting around that he was already sure those clothes belonged to Miss Bettie. He just didn't want to say it out loud. I felt my hands begin to tremble.

"Can any of you identify the dress?" he asked.

"Oh my God, Larry!" Nee Nee shrieked, pointing at the hodgepodge of clothes. "Look at the material. That's the apron your momma was wearing."

Larry leaned over, studying the cloth as he picked it up. He glanced over at LC and Lou, closing his eyes as he let the material slip from his fingers. "Fuck! She's right. That is Momma's apron. It's got those ugly-ass ducks on it."

LC looked like he was in a trance. I took hold of his hands, which were now shaking, just like mine.

"Were there any remains found with the body?" Lou asked. He seemed to be the only calm person in the room.

"We did find what appears to be a colored woman's arm about twenty feet from the clothing. We sent it to the lab to see what they could find."

"Is she dead? Do you think our momma is dead?" LC finally snapped out of his trance to ask.

"If that's her dress, then yes, Mr. Duncan, I believe your mother is dead." His voice, although soft spoken, blared like a bull horn in my head.

"Oh, no!" Nee Nee cried.

"Dear God, she's really gone. Miss Bettie is really gone," Shirley mumbled.

"M—M—M—Momma? G—g—g—gone?" Levi stuttered sadly. Shirley reached over and put her arms around her man's shoulders. As big as he was, he seemed to shrink in that moment.

"No, no!" Lou cried out as real tears ran down his face. He dropped his head on the table, muttering, "Momma can't be gone. Not like this. Not like this."

LC

8

"My condolences. . . . Sorry for your loss. . . . She was a good woman." The words pouring in from people at the service did little to comfort me.

I hadn't really been in favor of a big funeral, but Larry, a man of few words, had insisted and actually came out his cheap-ass pockets and paid for it. It seemed like half of Waycross was at Momma's funeral, which was a good thing, except for the fact that I knew one of them was probably the son-of-a-bitch who had thrown her into the swamp to be eaten by the gators.

"Your momma would have appreciated this," Shirley told Larry, placing a hand on his shoulder. He'd been sitting in a chair in the corner during the entire repast, sniffling back tears. I'd known that man all my life, but I'd never seem him cry like he did at that funeral. Seeing my brothers so emotional broke my heart, but I still couldn't bring myself to cry. The fact that we were even having a funeral seemed surreal to me. I mean, how could she be dead? She'd just come home to us.

"Yeah, well, she's home now," Chippy added. We had all gathered back at the farm after the funeral. The kids were outside playing with Levi, while everyone else was sitting in the living room. The mood was still somber. "Now she can finally rest."

"What if she ain't dead? What if that ain't her body the police gave us?" Lou said to no one in particular.

"What the fuck is wrong with you?" Larry snapped.

"Lou, that was totally uncalled for." Chippy frowned. "Even for you."

Lou persisted. "I'm just saying. What if she's still alive? What if the cops are wrong?"

"Man, give it a rest," Larry said angirily.

"Come on, Larry. You of all people know how these crackers can be." There was no backing down in his voice.

"Lou, don't." I sat up in my chair, shaking my head. "She's gone, man."

"But what if she isn't?" Lou sounded like he was pleading with me to make his wish reality.

The more Lou tried to rationalize the possibility of her being alive, the crazier he sounded, and the more angry I became. Here I was, trying to accept that she was gone, and he just wouldn't shut the fuck up with his conspiracy theories. Coming to terms with her death would be hard enough, and he was making it harder not just for me, but for everyone else. I had hoped that her memorial service would give all of us some closure, but here he was reopening the wound with his stupid false hope.

"Will you just shut the fuck up? She's dead! We just buried what was left of her!" Tears were streaming down my face as I stood up and started pacing to release some pent-up energy.

"I'm just saying, what if—"

And that's when I lost it. It was too much for me to handle any longer. I threw my glass of whiskey across the room and watched it smash against the wall; then I headed into the kitchen and flipped over the table. It was as if the entire world went black as I grabbed whatever I could find and demolished it. I wanted to destroy anything I could get my hands on, the same way my world had been destroyed when my mother went missing.

CRASH!

The sound was so loud that it caused the entire house to shake, and I blinked, suddenly realizing where I was. I looked over to see my family standing in the doorway and the refrigerator overturned. No one moved. They all stood there, staring at the damage I had caused. In addition to the flipped fridge, there were broken dishes, silverware, and pots and pans everywhere. I had destroyed the kitchen, but I had barely any recollection of doing it. My shirt had come undone, and my face was soaked with sweat and tears.

I felt Chippy's hand on my arm. "Baby, listen . . ."

"No, that's the problem. I'm tired of listening to this bullshit he keeps saying." I brushed her away and walked past her into the living room. "Momma is gone. We buried her and laid her to rest today. Now, everyone leave it fucking be."

"I can't and I won't. Not until I find out the truth for myself. We ain't even have a body. Just an arm, thanks to you and the mighty State Police." Lou's voice was louder and more aggressive now as he came to stand right in front of me. He was pushing it and he knew it.

"Fuck you, Lou!" I took a step back to keep myself from punching him in the face the way I wanted to.

"No, fuck you. And fuck you too for all your support, Larry!" He whirled around to face Larry. "You claim you love her so much. Why the big rush? We shoulda waited to bury her, but you wanted to have a service. You wanted closure."

"You questioning my love for Momma?" Larry asked as he puffed out his chest and stepped toward Lou.

"I'm questioning everyone." He looked around the room. "Seems like we all gave up pretty damn easy."

"I think everyone needs to calm down. This has been a long, hard day," Nee Nee said with a sigh as she went to pull Larry away from Lou. Larry shrugged her off.

"Y'all need to relax. None of you are thinking straight." Shirley stepped in between us.

"I'm thinking fine. Shit, I'm thinking this thing out clearer than everybody else. LC, you're supposed to be the brains of the damn family, remember, but it's like the cops showed up and all of a sudden y'all were ready to believe whatever fucking story they gave you. Shit, you already know your cops can be bought and paid for, so who's to say they ain't been paid by someone else this time? I'm telling you, I'm right about this." Lou pushed his way past Larry.

I was becoming more agitated by the minute, and I wasn't alone. The more he talked, the tighter the room became. Anger, sorrow, frustration—my emotions were all over the place, jut like my thoughts.

"She's dead, Lou!" I shouted, desperate for a way to shut him the hell up.

"Y'all can say whatever you want, but I'm never gonna believe Momma's dead," he shot back. "Do you hear me? Never!"

"Do you hear yourself?" I grabbed an ashtray and threw it against the wall.

"Calm down, LC. You're upsetting your wife," Larry warned me.

I glanced over my shoulder. "Oh, shit. Chippy, are you okay?"

She was inhaling and exhaling very slowly and deliberately, with a proteective hand placed over her big belly. "I'm okay."

"Go get her some water!" Shirley commanded me, and I quickly headed to the kitchen, stepping over the mess I'd made in search of a glass I hadn't broken.

I heard Larry speaking. "Damn, I didn't expect this type of drama. I just wanted to give Momma a nice send-off."

Nee Nee chimed in. "Having the memorial was the right thing to do so Miss Bettie could rest in peace, right beside her husband. All y'all's parents are finally together."

"Unh-uh. Believe what you want, but I know what I feel, and my momma is still alive." Lou's stubborn ass just would not give it up.

"I'm done," I said, coming back into the living room without even getting the water.

"I know, baby." Chippy came face to face with me, using the sleeve of her dress to wipe my face.

"No, I'm done. There's nothing else to talk about. We're leaving." I took my wife's hand and headed for the door.

"Look, LC, I'll shut up," Lou said, finally willing to change the subject. "We haven't finished discussing all the business—"

"Fuck whatever other business you wanna discuss. I'm done, and we're leaving for good."

"What's that supposed to mean?" Larry asked.

I stared into my wife's eyes as I made my announcement. "I love you guys, but I'm done with Waycross. There's nothing left here for me now that Momma's gone. Y'all always knew I planned on leaving one day. So me and mine, we're moving to Atlanta."

Donna

9

To say that I was tired and hungry was an understatement. I had been working double shifts for the past week and a half and just picked up another shift on my day off. Although I was exhausted, I enjoyed working. Not only did I make decent tips, but it kept me busy and kept my mind off the past and what could have been. Don't get me wrong; I took my responsibility for my fuck-ups, but there were times when I was home alone in my apartment that I found myself wondering what the hell had happened to me? 'Cause this damn sure was not the life I had planned.

I had grown up privileged, the daughter of the most successful black physician in Ware County. My parents made sure I wanted for nothing. I had every material possession a girl could ever ask for, and a healthy dose of self-confidence to go along with it. The one thing their money couldn't buy, I went out and got on my own. LC Duncan was the man every woman on campus wanted, and within a week of being formally introduced, he was mine. Well, at last until my world started spiraling out of control.

It all started when my daddy was federally indicted for Medicaid fraud. Our family was shamed, and Daddy skipped the country, but at least I still had LC. He was a college boy with a lot of ambition, and I knew that eventually he would make something of himself and take care of me in the way I was accustomed to. That security didn't last long, though, because LC became infatuated with a real life whore named Chippy. His family had always been from "that side" of the tracks, and although he was such a nice boy when I met him, I guess he couldn't resist the temptation but for so long. When I figured out he was slipping away from me, I fought like hell to hold onto him. In the end, I lost the fight and she won. LC left me standing at the altar. I was devastated, crushed, all of those things you would imagine a jilted bride to be, but most of all, I was embarrassed. I pretty much walked out of the church and roamed the Southeast until I hit the bottom.

I finally got my shit together about six months ago. I found my mom, who was living in a one-bedroom apartment in Brunswick. She let me move in, and I found the job at the Waffle House a few days later.

The more I worked, the less I thought about what happened, what could've been, or what should've been. And it had been working fine until Lou showed up. Seeing him reminded me of LC and brought up some unresolved emotions that I wasn't ready to deal with.

Since then, I'd hardly slept, and when I finally did drift off, I'd have nightmares and wake up covered in sweat. Tonight, though, I was determined to get some much-needed rest, so I bought a bottle of wine, which I planned on finishing. My mom was back in Waycross visiting with some relatives, so it was going to be me and my bottle.

I was halfway through my second glass when the phone rang. I let it ring several times, hoping whoever it was would get the message and stop calling. Unfortunately, they seemed to be just as determined to talk to me as I was to ignore them. Every time it would stop ringing, it would start right up again, so I finally answered.

"Hello," I mumbled, not even trying to conceal the attitude I had.

"Got damn, what the fuck took you so long to answer the phone? You must have a nigga up in there!" a gruff male voice shouted. Clearly whoever it was had the wrong number, so I hung the phone up without responding.

The phone began ringing again. Just like the first time, I let it continue ringing until I couldn't take it anymore. Then I answered with even more attitude than the first time.

"Hello!" I yelled.

"Got dammit, Donna! You hang this phone up on me one more time—" The voice was still demanding but less gruff this time, which gave me a chance to recognize who it was.

"Lou?" I squeaked.

"You was expecting maybe the boogieman? Yeah, it's me," he replied.

"Why the hell you calling my phone acting like some crazy man? What the hell is wrong with you?" I asked.

"I told you I was gonna call you when I came back through Brunswick. Well, dammit, I'm here."

I knew I had given him my number, and I knew that was what he said, but I truly hadn't expected him to call. "Okay, so what do you want?"

"We need to talk," he said. "Meet me at the Waffle House in twenty minutes."

"No!" I snapped into the phone. "I'm not going to meet you at my job."

"Girl, I'm hungry and you playing. Now, unless you want me to show up in the middle of one of your shifts, then—"

"Okay, listen. There's a new seafood place called Red Lobster off Ninety-five. I'll be there in a half hour."

Forty minutes later, I pulled into the parking lot of Red Lobster. Lou was already there; I could tell by the baby blue Cadillac parked in front. I looked into my rearview mirror and checked my hair, dabbing on a bit of lipstick. The fact that I had showered, put on the only decent dress I owned, and even dabbed some perfume made it seem more like I was going on a date than having a sit-down with a man I loathed—who also happened to be the brother of the man I loved once upon a time. But I did not want him going back to LC and Chippy telling him I was looking raggedy.

"About damn time you showed up." Lou greeted me in his usual tactless way when I arrived. He was seated at a booth and nursing a half-full glass of what looked like Johnnie Walker.

"I see you didn't leave," I said, easing into the seat across from him.

He responded by glaring at me.

"Hello. What can I get you to drink?" The waitress smiled and put an oversized glossy menu in front of me.

"I'll have a glass of red wine, please. Also, can I have a shrimp cocktail to start, along with a Caesar salad, extra dressing on the side? Oh, and I'll have the biggest lobster you have for my meal, with broccoli and a baked potato with sour cream and butter." I smiled contentedly.

The waitress looked over at Lou for confirmation because that was no small meal I had just ordered. I knew he wanted to object and cuss me out, but to my surprise, he didn't.

"And what about you, sir?"

"I'll have some shrimps and some fries, and bring me another one of these." He lifted his glass.

"Yes, sir, right away." She nodded and hurried away.

Lou shook his head and frowned at me. "What the hell, Donna?"

"What? You asked me to dinner. Said you was hungry. Am I not supposed to eat?"

"Eating is one thing; ordering shit like you 'bout to give a nigga some drawers is another."

I leaned over and gave him a seductive smile, making sure he had a great view of my breasts. "You want some drawers, Lou?"

The expression on Lou's face quickly changed from irritation to surprise as his eyes traveled to my bosom. "Hell yeah, I want some drawers!" I watched him swallow hard, like a nervous little boy.

"Then carry your ass to JC Penney and buy some!" I laughed, twisting my head as I sat back and closed the top of my dress.

"Aw, damn, that's fucked up."

"So is the fact that you actually thought I would give you some. I may have fallen off, Lou, but I'm not desperate."

"No, you're destitute." He laughed at his own cruel reply.

"Fuck you." I gave him the finger. "What the hell do you want, anyway?"

"A couple things." He sat up in his chair as if to signal that it was time to be serious. "I want to make sure you understand that you need to stay away from my brother and his family."

"Why would you think I wouldn't? Because I saw you?"

Lou sat back and looked at me. There was something solemn about his demeanor. "No, because you asked about him.

I could see in your eyes you still love him, despite everything that's happened."

I had told myself I wasn't going to cry, but it was suddenly getting hard to hold back the tears. "Is it that obvious?"

"It's written all over your face," he said with more tenderness than I knew he was capable of. He handed me a handkerchief to wipe away my tears. "But this is not a road you want to travel."

"I'm not trying to bother him, Lou, but I do want to know how he's doing. I have a right to know, don't I?"

He stared at me for a second, looking almost sympathetic, then he shook his head and said, "I'm just trying to avoid World War III and a lot of people getting hurt."

"Why are you really here?" I asked. "You could have warned me over the phone. And I know you didn't really think you had a shot at having sex with me just because you're buying me dinner."

"It's customary when a woman eats like you, but you don't have to worry. You may have big titties, but I like my woman with some meat on her bones. Skinny bitch like you, I'm sure I'd break your ass in half." He was laughing, and I felt insulted. I hated when people joked about my flat ass. It was the only part of my body I was insecure about. "Maybe you should order a couple of cheeseburgers with that lobster."

"Finished with the jokes?" I asked angrily. "Now, can you tell me why the hell I'm here?"

He calmed his giggling ass down and went back to being serious. "I need a favor."

I sat back, surprised. "What kind of favor?"

"You heard about my momma?"

"Yeah. My condolences," I said sadly. I'd never met Bettie Duncan, but from all the stories LC told me about his childhood, she must have been a nice woman. I'd read in the newspaper that after being in prison almost thirteen years, she had been released only to be found in the swamp half eaten by alligators. That was the official story, at least, but the word through the grapevine was that the family of the white man she killed had snatched her and threw her in the swamp to be eaten.

"I don't need your fucking condolences," he snapped. "My momma ain't dead. At least I don't think she is."

"Oh my God, I'm so sorry. I read in the papers—"

"Stop believing everything you read in the papers. Isn't that what you told us when they was saying all that shit about your precious pappy?"

I nodded my understanding. They'd said a lot of shit about my father, some of it true, but most of it was half-truths and outright lies—especially the part about him leaving me and my momma half a million dollars cash in a suitcase. He didn't leave us shit!

"Fair enough," I said, "but what does this have do with you needing a favor?"

"You know that paranoid nigga Eddie that was in the diner the other day with me?"

"Not really." I shrugged.

"Well, he knows you. He told me he's come by every day since and leaves you a dollar tip with his phone number on it."

I remembered who he was talking about. "Oh, yeah. He comes through on the regular now. Mr. Grits-with-one-slice-of-cheese. I got one of his dollar bills in my pocket right now. He's a little strange."

"A little? No, he's a lot strange, but he has something I need, and I need you to get it for me."

"How am I gonna get it from him? I don't even know the man."

"Maybe not, but he wants to fuck you."

I scrunched up my nose at the thought. "Well, I am the best-looking waitress in the place. A lot of men who come through that place want to fuck me. It's part of the job. But a dollar tip ain't gonna get them more than a smile and a thank you, that's for sure."

"What's five hundred dollars gonna get him?"

"Did you say five hundred dollars?" Truth be told, I was broke, and that was almost a month's salary at the Waffle House. The thought was intriguing, but the messenger was not. I sat back and crossed my arms over my chest. "I'm not one of your whores, Lou. I don't work at Big Sam's, or Big Shirley's, or whatever you call it these days. I'm not fucking your friend for five hundred dollars."

"I didn't say I wanted you to fuck him, but that would be the most logical way to gain his confidence. That little shit took my money and was supposed to find out who took my momma. Now all of a sudden he's hearing the same shit that's in the news and won't take my calls. He knows something. I can smell it."

"Maybe he just hasn't heard anything," I suggested.

"You don't know Eddie. He has a knack for finding shit out. If he really didn't hear anything, he would have at least made it sound like he did, but he was just outright ignoring me until I confronted him this afternoon. I should have never let him slip away."

"So what did he tell you?"

"He didn't tell me jack, just some basic shit that the cops had already told us. But I could tell he knew more than he was saying when he returned my money. Eddie don't give refunds."

"So why not strongarm him in that typical Duncan way?" I asked.

"Why does everyone keep acting like all we do is go around beating people up? That's not our way."

I stifled a laugh at his obvious lie. "Tell it to somebody who doesn't know, Lou. I've seen you and your brothers' work firsthand, remember? But if you don't want to do that, then why don't you just use one of your whores?"

He gave me a dismissive look. "He'd spot a whore a mile away, and you can't strongarm a guy like Eddie. People have tried. He'd rather die. The way to his mind is through his dick." He leaned in close and let his eyes travel to my chest again. "He seems to like you a lot."

"I'm not going to fuck him," I said just as the waitress returned with our food and placed it on the table. Her tense body language told me she'd heard what I said. Before she could open her mouth to ask if we needed anything else, Lou dismissed her.

When we were alone again, he leaned over the table looking more vulnerable than I ever would have thought he could be. "Donna, I really need your help. This is my momma we're talking about."

I couldn't believe it, but I felt myself sympathizing with this man who'd given me nothing but grief over the years. Besides, it wasn't just his momma we were talking about. She was LC's momma too.

"All right, I'll see what I can do to get the information, but I'm still not fucking him."

That wasn't good enough for Lou. "You gotta fuck him or he won't tell you shit."

I chuckled. "I don't have to fuck him to get what I want. Ask your brother. Not fucking him is going to get us what we want way faster than if I give him some—which I'm not. "

There was an eternity of silence during which Lou didn't move.

"Your food is getting cold," I finally said.

"I need that information, and I don't think you realize who you're dealing with," he said as he picked up his fork.

"Yes, I do. I'm a woman. I know how to get what I want out of men," I said. I wasn't bragging; just stating facts. Until Chippy came along, I'd never failed at getting what I wanted. "But, Lou, if I do this, if I help you, you have to help me too."

"Name your price," he said, mistakenly thinking I meant money.

"I want to see him."

Nee Nee

10

"So, what do you think?" Shirley asked me. She was walking around like a peacock.

I looked around the large open space, full of dust and dirt. The peeling paint on the walls, the cracked floors, and broken windows didn't exactly give me a reason to be too excited. The building, located diagonally across from Big Shirley's, had been sitting vacant for a few years. How she had gotten the key was just as much a mystery to me as the reason she had brought me there. But I had learned long ago that when it came to Duncan business, the fewer questions you asked, the better.

Technically, Shirley wasn't a Duncan because they weren't legally married. She had been Levi's woman for years now, however, and truth is, if she'd wanted him to marry her, he'd do it in a minute. He wasn't going anywhere, and neither was she.

"Umm, I guess it's okay," I told her, turning around and slowly taking it all in. To be perfectly honest, the place was a damn dump. I just didn't want to bad mouth it because of how excited Shirley seemed to be. She probably had grand plans to do something with it, or at least attempt to.

"But can I ask one question?"

"Sure, ask away," she answered.

"What exactly is it supposed to be?" I guess I couldn't judge until I knew what she planned to do with the place.

"Girl, it's your new restaurant!" Shirley announced with excitement.

"My new restaurant? What are you talking about?"

"I know it ain't really that big, but think about it. We can put some tables and chairs in here and make a small dining area. We can knock out this wall over here and put a small counter with a couple of stools and a takeout window. And come back here." She grabbed my hand and pulled me through a small doorway, into a kitchen that was surprisingly larger than I had expected. "This is your kitchen. And this back room can be a storage area."

"Shirley, I never said I wanted to open a restaurant," I said, totally confused by this whole situation.

"Sure you have."

Well, technically I had, but that was mostly talk. The truth was, I had never seriously considered it. The fact that I could cook was no secret. I was by far the best cook in Waycross. People told me that all the time. Cooking was my passion, the only thing that I loved almost as much as Larry and my son Curtis. Providing sandwiches for LC's customers at the station and cooking for First Fridays was something that made me happy, but that was as far as my dreams went.

"Nee Nee, you been cooking for Larry, LC, and the boys for long enough. It's time to take your gift to the next level. I was gonna tell you after the service the other night, but after LC made his big announcement, I ain't never got a chance."

"I appreciate what you was thinking, but I don't know. I'd have to talk to Larry about it. Restaurants cost money to open," I said.

She waved off my concern. "Talk to Larry about what? Don't worry about Larry. I got some money saved up. I'll be your partner. Don't you wanna be your own boss?" She swept her arm in the air, gesturing as if there was a big sign on the wall. "Nee Nee's Soul Food Cafe."

"That does sound good, Shirley, but I still gotta talk to Larry."

Shirley kept pushing. "I thought you were your own woman. You can't make a decision without Larry?"

"Yes, but I still have to go home and lay in that bed with him." This was something Shirley wouldn't necessarily understand because in her relationship, she made just about all the decisions for her and sweet, simple Levi. "Besides, what about Atlanta?"

Shirley rolled her eyes. "What about it?"

"I don't know. With LC and Chippy moving to Atlanta, maybe we should too," I suggested.

She had been standing there along with everyone else when LC and Lou almost had it out over their momma's death. LC's announcement about Atlanta had taken us all by surprise, but since then, Larry had been helping LC put things in motion.

"There's a lot of opportunity up there. Larry thinks it could be good for all of us," I explained. "He's talking about splitting time between Waycross and Atlanta until LC gets things settled."

"Unh-uh. I ain't going nowhere, and neither is Levi."

Shirley put her hands on her hips and shook her head. She was pretty for her age, once you looked past the scars on her face. I had a lot of respect for the woman who had started out being one of the original ladies of Big Sam's and now ran the place.

"Going to Atlanta makes no sense to me. We're doing fine right here in Waycross. We're already set up, making plenty of money. Folks know who we are and what we're capable of. The Duncan name is powerful here. Why the hell should we leave all this to go somewhere and start all over? For years, I worked and helped to make Big Sam's place what it is. Now I'm running it. Ain't nothing in Atlanta for me or Levi. And if you know like I know, you'd stay here and make something of what you've built here," she said.

I considered her words. On one hand, what she was saying was downright inspiring. I knew that as crazy as it sounded, if I did put a little blood, sweat, and tears—along with a lot of TLC—into the raggedy place we were standing in, it could be a success. On the other hand, I knew that there was no way in hell that Larry would allow me to stay here if he decided to make a move. And the thought of my man being in Atlanta without me and my son didn't appeal to me either. I trusted my man, but I didn't know how much I trusted those big city women.

"I don't know. I think they're planning for all of us to go," I told her.

"Listen to me. I've got my business, I got my man, and now I got my baby. My black ass ain't going nowhere!" She placed a hand on her belly.

It took a few seconds for me to comprehend what she had just said. When it hit me, I let out a squeal. "Your baby?"

"Yes, that's right, girl. I'm pregnant!" Her face beamed with pride, and she rubbed her stomach, which didn't seem any bigger than usual.

I couldn't believe it. It was no secret that Shirley and Levi were having sex. After all, that was her man. But the fact that they were about to have a child together was downright . . . surprising, for lack of a better term.

"Well, um, congrats." I finally found the words I was looking for. I reached over and gave her a hug. I really was happy for her.

"Thanks. So, you see, I'm not leaving everything I worked hard for here just to chase some grand delusion LC has up there in Atlanta, and neither should you."

"But they're our family, Shirley. You, Levi, and the baby; me, Larry, and Curtis; Chippy, LC, Junior, and their soon-to-be new baby. And let's not forget Lou. We're all family. We're the Duncan clan. Nobody fucks with our family, and nothing should separate us."

"Really? We're all family, huh? The Duncan clan!" She let out a hearty laugh. "So, how come Larry hasn't given you his last name like LC did for Chippy?" She was starting to make me angry, but she didn't notice the expression on my face, so she just continued right on needling me. "You ain't a Duncan, and neither am I, but at least mine's by choice. So, let's be honest. We call each other whatever we want"—she patted her belly gently—"but we're not really family."

LC

11

"Mr. Peterson, please," I said into the phone as I stared out my office window at an empty lot. I had decided not to give my name this time in hopes that it would get the owner of the trucking company to answer the phone.

It took a moment, but my prayers were finally answered when I heard his gruff Southern accent. "Don Peterson."

"Mr. Peterson, this is LC Duncan, from Duncan Motors." There was silence on the line for a second, and I worried he might hang up. "Mr. Peterson?"

He sighed. "Yes, Mr. Duncan, how can I help you?"

"You can start by telling me when I'm going to receive my cars. The manufacturer says they're still at their facility." I got up from my seat and began to pace the obstacle course of half-open boxes that were scattered around my office.

"That is absolutely correct, Mr. Duncan, but we plan on getting those cars to you as quickly as humanly possible."

"And how long would that take?"

"Give or take a day or two, probably about three weeks."

"That's unacceptable," I growled into the phone. "I have a grand opening in two weeks."

"Well, you might want to push that back." I could almost hear this motherfucker snickering under his breath.

"I don't understand. I've done my research. You're the biggest car carrier company in the South. You have more trucks hauling cars outta Detroit into this region than anyone in the country. It only takes two days to drive from Michigan to Atlanta. Why is it going to take me three weeks to get my cars?"

"Well, Mr. Duncan, unfortunately, that's how long it takes. I apologize for any inconvenience." That was definitely not the answer I wanted to hear.

"This is some bull. I bet this wouldn't be a problem if I was white," I said angrily. If he was going to jerk me around like this, then why the hell should I bother to be polite?

"Mr. Duncan, I know you're anxious, but you're new to this, so I'm not going to take exception to your words. Of course, if you don't like our service, we can issue you a refund, and you can try one of our competitors." He sounded smug, like he knew damn well I wasn't going to cancel the contract.

"Well, I just might do that!" I hung up the phone in frustration, feeling overwhelmed. As much as I didn't want to have to do it, my next move would most likely be to call Mr. Mahogany for help. I seemed to be doing that on a regular basis, and I didn't like it one bit. He was so damn calm under pressure and always seemed to have the answer, and it was sickening.

I'd left Chippy and Junior back in Waycross while I looked for a house and tried to get the dealership off the ground up here in Atlanta. Things were moving forward thanks to Mr. Mahogany, but I missed the days when Lou, Larry, and I would just sit around and talk things through until we came up with our own answers, right or wrong. Talking to Mr. Mahogany made me feel like he was calling all the shots, and this wasn't even his business.

I hated to do it, but I needed those cars, so I reached for the phone to call him. That was when I heard a *tap tap tap* on the glass in my office door. I looked up and burst into a smile.

"Larry! What are you doing here, man?" Then I panicked for a moment. "Shit, everything all right at home?"

"Everything's fine. You said I had an open invitation, so I figured I'd drive up and see what all the fuss is about in Atlanta." He bopped into my office, and we embraced. "I know it's only been two weeks, but I miss you, little brother."

"I ain't gonna lie, I miss you too. How are things back home?"

"Things are good. Title company's doing well, and so is the service station," he replied, taking a seat in front of my desk. "There's a few people still bitching about you being gone. Say they only let you work on their cars. But they'll get over it, or their shit will be sitting on the side of the road," he said with a laugh.

I smiled. It was nice to know that some people really appreciated the work I did on their cars. "What about Lou, Levi, Shirley, and Nee? How they doing?"

"Levi is Levi. Nee and Shirley are fine, and well, Lou is still searching for Momma's killers."

"He find anything?"

"He keeps saying he's close." Larry shook his head. "I'll say this much: I've never seen him this passionate about anything in his life."

"Maybe he's right," I replied. Larry lifted his head and stared at me, frowning. "Not about Momma being dead," I explained, "but about finding her killers. Maybe we should be out there looking for them."

"LC, I'm never gonna stop looking for them, but I got a hardheaded little boy I got to raise. If I become obsessed with trying to find Momma's killers, I'm gonna have to become the old Larry, and then I'm gonna lose him. I can't lose him." His face said everything I needed to know. As a father, I understood where his priorities had to lie.

"It's always something, isn't it?" I said, letting him know I didn't fault him for his decision.

"Tell me about it." He laughed, and we let that conversation drop.

Larry looked around my office for a minute, surveying the mess, and said, "I'll be honest with you, little brother. When you first said you was coming to Atlanta to open a full-fledged dealership, I thought you was full of shit. But I can see you're on your way to making it happen."

"Well, as much as I hate to admit it, I couldn't have done it without Mr. Mahogany. He vouched for me with the banks on the business and the real estate loan," I replied, giving my new mentor his props. I really wanted to tell Larry about the Council, but I couldn't risk losing everything that I was putting in place by pissing off Mr. Mahogany now. Besides, I hadn't even been to my first meeting yet.

"Yeah, he's sure taken a liking to you." Larry kind of half-smirked. "I just hope he kisses you first."

"What the hell is that supposed to mean?"

"It means I hope to God he kisses you before he fucks you, 'cause don't no man hook another man up with a business like this without ulterior motives. He's up to something, I can feel it in my bones."

"Larry, you're wrong about him."

"Am I? Then give me a good reason why he's doing all this for you? From what I hear, he don't even treat his own sons this well." Larry sat back in his chair, smug.

I hated feeling challenged by my brother like this. He might have been older, but I was the one who went to college, so I didn't appreciate him trying to make me feel stupid.

"Have you ever heard of something called the Council?" I blurted out.

"The what?"

I wished like hell that I could take back the words, but it was too late. The best I could do was distract him by giving him another tidbit of information. "Listen, Larry, you're right. He does get something out of it. He silently owns thirty percent."

"I knew it!" Larry shouted confidently. "You should have only given him twenty percent."

I didn't even care that he was trying to lecture me about my choices, as long as he forgot I'd brought up the Council.

"But I guess thirty's not bad, considering he's a silent partner," Larry finished. To my surprise, he seemed to be okay with me taking on Mr. Mahogany as a business partner. Then he took it one step further by giving me a great compliment. "You doing really good, LC. I'm proud of you. Seems like you got everything under control."

I shook my head. "I wish you were right. I got everything but the fucking cars."

Larry raised an eyebrow, looking around again. "I wasn't even thinking about that. I just figured the cars were on their way. What's going on, LC?"

"Nothing. I was just thinking out loud," I said, trying to dial it back. I usually liked to talk things through with them, but I didn't want my brothers thinking I had bitten off more than

I could chew with this dealership situation, especially after leaving Waycross the way I had.

"Don't fucking lie to me," Larry said. "I've known you longer than you've known your damn self. I know when something is wrong. Now, tell me what it is." He spoke to me like I was a boy and not a grown man. Had it been anyone other than him, I would have addressed his tone, but I knew that my brother didn't mean anything by it. This was his way of showing concern.

"Why don't you have any cars?" he asked when he got tired of waiting for my response. I had to tell him because he wasn't going to stop asking questions until I did.

"Man, it's minor, really. I've been waiting on a shipment from Detroit."

"So, what's going on? You running outta cash? You know you can't go to Mahogany 'cause he's just gonna want a bigger percentage."

"It's not the money. The cars are paid for and waiting for transport. It's the shipping company. A bunch of good ol' boys who keep giving me the runaround about shipping them, that's all. I've been waiting damn near two weeks, and they haven't shipped one car. They're talking about another two or three weeks 'til they arrive."

"That's some bullshit! What are they saying?" Larry snapped.

"It's just one excuse after another. You know how these good ol' boys do. Everything was cool until they found out we were a black-owned company. But I'm gonna call Mr. Mahogany. He'll get it strai—"

"Why the fuck you gotta call him?" Larry yelled.

"Because he has a way of getting around red tape when it comes to situations like this and—"

"Fuck that. We'll go get the cars ourselves." Larry said it as if picking up forty cars and bringing them halfway across the country was as easy as going to the store and buying a loaf of bread.

I shook my head. "You crazy as hell. We have two tow trucks, one of which is in Waycross and probably wouldn't even make it to Atlanta if we tried to drive it that far. We don't have a way of going to get 'em."

"So let's buy a rig and trailer big enough to haul them. Isn't that how they were gonna get them here? On one of those trailers?" he asked.

"Yeah, but—"

"But what? I got a CDL, so I can drive. Since when have we ever relied on a white man to do anything for us? I'll buy one of those and go get them bitches myself. Hell, why pay them when you can pay me, Duncan Trucking? I can go pick up cars from all over the damn country." His eyes lit up. He always got this way when he was formulating a plan that he knew could make him money. I liked seeing it because Larry was a serious dude who rarely showed excitement for anything.

"You're serious?" I asked.

"Since Momma died, I've been looking for a purpose, LC. I think maybe I found it. I like driving trucks, and I like working with you and Lou. This might be the best of both worlds."

I loved the idea of my brother being around, but even if I didn't, his mind was made up. I just prayed he didn't go nosing around and end up causing problems between me and Mahogany and the Council.

Donna

12

Seventeen whole dollars. That was my tip total so far, and I only had fifteen minutes left on my shift. I folded the crinkled bills and put them back into the front pocket of my apron, trying not to be mad. Stepping out from the restroom, I scanned the dining area. My table section was still filled with the same customers, but I noticed a familiar face sitting near the front where Izzy was assigned.

"Girl, I need you to let me get that table." I walked over to Izzy, who was behind the counter, and tipped my head in the direction of the table where Eddie was sitting, looking uneasy. I was relieved to see him, because he hadn't been around in almost a week. I was determined to get the information Lou wanted so I could get paid, but I couldn't exactly do that if the guy never came around. Lately I'd been feeling desperate enough that I considered picking up the phone to call Eddie—not exactly the best way to play hard to get.

"Why?" Izzy asked. "He some type of big spender? 'Cause, girl, I need every tipping customer I can get. My rent's due Friday."

"Come on, please. It's personal," I begged, raising my eyebrows suggestively a few times.

She looked over at Eddie and turned back to me with a horrified look. I didn't care if she believed I was interested in fucking him. In fact, I was so desperate for my payday from Lou that I reached into my apron and pulled out five precious dollars from my day's stash.

"Here," I said, handing the money to her. "This should cover the tip he would have given you. Just let me have him."

She snatched the five out of my hand with a smirk. "Fine. But you need to get out more, 'cause your standard in men has seriously declined."

"Thanks." I strategically adjusted my uniform while she stared at me like I was nuts. "What? Can't catch fish if you don't have bait," I said.

She shook her head and handed me the coffee pot. I headed over to Eddie's table.

"Here you go, stranger." I gave him a broad smile as I filled the coffee cup on his table. I could almost see his transformation from skittish loner to self-imagined Casanova when he realized it was me.

"I was starting to think you'd forgotten about us, Mr. Eddie," I said flirtatiously.

"I could never forget about you, Donna. I was just caught up with work."

"You gonna have the usual grits and cheese, or you want something else?"

"Come on, now. You already know what I want," he said boldly, giving me a not-so-innocent look.

I shook my head. "You're cute, but that's not on the menu."

"That's too bad, because I'd pay whatever it took to have a taste of that." He laughed, and I forced myself to chuckle as he grabbed at my waist. I didn't pull away. Not at first, anyway.

"Let me take you out and show you a good time," he said.

The thought of being with him was about as inviting as kissing Old Fred, the fifteen-foot alligator they advertised over at Gator World, but I had to do this in order to get what Lou needed. If Lou got what he needed, then I would get what I wanted.

"Mr. Eddie, you need to stop playing so much," I said, trying to sound playful as I pulled out of his grasp.

"Call me Eddie. And I'm not playing, Donna." He reached for me again.

"Seriously, Mr. Eddie, you're gonna get me fired. They don't like us fraternizing with customers. That's a no-no. I need this job. I can't afford to get fired." I slapped his hand.

"Fuck this job. You need money? I got enough money to take care of you." He gave a very confident smile. "Let me prove it to you."

I shook my head and lost the playful tone from my voice. "Don't let the uniform fool you. I may work as a waitress, but I'm not a cheap date. I'm very high maintenance."

"Oh, I know." He sat back in his chair with an amazing aura of confidence I'd never seen before. "I know all about you, Donna Williams. I know about your rich doctor daddy who's on the run. I know about how you were left at the altar by LC Duncan." There was cruelty behind his words, but a hint of joy in his eyes. He was clearly enjoying this as he went for my most vulnerable spots. The guy was a fucking sadist. As I unraveled inside, he remained calm, continuing with, "I know about that little one-bedroom apartment you and your momma owe two months' back rent on. I even know about your stay down in Jacksonville and up in New York."

I took a step back. To say I was surprised and creeped out would be an understatement. "How do you know about all that?"

"It's what I do. It's my business to know shit." Eddie pulled out a wad of cash and flashed it at me. My eyes got big. It looked like it was all brand-new hundreds. "Now, are you high maintenance enough to help me spend some of this?"

"Where the hell did you get all that money?" I glanced around to make sure no one was looking.

"You didn't answer my question." He fanned himself with the money. I wasn't quite sure what the question was any- more, but I gave him an answer.

"Yes." I sighed. "I'll go on one date with you. Now, put that money away before someone sees it and you get robbed."

"That's all I need." Eddie grinned as he tucked the money back in his pocket. "Ain't you 'bout to get off? Come on. We can go right now."

I shook my head. "No, fool! We can't go right now."

"Why not?"

"Because I just told you my boss don't like us dating customers. And you need to plan this thing out right. It's one thing to talk about taking care of a woman properly; it's another thing to do it. You will only get one chance to make a first impression. You want a second date, don't screw up the first one." I took out my notepad and wrote my number on it. "Here's my number. Call me later on tonight and we can make plans. I've got a few nice ideas. And you might want to leave a nice tip. A girl's gonna need to get a proper dress if a man's gonna spoil her."

Eddie took the slip of paper from me and slid it into his front pocket then stood up. "I'll call you later, sexy."

"Wait. Where are you going? You didn't even order any food."

Eddie took out a hundred-dollar bill and placed it into my hand. "Like I said, what I wanted ain't even on the menu. But I got it anyway."

He walked away, leaving me feeling slightly dirty as I stuffed the hundred in my pocket and wondered how the hell I had let that get so out of control. So much for playing hard to get. I would have to be better prepared when we went out on our date.

Nee Nee

13

"Momma!"

Larry and Curtis were sitting on the front porch playing when I pulled into the driveway after helping LC and Chippy pack for their move to Atlanta. Curtis came running and jumped into my arms the second I stepped out of the car. I gave him a big kiss and carried him toward the porch, where Larry met me with a wet, passionate kiss of his own.

"How'd it go?"

"Well, the truck is all packed and loaded for you and Remy to drive up in the morning. LC has some big meeting with Mr. Mahogany, so he's already on his way back to Atlanta. Chippy and I are going to follow y'all in her car with the boys." I let Curtis down, and Larry and I took seats in the two porch rockers. "I still can't believe they're moving."

"Well, if shit goes as planned, we're not gonna be far behind them. I want you to start looking at houses while you're up there helping Chippy."

"Larry . . ."

"Yeah?"

I took a nervous breath. "What if I don't want to move to Atlanta?"

Larry stopped rocking. "What the hell are you saying, Nee? We been talking about moving up to Atlanta for almost a month now."

"No, you been talking about it. All I been doing is listening. Not once did you ever ask me what I wanted to do. Shit, Larry, you didn't even ask me if I wanted to go."

"Curtis, go play in the yard," Larry snapped.

"Can I get my ball?" Curtis asked.

Larry nodded. When our son ran off, he turned his attention back to me. "What's the problem, Nee? What's wrong?"

"Nothing's wrong. I mean, I'm just trying to understand, that's all. Why exactly are we moving to Atlanta? LC's the one who has the problem with Waycross. Not you or me."

"Because he's my brother and we're family." He said it like that should be the end of the discussion, but I wasn't finished speaking my mind.

"And if we stay here, you'll still be brothers," I said, shifting from one foot to the other. When he didn't answer right away, I started getting a little nervous. Larry could have a short fuse sometimes, and I didn't want to be on the receiving end of his temper at the moment. I eased past him, opened the front door, and walked into the living room. By the time I sat on the sofa and took off my shoes, Larry was standing in front of me. He didn't have that telltale vein in his forehead that usually popped out when he was really upset, so I figured it was safe to keep talking.

"Shirley and I are talking about opening a restaurant together," I said.

"It figures Shirley planted all this in your head." He sat down next to me. "Nee, if you wanted to do all this, your ass shoulda said something before now. We done made all these plans—"

"You've made plans, Larry. And don't act like I didn't mention opening my own restaurant to you. We talked about it."

"So, you wanna stay here." It sounded more like a statement than a question.

The truth was, I didn't know what I wanted to do. On one hand, the thought of moving to Atlanta and living in a new house in the big city excited me. But, I was born and raised in Waycross. It was all I knew. My family was here, and if I stayed, I would be my own boss, doing something I loved to do. For the past month, I had gone back and forth in my mind, oftentimes tossing and turning in bed while trying to decide. I hadn't spoken up whenever Larry mentioned it because he was so excited about this new trucking company, and seeing him smile was something I rarely saw, especially since Miss Bettie was gone.

"I'm saying I want us to talk about it. Together." I reached for his hand, but he pulled away a little.

"Fine, talk," he said.

I could see that Larry had an attitude, but now that I'd spoken up, I was determined not to be intimidated. We had been together long enough for me to know the real Larry. He was used to people jumping when he said jump, and he could fly off the handle every once in a while, but deep down, he was a teddy bear. I just hoped he'd be willing to listen to my side, because I guess I was kind of asking him to choose between me and his brother.

"I know why LC wants to go to Atlanta, but why do you want to? What am I gonna do when we get there?" I began cautiously. "At least here in Waycross we have the service station and the other businesses, and then, hopefully, my own restaurant. We have to look at the big picture. We have a son. This is our home."

"Do you think I would take you anywhere and not make sure you're taken care of?" Larry asked me.

"It's not about that, Larry. I know we'll be taken care of whether we leave or stay. I'm just saying . . . I want something to say about it. I'm not your puppet."

"No, you're my woman." It felt good to hear the words, but there wasn't really any passion behind the words.

"Yes," I said sadly, "I'm your woman, but being your woman doesn't give me the privileges of being your wife."

"Are we back to this marriage shit again?" His entire demeanor changed. He stood up and put some distance between us. "Stay here then, Nee Nee, if that's what you want to do. But I'm asking you to come with us."

"You're asking me to walk away from a lot. Do you even see that?" My eyes were starting to fill with tears, but that didn't earn me any sympathy from him. Matter of fact, he seemed to become even more annoyed.

"What's the problem? Fuck, I coulda easily went without asking you to go with me, but here I am trying to do the right thing, and this is what I get."

I felt anger rising from within, and I snapped at him. "You're damn right. And going without us is still an option. Don't you see that's part of the problem, Larry?"

He exhaled loudly. "This is some bullshit."

"You always talking about family and being together, but is that really what you want? Be honest."

"Of course it's what I want. Do you think I would even be here talking about this if it wasn't what I wanted?"

"What about Curtis and me?"

"What about y'all? Y'all are my family. I love you, Nee Nee." His tone softened a little when he said he loved me, but there was still plenty of tension in the air.

"And I love you too, Larry, but this ain't about that. I need more than love."

Larry gave me a frustrated look and then shook his head. "Here we go with that bullshit again."

"It's not bullshit."

"Nee Nee, you already know how I feel about this whole marriage thing. There is nothing a piece of paper can do to make me love you any more than I do now or ever will. And if you can't see that, then maybe you don't need to move to Atlanta."

There it was. He was giving me an ultimatum, threatening that if I didn't see things his way, I might as well not be with him. Well, I was going to call his bluff this time. I stood up and faced him. "You know what, Larry? You're absolutely right. I don't need to move. Anyway, I would be a damn fool to go running off to Atlanta behind a man who claims to be all about family but refuses to make the mother of his son an honest woman. Ain't no telling what'll happen when you get there."

"Ain't no telling what'll happen when you stay here!" he yelled back at me.

"You better hope I don't meet a man who wants to be a husband and a father to your son."

Before I knew what happened, Larry had yanked me toward him, squeezing my arms so tight that I couldn't move. What I said had been hurtful—I'd meant for them to be—but I didn't expect him to react so violently.

"Don't you ever fucking say that again. And if I hear about my son being around another man, I will kill you. Both of you."

Tears spilled out of my eyes, and he finally loosened his grip. Larry had never put his hands on me. We stared at one another, both breathing heavily and neither one moving. The tension in the air felt like it could smother me.

"Momma, can I have some ice cream?" Curtis yelled as he burst through the front door.

Grateful for the interruption, I shook myself away from Larry and looked down at my son. "Of course you can. Come on, let's go and get both of us some."

He turned and asked Larry, "You want some ice cream, Daddy?"

Larry glanced at me and said, "Naw, son. Daddy ain't in the mood for nothing sweet right now."

As I turned to go into the kitchen, I felt Larry's hand on my shoulder. I twisted my torso to look at him. I could see the apology in his eyes without his saying a word, but I resisted the urge to touch his face, for fear that it would give him the impression that he had won and I was giving in. We rarely, if ever, argued, and this wasn't one that I had planned on having, but now that it was all in the open, I realized that this move to Atlanta wasn't the only decision I had to make in my life.

14

True to his word, Larry had bought two Mack trucks and rented two car-carrying trailers to transport my vehicles from Detroit to Atlanta. They weren't the best-looking trucks I'd ever seen, but they did the job. He'd already made his first pickup and dropped off fourteen cars this morning and then was back on the road to Detroit about ten hours later.

I appreciated what he was doing, but I was glad he was gone, because right after he left, Mr. Mahogany called and said he was coming to pick me up in ten minutes. One thing I could say about this brother was that he had no idea what CP time was, because he was in front of my place exactly ten minutes later. I jumped in his car, and we went for a long drive out to the country. There was a strange tension in the air, and neither of us spoke a word, which was unusual because both of us were pretty chatty individuals.

About forty minutes into the drive, he stopped the car at the entrance to an old plantation and turned to me. "I'm sure you know why I wanted to meet with you tonight. This doesn't need any more explaining, does it?"

"No, I'm pretty sure I know why I'm here and what we are about to do."

"Good. Have you made your decision? Are you ready to continue the legacy of your father and take your rightful place at the table?"

I stared at Mr. Mahogany. Here was a man of wealth and knowledge, a family man who seemed to have worked hard, achieved success, and was enjoying life in a way that Chippy and I aspired to live. My father had been a sharecropper and a loan shark, and now I was sitting across from a man who respected and held him in high regard. I couldn't think of a better mentor to guide me. The answer was simple.

"Yes, I'm ready."

A wide grin spread across Mr. Mahogany's face. He looked like a proud father, and for a split second, I felt like his long-lost son.

"I knew you were a smart man. But understand there is no turning back after this." He continued to drive up the long driveway until we were in front of the house, where he parked next to several other cars. "Follow me."

I stepped out of the car into the darkness to follow him, and for the first time since we'd left the dealership, I could feel myself getting cold feet. My mind raced through fifty different thoughts. Was this all for real? What the hell had I gotten myself into? I froze in place, and he didn't notice until he was halfway up the stairs.

"Breathe, boy. Take a deep breath. You're not the first person to be overwhelmed by this experience."

It was as if he was reading my mind. I sucked in some air, letting it fill my lungs. The oxygen revived me, and I exhaled, doing it again and again until my brain seemed to function normally and take control over my body again.

"You all right? You coming?"

I nodded, following him inside the house and down the hallway into a large room that looked like an old-fashioned study, with shelves full of books on the walls, comfortable antique furniture throughout, along with a very expensive chess table off to the side. Also in the room were seven well-dressed individuals, five men and two women.

"Ah, Mr. Mahogany, I see you have brought out our newest member. Welcome, LC Duncan, welcome," a deep-voiced, older gentleman said as I entered. He was thick, with a face full of well-groomed hair.

"He's much more handsome than his photograph," a very well to do–looking woman in her late forties said as Mr. Mahogany and I took two empty seats by the fireplace. "We are so happy you've decided to join us."

"Thank you," I replied.

"I believe we should start with introductions." Mr. Mahogany stood beside me. "Fred, why don't we start with you?"

"Good evening, Mr. Duncan. My name's Frederick Johnson." He was a dark brown man, like myself, in his late sixties. "My sons and I run Parker Family restaurants since 1959. Right now we have fifty restaurants throughout the Southeast. Matter of fact, we have a restaurant right across from the mall in your hometown of Waycross."

"Yes, I've eaten there several times," I replied. "I just never knew it was black owned."

"Neither does anyone else outside of this room and my family," he answered.

I wanted to say, "Shit, that is fucking ingenious!" but I didn't know the people in the room well enough yet to know how they'd react to my colorful language.

The introductions continued. "LC, I'm Tommy Rawls. I live in Charlotte, and I make funds available for folks in need who aren't able to get money from the banks—if you know what I mean. Your father was a good man and taught me everything I know. It's a pleasure to make your acquaintance."

"Thank you for the kind words about my father," I replied. "Nice to meet you, too, sir."

The woman who had originally complimented me waved. "Hi, handsome. My name is Lula Landry. I'm the secretary for the largest real estate developer in the South, and I also happen to run the best whorehouses in North and South Carolina."

"Yes, she does!" another man confirmed enthusiastically, and everyone laughed. Then he said, "LC, I'm Major Gary Holmes out of Fort Bragg, North Carolina. I provide weapons and manpower for those who need a helping hand. Oh, and I help out Lula." He gestured toward the woman who spoke up next.

"Hi, I'm Catherine, or Cat, as they call me. My brother and I control narcotics in Memphis, Nashville, and most of Alabama. We need to talk about your New York connection."

How the fuck did she know about our New York connection? Obviously the members of the Council knew a hell of a lot more about me and my business than I knew about them. I was at a distinct disadvantage, and I didn't like it one bit. Still, I maintained a poker face and greeted her kindly.

"Yes, we should do that real soon. Nice to meet you," I said.

"I'm Abe Jenkins. I run the bank you received your loans from. In addition, I own several car washes here in Atlanta. We need to sit down and talk business real soon."

The next man to introduce himself was the brother with the deep voice. "I'm Reverend Percy Hawkins, the pastor of First Baptist Church, one of the largest churches in Atlanta. I'm also the head of the National Baptist Union. Pleased to meet you, son."

Damn, they even have a preacher, I thought with amazement.

The last man walked up to me and shook my hand. "LC, I'm Walter Matthews. I'm the assistant Deputy U.S. Attorney for the northern district of Georgia."

I let go of his hand like it was a hot potato. "U.S. Attorney! You're a fucking fed?" The words escaped my mouth before I could stop them.

Fortunately, everyone laughed.

"Yes, LC. Ol' Walt here is a fed," Mr. Mahogany said with no further explanation. "Now, ladies and gentlemen, why don't we retire to the board room so we can get down to business."

They all moved from their respective spots toward a pair of double doors. I followed them into another well-decorated room with a large oval table with nine chairs seated around it. I sat in the empty chair beside Walter and waited as Mr. Mahogany took his seat at the head of the table. Everyone turned their attention to him.

I glanced around the room. These folks were no joke, and I was not sure yet if I was in over my head. I could definitely see how a group like this could work, and I was going to try my damndest to be a productive member of the Council. I just didn't know how long I would be able to keep something like this from my brothers.

"Well," Mr. Mahogany said. "Now that we are all here, let's get down to business."

And just like that, with very little fanfare, I became the newest member of the powerful Black Council.

Lou

15

I was just finishing up some eggs, bacon, and coffee at the bar at Big Shirley's when I spotted Shirley coming down the stairs, followed by Levi. I'd spent half the night breaking in two new girls, but I was up early so I could head over to Brunswick and check on Donna's progress with Eddie.

"Morning," I said as they approached.

"Morning, Lou." Shirley reached for the coffee and poured herself a cup then poured Levi a glass of milk.

"You're up pretty early," I said to Shirley. "I know Levi gets up to take care of them animals, but I don't expect you up until at least eleven."

"Who you telling? But I guess you didn't hear the news. Miss Chippy had her baby last night," Shirley said with a smile.

"Get the fuck outta here! What she have, a boy or a girl?" I was grinning from ear to ear. I was so proud of my little brother and the family he was creating.

"A little boy, but he wasn't so little. He was nine pounds, six ounces."

"Oh, yeah, that's not so little at all. Did they name him yet?"

"Yep. Named him Vegas."

"Leave it to Chippy to give him an original name—although I must admit I like it. Vegas Duncan is a strong name. Guess I gotta get up there before I go to Brunswick."

"Mm-hmm, that's why I'm up. If I don't get up there to Atlanta today and see that baby, I'll never hear the end of it."

I raised my coffee cup as if offering a toast. "I know that's right. I still can't believe they're really moved up there."

"Me either," she replied.

Levi stayed silent as he drank his milk. He had his routine that he stuck to every morning, and I guess he wasn't going to let talk of a baby steer him off course. He set down his glass then headed toward the back of the building to feed the dogs.

"So, Lou, can I ask you a question, hypothetically?" Shirley said when Levi was gone.

"Sure, as soon as you explain to me what hypothetically means." I laughed.

She ignored my little joke. "With Chippy and LC up in Atlanta, I guess you and Larry will be moving up there soon?"

"Might be some money to be made up there, but I ain't packing my bags quite yet. Larry's the one talking about buying a fleet of trucks and making a move. I'm not going anywhere until I find out what happened to my momma," I said seriously.

"Well, if you do move up there, what does that mean for me and Levi?" she asked. Personally, I thought it was a dumb question. I didn't have to think about my answer.

"You move up there with us."

"And what if we don't want to move?"

I raised an eyebrow. Where the hell was this coming from? "We? Or you? 'Cause our brother goes where we go."

She hesitated, probably making sure she chose her words correctly. "There's nothing up there in Atlanta for me, Lou. I'm a whore past her prime. Here, I'm a Madam, a boss. I'm Big Shirley of Big Shirley's whorehouse. Here, I'm somebody."

I knew where she was coming from, but she was fooling herself if she really thought she was that important. I had to put her back in her place. "You do understand that it's Big Shirley's in name only, right? That this place is owned by LC, Larry, and me. That the ten percent you take down each week is a courtesy we give you for running the place and looking after our brother."

"Yes, and I do both well, and I make you money every week. This place is not just about the money for me, Lou. This place is my life." She played it smart by keeping her tone respectful, but that still wasn't going to make me change my mind.

"Look, Shirley, I understand how you feel about this place. I love it too. I practically grew up in it, but there is nothing more important than my family, and if me and my brothers go to Atlanta, Levi's going with us. You need to understand that."

She pushed back, her voice cracking with emotion now like she might start crying or something. "And what if he don't want to go with you? What if he wants to stay with me? He's a grown man, Lou."

"This is my brother Levi we're talking about. You know, six foot eight, strong as an ox, with the IQ of a box of rocks." I took hold of her arm and we locked eyes. "So, I want you to tell me: what constitutes him being grown?"

She stood up and placed her hand on her belly. "How about the fact that he put a baby in my belly?"

I just about fell out of my chair. "Get the fuck, outta here, you're pregnant?"

She nodded proudly.

Fuck! Well, that sure complicated things for us Duncans.

Nee Nee

16

"Wow. This is so nice," Shirley said when we arrived back at LC and Chippy's house after leaving the hospital, where we had all gone to see baby Vegas. The boys immediately ran into Junior's room to play. Lou and Larry settled in the den to watch some game on the color TV, while Shirley and I started preparing dinner. LC had some work to take care of in the city, so he stayed behind at the hospital to spend some time with Chippy before his meeting.

"Girl, is that a dishwasher?" Shirley's eyes widened, and she walked over to see for herself.

"Yep, and guess what else they got?"

"What?" she asked as she opened the dishwasher door and peeked inside.

"A brand new washer and a clothes dryer. They don't even have a clothes line outside at all."

Shirley stood up straight, making a dramatic face. "Shut your mouth. Damn, almost makes me wanna move to Atlanta."

"Me too. Just don't tell Larry." I took out pots and pans and put them on the stove. "I mean, I told Larry I didn't want to leave Waycross, but I tell you, staying here these past few weeks has made me see life in a whole 'nother way. Now I don't wanna leave. And my son loves staying here too. There's a park right down the street, and the people here are so nice," I said. "Larry told Chippy that if we move, he'll buy the house they're building up the block."

"You believe that?"

"I'm trying not to. A house like that is like a dream come true," I said wistfully.

"He's starting to wear you down, isn't he?" Shirley shook her head.

"Him and Curtis."

"Curtis?"

"My baby's not stupid. He knows what's going on. He wants his mommy and daddy together, and so do I. The fucked up part is that Larry's moving forward with this trucking company whether I move up here or not."

"What you gonna do? Sounds like trouble in paradise."

I'm sure she didn't mean anything by it, but I did not like the sarcasm in her voice.

"I don't know." I sighed, rubbing my hand through my hair. "We've barely spoken to each other the past two weeks I've been up here."

Shirley's facial expression changed drastically. "Wait a minute. I thought y'all was up here helping Chippy and LC together."

"We were. He was helping LC by driving back and forth picking up cars from Detroit, and I was helping Chippy with the house and getting ready for the baby. But we ain't slept in the same bed since we left Waycross. Hell, he slept in the truck last night."

She shook her head. "That's a damn shame. You have to stick to your guns, otherwise these men will walk all over you, Nee Nee."

"Ain't nobody walking over nothing," I snapped back.

"Good, 'cause we have a restaurant to open when you get back."

When Shirley had first come to me about opening my own restaurant, I was excited about the idea. But then, LC and Chippy asked if I would come with them to Atlanta for a few weeks to help them get settled in. It seemed to make sense, especially with the new baby coming. Chippy was definitely going to need someone to help out with Junior. I didn't mind at all. I assured Shirley that I was only going to be gone a month, two at the most, and we would be moving forward with our business plans as soon as I got back. But I was beginning to enjoy Atlanta much more than I ever thought I would.

"I haven't forgotten about that," I said tentatively. "But . . ."

"But what? This is real important. Don't be stupid. Not over a man." Shirley stood directly in front of me like she planned on making me see things her way.

"Loving someone isn't stupid, Shirley," I protested, though I told myself I would hear her out before getting mad. "What's wrong with wanting to be married and a have a beautiful house with a white picket fence? I'd gladly give up opening a restaurant for that. Look at LC and Chippy."

"Girl, please. You and Larry are not Chippy and LC. They have always had these high hopes of living this uppity lifestyle, and that ain't us. We don't need all of this to be happy. Our lives are fine back in Waycross, and we got dreams and plans of our own," she said. "We ain't them."

"I never said we were them, Shirley. And there's nothing wrong with wanting and getting nice thi—"

Shirley cut me off. "You right, but how come me and you and our kids always seem to get the hand-me-downs, and she and hers is always wearing new shit?"

"That's not true."

"Ain't it? When I got to the hospital and told everybody I was pregnant, what was the first thing Chippy said?" She answered herself before I could even recall the conversaiton. "That she had a box of baby stuff I could have."

"She was just being nice," I suggested.

Shirley laughed mockingly. "Really? 'Cause I find it kind of offensive that a woman who just had baby last night is giving me her first child's shit because she already has too much shit for the new one."

My mouth fell open, but I didn't even know how to respond. I'd never heard her sound so bitter, especially about family.

"Nee Nee!" Lou called from the den, saving me from this uncomfortable conversation. "They got any beer in there?"

I opened the refrigerator and took out two beers and wrapped a paper towel around them. I didn't say anything else to Shirley, who followed me out of the kitchen. I never really thought of myself in competition with Chippy, Shirley, or anyone else, but the more I thought about it, her point about the baby clothes made a lot of sense. Chippy was always giving me Junior's old clothes because he was so much bigger than Curtis. I always saw it as generous, but maybe there was something else to it.

"Here you go." I passed a beer to each of the men.

"Thanks," Lou said, opening his and taking a swig.

The front door opened, and LC walked in.

"Hey, little brother," Larry said. "Me and Lou was just talking about you."

"I hope it was good," LC answered.

"Yeah, I think so." Larry turned to Lou and smiled. "How'd you like it if the Duncan brothers all moved up here to Atlanta?"

I guess I wasn't the only one surprised by Larry's announcement that everyone was relocating because LC was speechless for a minute. When he finally answered, LC said, "It would be a dream come true."

"So why don't you grab a beer and help me convince our brother that it's the right thing to do?" Larry said.

I sucked my teeth loud to get Larry's attention. When he was looking at me, I said, "Humph. Lou ain't the only one who's gonna need some convincing."

"I know that's right," Shirley chimed in from behind me.

Donna

17

"I had a nice time tonight. Thank you."

"I always have a great time with you, Donna," Eddie said, giving me that grin he seemed to always have around me.

"I feel the same way," I said politely, digging in my purse for my keys.

Eddie got out of his Continental and walked around to open my door. It had only been ten days, but I'd already trained him well. He had taken me all the way to the Landing in Jacksonville for dinner. It was a nice area near the beach, full of nice restaurants and shops. My warning to Eddie that he was going to have to impress me if he planned on dating me had been heeded, and he had been attempting to do just that.

After helping me out of the car, he opened the trunk and took out the large shopping bags, which held the cashmere sweater and silk scarf that I'd admired in one of the shop windows and he had gladly purchased.

"Aren't you going to invite me in?" he asked when we arrived in front of my apartment door.

I shook my head. "You already know that I'm not, Eddie."

"Damn, Donna, come on. I've been wining and dining you for two weeks. You giving me the run-around?"

His attitude was just the reaction I was expecting.

"So, you think because you take me out for a couple of meals and buy me a few things that I'm supposed to just let you have your way with me? That's all I'm worth?" I snapped.

"That's not what I'm saying. It's just—"

I sighed loudly to shut him up. "I swear, every time I allow myself to start getting close to a man, this is how they act.

Whatever happened to chivalry and romance? I thought you were different from all those others. I see I was wrong." I forced tears to form in my eyes and allowed my bottom lip to quiver for added effect.

"I am, Donna. You know how I feel about you. This ain't a game for me." Eddie put his arm around my shoulder. "And you're worth way more than anything in my life right now. That's why I try and show you that by taking you to nice places and buying you nice things."

"So, you are trying to buy me." I pulled away.

"No! I'm—Come on, Donna. I like you a lot. I more than like you. I just wanted to come inside and enjoy your company a little while longer, that's all. Maybe sit on the sofa and hold you close to me. I bought you that Commodores album you wanted because I thought we would listen together. Can't we at least do that?" Eddie pleaded.

I felt kind of bad because he was right. For the past two weeks, he had been spoiling me and treating me in ways that I hadn't enjoyed since my father left. We ate at fine restaurants, he took me shopping in Savannah and Jacksonville, and he even talked about taking me on a vacation. Although my mission was simply to get information for Lou, I was glad that it did come with some fringe benefits. I knew I had Eddie wrapped around my finger, but as much as I liked being treated like the queen I was, I was just not attracted to him, at all. Sooner or later my hard-to-get routine would get old, and he would figure out that he couldn't buy me. This was not a moment I was looking forward to, because Eddie was not the type to take no for an answer.

I eased my arm around his neck, closed my eyes, and held my breath as I gave him a kiss with as much passion as I could muster, which wasn't much. Luckily, it was enough to satisfy him. When I pulled away, he looked like he was in a trance.

"Eddie, baby, just give me a little more time to get to know you. Like you told me when you first asked me out: you know all about me and all the things I've been through over the past couple of years. Getting close to someone isn't something I do easily, especially after what happened with LC." I batted my lashes and caressed his chest with my fingertip.

"Fuck LC. I ain't him. Hell, fuck all them Duncan bastards."

"Look, it's late, and I have to be at work early in the morning. A lady's got to get her beauty rest. Thank you for a wonderful evening. Give me a call tomorrow, okay?"

"Donna, you're already the most beautiful woman in the world to me. Shit, you can quit that job and never go back there. I make money to take care of you. To be honest, I can take better care of you than that Duncan motherfucker ever could." Eddie reached in his pocket and then flashed his fat wad of cash that I had become accustomed to seeing.

"Will you put that damn money away? You ain't gonna be satisfied until someone robs you. Now, good night." I took my bag from him, turned, and put my key in to unlock the door.

"Donna, wait." He called my name just as I turned the knob to go inside.

"What is it?"

"Can I get another kiss, please?"

I fulfilled his request, kissing him lightly on the lips. I felt his hands move from my waist to my ass, and I allowed him to enjoy the moment for a few seconds before I quickly took a step back into my doorway and waved to him as I closed the door. Once inside, I put the chain lock on the door then tossed the bag on my sofa, where several other bags of gifts from earlier shopping sprees still sat. The pile was growing so big there was barely space to sit on the couch anymore.

I went to the kitchen and poured myself a drink, then came back into the living room to relax for a few minutes before I started putting away some of the gifts. I had just taken off my heels and was about to turn on the eight track player when I heard knocking at the door.

"Didn't I tell you we'd talk tomorrow?" I shouted.

He just started knocking harder and louder. I rushed over to the door to stop this fool before he woke my neighbors.

"Eddie, what the hell is wrong with you?" I snapped as I undid the chain and snatched the door open.

"Do I look like Eddie?" It was Lou. I quickly pulled him inside.

"What are you doing here?" I stuck my head out the door to make sure Eddie was gone.

"Man, I thought that motherfucker would never leave. What the hell were y'all talking about?" Lou asked as he went and sat on my couch.

"Are you crazy? What are you doing here?" I repeated.

"I came to get some kind of fucking update. I haven't heard from you in a few days."

"I told you I would call you when I had some solid information. I'm still working on it. I'm holding up my end of the deal. What about you? Did you set up the fucking meeting?" I stared at Lou with my arms crossed and waited for his answer.

"As a matter of fact, I got something I'm working on this weekend, but you gotta come with me to Atlanta." I noticed him taking in my body with his eyes, but I ignored his seductive glance. I was more interested in the details of what he had set up.

"Atlanta?" I asked.

"Yeah, Atlanta," he said, making it clear he wasn't giving up any more information. "And why is it taking so long for you to get info from this dude? Looking at all these shopping bags, I figured you would've been fucked him and got the scoop by now."

I wrinkled up my nose in distaste. Just the thought of sex with Eddie was disgusting. "I haven't fucked him. And I'm not going to fuck him."

"So, that's what the holdup is. Dammit, Donna, you do whatever you gotta do to get me what I need, or I ain't setting up shit for you."

I felt myself panicking, because I did not want him backing out now. "Look, I know what I'm doing. Trust me. I may not have all the info, but based on what I know so far, you've been more right than wrong."

"What does that mean?" Lou stared at me intently.

I inhaled deeply and told him, "I believe your mother is still alive."

"Eddie told you that?" Lou looked a little stunned.

"No, but he made it pretty damn clear that the arm they found in the swamp doesn't belong to your mother." Lou looked flabbergasted, and I felt sorry for him. "Someone is paying him a lot of money lately, and right now, he's more afraid of them than he is of you."

"Well, we'll see about that." Lou headed for the door, but I slid in front of it, stopping him.

"Where are you going?" I asked.

"To find that son of bitch!" He tried to push me out of his way, but I stood my ground.

"And do what?" I asked. "Beat the hell outta him? What good is that going to do? You already told me that he's so fucked up after being in the Army that torture doesn't affect him." I didn't need him killing Eddie, because then I would be of no more use to Lou—and I wouldn't get what I wanted out of the deal.

"Yeah, but I gotta do something."

"You have. You partnered with me. And if I can find this out, I can find out everything you need."

Bettie

18

"Get up, bitch!"

I flinched at the voice waking me. I was curled up naked in the corner of the room, my head on a flimsy sheet that I had balled into a makeshift pillow. I didn't have a blanket, but the thin piece of material wouldn't serve as any kind of warmth anyway, so I figured it could as least serves as a barrier between my head and the cold, nasty floor I was sleeping on.

"Did you hear what I said? Get your ass up!" the man growled again. This time his demand was followed by a kick in my back.

I grimaced in pain but didn't utter a sound. I wasn't as young as I used to be, but this wasn't the first time I'd been kicked. Slowly, I sat up and stared at him. This tall, ape-looking motherfucker got a thrill out of abusing me. He was a sadistic bastard, unlike the two men who had taken me from the house a few days ago. Or had it been a few weeks? The days and nights had begun to run together, especially since I had been moved around so much. There were times that I had been locked in rooms with no windows to even see daylight, and needless to say, I didn't have a watch. The ape pulled me up and placed me in a chair, covering my head with a cloth pillowcase or sheet.

"Don't you fucking move," he ordered. I could hear a gun being chambered.

Now, I was truly afraid. There was no doubt in my mind that the end was near. I had been left down here to die. I sat for what seemed like an hour until I heard the door open again and footsteps approaching.

"Bettie Duncan."

My heart began pounding as I realized who the voice belonged to. It had been decades, but there was no mistaking it. I could feel someone coming closer to me, and then, the covering was removed from my eyes, confirming what I already knew. I didn't say a word.

"It's been a long time, hasn't it, Bettie?" The voice was like gravel. It had always been distinctive, yet it now had a hoarseness to it. Time had changed jet-black hair to white, and although the hazel eyes were just as piercing, the skin around them was wrinkled with age.

"What the fuck do you want?" I asked quickly.

"Come now, Bettie. Is that a way to greet an old friend?"

"We're not friends," I spat, hatred boiling within me.

"We were friends at one time."

"That was before—"

"Before you and your husband messed it up."

"We just did what we thought was right. It was your—"

Slap!

My face stung from the palm of a heavy hand. I reached up to rub it.

"Don't you even go there. Don't you dare blame your mistakes on him!"

I was breathing so hard that I could see my chest rising with each breath. The will to fight was there, but the man guarding the door looked way too strong, and he was carrying a gun.

"What is this all about?" I asked.

"Don't act stupid, Bettie. You've always been a smart woman. There's only one reason I'd be standing in front of you after all these years in this godforsaken place."

Everything clicked in that moment and I understood why I had been taken and by whom. It all made sense. As terrible as this all was, at least now I understood why I was taken from my family. It had been so long I'd almost forgotten. I had been holding this secret for over two decades, and for two decades, it appears my captor had wanted the secret I held.

"Jesus Christ, is that what this is all about? Why not let sleeping dogs lie?"

"Did you think that just because you went to jail it would be forgotten?"

"I never really gave it much thought," I replied. "Prison was hard enough without worrying about y'all. To be honest, now that I think about it, I'm surprised you let me get out of prison."

"You slipped through the cracks, but it's better this way. Now we can put this shit to bed forever." There was so much hate in that voice. "Now, start talking. There's a lot of shit I need to know."

I shook my head, refusing to speak.

Bam!

This time, it was a fist from the ape that struck my jaw. I covered my face to block the blows as I tried to scurry away from the repeated kicks to my legs and torso.

"Tell me what I want to know, Bettie, or we're going to hurt you much worse than this."

"No!" I shouted repeatedly, and with that, the kicks continued. "Go ahead and kill me now, because I will never tell you."

The sound of my sudden laughter must have been a complete surprise, because the assault stopped. I turned to stare into the eyes of the monster in front of me and smiled.

"You can't kill me, can you? You're not just after the secret, you're after the—" I was given one more kick to stop my sarcastic rambling.

"This is not over." They left, slamming the door behind them.

There was a series of clicking sounds, and I knew that the door was locked. Just as I stood up and began looking around, everything went dark. The lights had been turned off. I leaned against the wall and slid to the floor. I now knew what they wanted, and they would hold me there until I told them. But there was no way I could tell them. It was the only thing keeping me and my boys alive.

Tears that I had been holding onto for days, weeks, months, years came flowing from my eyes. I felt helpless.

"Hello?" I heard a small voice cry out to me. "Are you okay over there?"

At first I thought I must have fallen asleep and was dreaming. I sat up and listened closer.

"Hello, can you hear me over there?" someone called out again. I wasn't dreaming. The voice was coming from the other side of the wall I was leaning on.

"Yes, I'm here," I answered.

"Okay. I'm just making sure you're okay. I'm Lisa."

"I'm Bettie." I put my ear against the wall so I could hear better.

"Hey, Bettie."

"Hey, so how long have you been down here?" I asked.

"I stopped counting the days after about six months," she replied, and although she did sound sincere, my first thought was that this was a trick. Now that I knew who I was dealing with, I couldn't put anything past them. They were ruthless if they were anything. But I'd go along with it for now. Trick or not, I'd learned from prison that comradery made the time go by faster.

Lou

19

I pulled open the glass doors with the words *Duncan Motors* painted on them and walked inside, looking around to take it all in. To say I was impressed would be an understatement. From the fleet of cars for sale in the front lot to the carpeted, air-conditioned office space complete with a water cooler and a reception area, this place was more than I could have ever expected. To top it off, my younger brother was the owner. I knew that LC had a plan when he moved to Atlanta, but I never expected this.

"Can I help you?"

I smiled at the young woman behind the desk, and my eyes traveled down farther. Her breasts were a bit smaller than I would have liked, but her pretty face more than made up for it.

"Hey there, beautiful. I'm Lou Duncan. I'm here to see my brother, LC," I replied.

"Of course. I'll see if he's available." She reached for the phone, but I stopped her.

"He's always available for me. No need for all the formalities. Just point me in the direction that he's at and I'll find him myself." I walked past her desk toward a long hallway, "Is his office this way?"

She quickly jumped up behind me. "Sir, wait one second."

I kept walking. There was an open office door with LC's name on it. I peeked inside, expecting to find him, but it was empty. I continued down the hallway.

"Lou!" LC called my name, and I turned around to see him coming from the opposite direction. "Hey, man!"

"What's up, LC?" I said when we met in the middle of the hallway and embraced.

He was dressed in a suit and tie, carrying a clipboard, which he handed to the receptionist. She was looking at me like I'd stolen her first born.

"Vivian, make sure you make duplicate copies before you file these, please," LC said to her.

"Right away, Mr. Duncan. You need anything else?"

"No, that's all," LC told her.

I checked out her ass as she walked away. She may have been lacking up top, but she had enough in the back to keep me interested. I was going to have to stop by the dealership more often.

"I like her. She got spunk!" I laughed. "What's going on?"

"Nothing much. Just handling some paperwork for some vehicles that just came in."

"This is some place you got here," I said.

"Thanks. It's coming along nicely. Taking care of some final details. Let me give you the grand tour."

LC showed me around the dealership. The place had everything: a garage, a space for auto detailing, office space. My brother was definitely doing well for himself.

"So, what are you doing here?" he asked when we headed back into his office and took a seat.

"Well, I was actually just passing through on my way to New York to handle some business with Sal Dash." I tapped the briefcase I was carrying. "I was hoping to catch you. I got few things on my mind."

"I see." LC looked concerned. Both LC and Larry had been lecturing me lately about looking into what happened to Momma. They told me I was letting it get the best of me and I should try to relax a little. Personally, I thought they weren't taking shit seriously enough, waiting for some lazy-ass cops to figure it out when we knew they never would.

As much as I wanted to blurt out what Donna had told me about the arm that wasn't Momma's, I had to treat this carefully. First of all, LC was not exactly gonna be happy to find out I'd been talking to Donna. Also, I had to prove to him I wasn't totally obsessed, and that I still had my mind on business too. If I jumped right into talking about Momma, he'd tune me out in a hurry.

"Seeing as you've got the dealership and Larry's got the trucking," I started to explain, "Why don't you let me put a title company up in here like we have at home? That way, people who can't get regular financing or need short term money can do business too."

He leaned back in his seat, looking a little more relaxed. "You finished searching for Momma's killers?"

I had to stop myself from blurting out, "Momma's not dead!"

Instead, I said, "I got a few more leads that I'm checking out, and if they don't pan out, I'm gonna just have to accept it." I didn't tell him, but I was already convinced those leads would prove to be true now that Donna had confirmed my suspicions.

"Fair enough."

"So, we good to open the title company?"

"Sounds like a good idea. Let me run it by Mr. Mahogany and see what he says."

"There you go with that Mr. Mahogany bullshit again. Why do you have to involve him? This don't have shit to do with him." I had yet to understand why LC had this "relationship" with this dude. It was as if Mr. Mahogany appeared out of nowhere and cast some kind of spell on my brother, and I didn't like it one bit. He may have sold Larry on this shit, but I sure as hell wasn't sold. "This is between you and me."

LC sighed. "Listen, Lou, I already explained this to you before. Mr. Mahogany is the reason I'm able to open this dealership. He's helped me out a lot."

"Well, explain it to me again, because I don't understand this. Supposedly he's a minority partner, but he calls all the shots."

"He doesn't call all the shots."

"Then why the fuck do you need his permission for your own brother to open a title company on your property?" I felt my temperature rising as my anger flared, but LC remained cool.

"Because this is his city, and what you're proposing isn't exactly on the up and up," he said evenly, "and he's well connected when it comes to business, and not only is he knowledgeable, he's resourceful. He's helping me establish a solid business foundation. That's way more important than money."

"Oh, so I guess I ain't teach you shit, huh?" I snapped. I couldn't believe he was standing there saying that. It was as if everything Larry and I had done and sacrificed meant nothing. Hell, we were the ones who paid for him to go to college, bought him his first car, even bought that damn garage in Waycross for him. Now, all of a sudden he was trying to tell me of all people about building a damn foundation. As far as I was concerned, family was the most important foundation he would ever have.

"Man, don't be like that. I'm sure putting a title office here won't be a problem at all. I'm sure Mr. Mahogany will—"

"Say, that sounds like a great idea. A title loan company is just the thing you need, LC. Not to mention having family around."

I turned around to see Mr. Mahogany standing in the doorway of LC's office. It seemed mighty funny that Vivian hadn't called and announced that he was in the building as she had done with me.

"Mr. Mahogany, you remember my brother Lou." LC nodded in my direction.

The older man stretched his hand out, and after a moment of hesitation, I shook it.

"Nice to see you again, Lou."

"Yeah, same here," I said.

"LC, I'll wait for you in the car." Mr. Mahogany tapped his watch before exiting.

"Hey, Lou, listen. We actually have a meeting we have to be at. How about you go on over to the house with Chippy and wait there for me? I won't be that long. Maybe a couple of hours." LC stood up.

"Uh, well, I did need to holler at you about something else right quick," I said, wanting to get to the real reason I had come to visit him.

"That's fine, Lou. We can chat when I get to the house."

"I just need a minute. It won't take that long. It's about Momma. I don't think—"

LC frowned and shook his head. "Lou, not now, okay? That's your fantasy, not mine." He looked down at his watch. "I gotta go. It's a big meeting."

"What if I can prove she's alive?" I blurted out.

He hesitated for a second. I had piqued his interest. "Prove it how?"

"I got this girl who's fucking Eddie Jenkins—"

He cut me off right away. "Crazy Eddie Jenkins? The motherfucker who is always talking about the walls have ears?"

I guess my facial expression said all that he needed to hear, because he didn't let me answer.

"Lou, are you out your mind? That dude is certifiably crazy. He's been in and out of Central State like five times." He walked over to a file cabinet and started shoving papers in a briefcase. "And how could you believe anyone who would fuck him? Bro, I think you're just looking for anything to believe in."

"Yeah, I guess you're right. Sorry I brought it up," I said, storming out of his office.

"Lou, wait!" He called behind me.

I ignored LC and kept walking out of the building, past Mr. Mahogany, who was sitting in his black Cadillac, staring at me as if he were waiting for me to say something. Instead, I stared back and said nothing as I made my way to my car.

When LC came out of the building, I watched him climb into Mr. Mahogany's car, which then drove out of the parking lot. When they were no longer in sight, I opened the door of my car and climbed in.

"Does he know I'm here? What did he say?" Donna asked, popping up from the back seat.

Turning on the engine, I sat in silence as I thought about my next move.

"Answer me, Lou! What did he say? Does he know I'm here?" Donna had a lot of hope in her voice.

I finally said, "He didn't say anything. Hell, shit got so complicated, I didn't even tell him you were here."

Nee Nee

20

"Girl, you right on time." Shirley was grinning from ear to ear as I entered her office. She was sitting behind her desk, talking to old man Butler. He did all the handyman work and repairs at Big Shirley's. He was kind of a jack of all trades and could fix damn near anything if you gave him the time. "Mr. Butler says it's only going to take about three weeks to whip that place into shape. We about to be in business."

"Is that right?" I smiled as I sat down next to Mr. Butler. I wasn't quite as enthusiastic as Shirley, but I had to admit it was good news considering the state of the rest of my life. I'd been back in Waycross almost a week after helping Chippy get settled with the baby and the new house in Atlanta. Unfortunately, Larry had made it clear by his actions that he wasn't going to marry me, and he wasn't going to beg me to move to Atlanta, either.

"So, Mr. Butler, how much exactly is this gonna cost?" I asked.

"Don't you worry about that." Shirley winked, smiling at Mr. Butler. "All we have to do is buy the materials and equipment, and Mr. Butler here will do the rest. Ain't that right, Mr. Butler?"

"Long as you stick to your side of the bargain, we got us a deal, Shirley." He got up from his chair, smiling like a Cheshire cat. "Let me know once you sign that lease so me and my boys can get started."

"We about to sign it right now."

He walked out, and as soon as the door closed, I asked, "What exactly did you promise him?"

"A free pussy card."

I fell out laughing. "You bartering pussy now, Shirley?"

"It's a commodity, and ain't that what business is all about, bartering and trading? And as far as money, we got that too." She reached into the bottom drawer of her desk and pulled out a large gray lockbox. Opening it, she turned it around so I could see its contents.

"Jesus, Shirley, that's a lot of cash."

"And there's more if we need it. See, while Larry is hell bent on following LC to Atlanta to make him a millionaire, I'm willing to help you become one. Your dreams and LC's dreams. If Larry was a real man, he would stay and help you make yours come true too," she told me. She was determined to make this work, and her enthusiasm was beginning to become mine.

I sat up in my chair excitedly. "Okay, let's do it! Call the owner. Fuck Atlanta and fuck Larry. We got this, and we got each other. We're gonna work together, create our own empire, and make our own dreams come true."

"Fuck LC and Chippy. They ain't thinking about our asses anyway." She walked over and pulled me into a big hug. "Fuck the Duncans!"

"Fuck all of them!" I shouted, laughing now.

"Mommy!"

We both jumped, startled by Curtis, who was in the door- way, in Larry's arms.

"What the fuck y'all got going on in here?" Larry demanded to know.

"Larry," I whispered.

"What are you doing here?" Shirley asked him. "You hate being in this whorehouse, remember?"

He ignored her and walked closer to me. "I just bought that house up the street from LC in Atlanta." He tried to hand me some papers, but I woulddn't take them. "We can move in whenever you're ready."

"I ain't going no damn where." I shook my head and plopped back down on the sofa. From the determined look on Larry's face, I could tell this was about to be one hell of a fight. I pressed on anyway. "Me and Shirley are about to sign these papers and open a restaurant. So, you have fun in Atlanta."

"You sure about that?" He let Curtis down, and he came running over to me. "You sure you don't want to go?"

"You damn right I'm sure. What do you mean?" I bent down and hugged my son, staring at Larry defiantly.

"Well, can you a least take a look at these papers before you go off all half-cocked?" He handed them to me, and this time I took them. "Just read the first three lines."

Reluctantly, I unfolded the papers and read the first three lines as he'd requested. "Why you playing, Larry? This isn't funny." I looked down at the paper and reread the same lines. "This isn't even real, is it?"

"Yes, it is." He nodded.

I dropped the papers. Truthfully, I'm surpised I didn't faint.

"What the fuck does it say?" Shirley reached down and scooped up the papers before either of us could answer. "Well, I'll be damned." She began to read out loud: "This land and dwelling are deeded to Mr. and Mrs. Lawrence and Anita Duncan."

Larry dropped down to one knee and reached into the front pocket of his shirt. "I know I'm not the easiest guy to get along with, but I love you and Curtis, and I want to spend the rest of my life with you. Now, I'm not trying to have some big, fancy-ass wedding. Fuck that. I ain't doing it. But what I will do is drive you down to the courthouse and get married right now and give you my name." He took a breath. "So, with that being said, will you marry me?"

Never in a million years would I have suspected that Larry Duncan would agree to get married, let alone get down on one knee and propose. It was one of the sweetest moments I had ever experienced.

"Momma, you gonna marry my daddy?" Curtis was standing on the sofa, his face three inches from mine.

"Yes, Curtis, yes! I'm going to marry your daddy. That's all I ever wanted."

Larry slipped the ring on my finger, and I fell to the floor beside him and threw my arms around his neck, nearly knocking him over. He grabbed me and kissed me so passionately that I would have made love to him right there if Shirley and Curtis hadn't been there.

"Well, congratulations. I guess I'm going to have to go look for a new partner." Shirley sighed half-heartedly. She looked like she was trying to fight the tears that were forming in her eyes, but she was losing that battle.

"Sorry, Shirley. You know how much I love you," I said, walking over to her when Larry released me

"It's okay. I know this is what you really wanted." She wiped away a single tear that was rolling down her cheek.

Larry didn't say anything to her. "Come on, Nee. The courthouse closes at four o'clock. We gotta hurry if we're going to get married today." He tugged at my hand then scooped Curtis up with the other, and we were out the door.

Bettie

21

"Noooooooo! Stop it! Get away from me!"

I could hear the screams in my dream. I was back in the penitentiary; it was dark in my cell, but I could make out the shadowy figures of two guards in the cell across from mine, grabbing another inmate and dragging her out. She was a pretty girl, young and curvy, with too much mouth. I had watched the guards eying her all week, and earlier in the evening, when she got into a fight with her cell mate, one of them made a comment about "handling her" if she didn't calm down.

"You'd never be able to handle the *thought* of me, let alone touch me," she had shot back with her smart mouth.

The guard reached for her, but she snatched away and walked off. Their eyes followed her, and one guard said to the other, "Man, what I would like to do to that ass . . ." I knew then that she was going to be in trouble.

"Leave me aloooooooone!" Her cries echoed now, sending chills down my spine. I shivered at the thought of where they were taking her and what they were about to do. Sexual assaults were a common occurrence in prison. It was part of where we were, a part of the hell we lived in day after day, the culture of living behind bars. Inmates raped other inmates, and there were times like now that guards took what they wanted from whatever inmate they wanted. There was no fear of anyone pressing charges, no risk of losing their job, not even a fear of catching a disease or getting anybody pregnant. They were the predators and had a plethora of prey to choose from. Tonight, they had chosen her.

"Shut the fuck up!" a man's voice growled. I heard the distinctive sound of his hands striking her body.

Suddenly, I was aware that I wasn't dreaming. I was in a prison, but this wasn't the penitentiary. My eyes fluttered open, and I strained to see in the darkness. I remembered exactly where I was and realized where the voice was coming from. I sat up from the cold floor where I had fallen asleep and scurried over to the wall. Pressing my ear against the surface, I listened.

"Nooooooooooo! Get away! Get away!" I could hear her fighting back. "Get off me!"

"Oh, you wanna play rough tonight, huh? Bitch, I'm not playing wit' you!" he yelled, striking her repeatedly.

"Help me! Somebody please help me!" she cried.

"Stop fucking squirming! Take this dick! Fine, I know what you want!" his sinister voice announced. "Turn that ass over."

"Nooooo! Please, no! Somebody please help me!" Lisa's screams turned to whimpers, and she whined, "Please, I'm begging you."

"Oh, yeah . . . yeah, bitch. That's what I'm talking about!" He moaned.

"God! Please, stop, please! Some—" She screamed even louder, which prompted him to beat her more viciously until she finally fell silent.

I beat on the wall as hard as I could and yelled, "Leave her alone, you bastard! Get the fuck away from her!" I'd been through a lot of horrifying things in my lifetime, but this had to be by far the worst because of how helpless I felt.

"Oh, yeeeeeeaaaaah," the man suddenly howled in ecstacy.

"Stop it! Get off her!" I continued beating until my fists hurt. Tears began to burn my eyes as I listened to him violate her over and over again.

Then, suddenly, it was quiet. I began to panic at the thought of what might have happened. *Is she all right? Is she passed out? Is she dead?*

"Lisa? Lisa, can you hear me?" I called out, but there was no response. "Lisa!"

Still nothing, until I heard the slamming of the door and then the sound of footsteps in the hallway. My heart was beating so fast that I could hardly catch my breath. The lock of the door in front of me slowly turned, and I began praying that I wouldn't be next.

The door creaked open, and I saw the shadow of the big burly ape standing in the doorway.

"What the fuck is the matter with you?" he growled at me.

"Where is she? Where is Lisa? Did you kill her?" I demanded to know.

"Listen, you old bitch. You better learn, your place or I'll give to you what I gave to her with a broom handle."

He took a step back and then opened the door a little wider. I squinted my eyes to see as I prepared for whatever he had planned for me.

"Here!" He pushed something into the room. I jumped back and then heard a moan as it hit the floor. "You so worried about this bitch. Here you go!"

"Lisa!" I rushed over to the crumpled woman and grabbed her into my arms. The light from the hallway illuminated enough for me to see that she was a shivering, crying, bloody mess.

"Now the both of you can die together!" He was laughing like a madman as he slammed and locked the door.

I didn't have time to even wonder about what he said. I was focused on comforting Lisa as she held on to me for dear life. I used my shirt to wipe her face.

"It's okay," I said, rubbing her back.

"Kill me!" She kept crying over and over. "Kill me, so he can't do it again."

"No, I'm not going to do that, baby girl, but I promise you this: we are gonna get the hell up out of here."

"No, we're not. We're gonna die in here."

"Look at me," I told her.

It was too dark to see much more than shadows, but I could tell she lifted her head toward me. "We ain't dying in here," I said. "I may not be the one to get us the hell up out of here, but I got four boys out there looking for me—some smart boys who know how to handle shit like this. Trust me, they gonna come, and we gonna be fine."

"But—"

"No buts. I know my boys. They ain't gonna rest until they find their momma. Trust me."

In my heart, I knew what I was saying was true. I knew that Lou, Larry, LC, and even Levi would search the entire world looking for me. But, I wondered if they even realized that I was still alive, because if they thought otherwise, then Lisa may be right, and there was a chance that we were going to die.

Shirley

22

"What's up, girl? How're things going?"

I was in the middle of my own personal pity party over Nee Nee and Larry getting married when Li'l Momma came over and sat beside me at the bar. She was a pretty girl who was one of the best whores we had, along with being one of my oldest friends. I'd known her ever since she started working for Big Sam about eight years ago.

"I'm fine. And don't come over here 'Hey, girl-ing' me. What do you want?" I knew Li'l Momma well enough to know that she didn't care how things were going. All she cared about was making her quota and having enough money to send back home to her five kids and her momma.

"Why you gotta be like that, Shirley? I can't take a few minutes and chat with the lady of the house to see how she's doing?" Li'l Momma asked.

I stared at her, dressed in a red silk robe tied at the waist, with red kitten heels on her feet. Her real hair was covered by a not-so-expensive wig, and she wore too much makeup. She always had, mainly because she wanted to look older. That made sense when she was seventeen, but I didn't understand why she still did it. As far as most of the men that frequented this establishment were concerned, as long as you were cute and were able to suck and fuck, it didn't matter how old you were.

"Like I already told you, I'm fine. Now, what is it that you want?" I asked again.

"Shit, I'm worried about you, Shirley, and so are the other girls. You've been in a real mood these past few weeks. I wanna know what's wrong." She stared at me long enough for me to figure out that she was serious.

"This place. That's what's wrong." I shook my head.

"But why?" she asked. "Business around here has been good. We got plenty of customers, and they been paying left and right. I heard Lou say we ran outta liquor Saturday night and that it was a good problem to have." There was a pack of cigarettes and a lighter on the bar, and she picked it up, taking one out for herself and passing one to me.

"No, thanks." I shook my head. I hadn't given up drinking completely since I got pregnant, but I had stopped smoking. Chippy told me she'd read something in a magazine about it being bad for the baby. Luckily, Li'l Momma didn't seem to think anything of me not smoking, because I wasn't really sharing the news with anyone yet.

I watched her light her cigarette as I asked her, "You ever think about what you gonna do when this is over? When our asses is just too old to hoe? When you gotta go home and face those five babies your momma raised, instead of you?"

Li'l Momma shrugged and took a long drag. "More times than I wanna talk about. I guess in a way that's why I wanted to talk to you."

"Mm-hmm. I knew you was up to something," I said, rolling my eyes.

"No, we really are worried about you. You got everyone walking on eggshells around here when you come in the room. You've been so mean lately, it's almost like working for Big Sam all over again." She paused for a second, I guess waiting to see if I was going to bite her head off for comparing me to Sam, but I kept it cool. I couldn't deny I'd been in a pretty foul mood most days. She looked relieved as she continued. "But we all know your family is going through a lot with Miss Bettie passing and everything. We understand."

"Whatever," I shot back. I wasn't about to get sentimental with her. After all, I was still the boss, and it would never be a good idea to show weakness around my girls. "You bitches is lazy, and I'm not putting up with it anymore. Shit, maybe Sam knew what he was talking about. Give a ho an inch and she want to take a mile."

She leaned back and scrunched up her face as if I'd hurt her feelings, which I really didn't care about.

"Now, what do you really want?"

She finally got to the point she'd been dancing around. "Well, you know my customer David? The one who comes down from Savannah to see me?"

"David? Can't say I do." Li'l Momma had so many damn regulars that it was hard to keep up. Men couldn't get enough of her short, petite ass.

"Nice-looking guy, always dressed in a suit and tie. He works as the bank manager up there," Li'l Momma chirped. "Got a little bit of a belly."

"Oh, him." I remembered who she was talking about. "What about him?"

"He's taking me on vacation. To the Bahamas." She was beaming with pride.

"Vacation?" I frowned. "Is he paying you for this vacation?"

"He's paying a lot of money for this trip. I figured that was enough," Li'l Momma confessed.

Going on vacation with a customer was not something I allowed or encouraged. It caused too much confusion, and the last thing I wanted in Big Shirley's was confusion over one of my girls.

"Li'l Momma, you a whore, and that nigga ain't taking you on no damn vacation. You sound stupid. He's just trying to get you away from here so he can get some free pussy, that's all. The only place he's taking you is probably to some cheap-ass hotel on the other side of Savannah. You've been a whore long enough to know that." I shook my head at the poor, naive girl.

"I know that David likes me. He more than likes me. And I like him," Li'l Momma huffed as she stabbed the cigarette out in the ashtray.

"You know how ridiculous you sound? The reason that man comes all the way from Savannah to see you is probably so his wife or his girlfriend won't find out. You're his whore, not his woman."

"You're wrong, Shirley. I'll be right back." She got up and headed off upstairs, where her room was.

I sat there and tried not to laugh. I didn't know what sounded crazier: the fact that this man was telling her that he was taking her on an island vacation, or the fact that she believed him. Li'l Momma had been in the game long enough to know better, but I guess some of these girls never learned.

She returned a few minutes later, holding out an envelope.

"Here."

"What's this?" I asked.

"Open it. Read it."

I took out the content. Sure enough, there was a set of airline tickets and another folded piece of paper with hotel reservations.

I looked at her and shook my head in pity for her foolishness. "Girl, I don't know what this man's planning, but these here tickets are for someone named Christina Caldwell. For all you know that's his wife's name."

She had the nerve to laugh out loud at me. "That's me! Christina Caldwell is my real name." Li'l Momma folded her arms. "And this is gonna be the first trip of many. I might even let him marry me."

"Now you really sound crazy." I put the tickets and the paper back in the envelope and passed it to her. "Does he know about all them children you got?"

"Yes, he does." She stared back at me defiantly. "Why is it so hard for you to believe that I can get a man who actually cares about me? Chippy got LC. I thought you'd be happy for me, Shirley."

"Why the hell does everyone think they can be just like Chippy?" I yelled so loud that other people in the room stopped and stared at me. I didn't care. I was sick and tired of hearing about Chippy and everything she had. It was as if she had all of a sudden become some hero or poster child for working girls who wanted to reform.

"Calm down, Shirley. I didn't say I wanted to be like Chippy. And why you so mad? You got Levi."

"Have you taken a good look at Levi lately? He's not exactly man of the year." I caught myself just as those bitter words slipped out of my mouth. "You know what? Take the damn week off. Hell, take the whole damn month if you want." I jumped off the barstool and stormed to my private office in the back of the house. I slammed the door behind me, startling Levi, who was sitting on the bed looking at a wildlife magazine. I had forgotten that his ass was even there.

"Sh–Sh–Sh–Sh–Shirley?"

"Yes, Levi?" I said, flopping into the chair behind my desk.

"I love you." He smiled at me.

I looked over at him and my heart swelled. Li'l Momma was right. I did have a man who loved me. Even with the scars on my face and the darkness of my past, Levi loved him some Shirley, and I loved him. But I couldn't lie; I wanted more.

"I love you too, Levi. Baby, you know what I was thinking?" I got up and sat beside him. "Why don't we get married before the baby is born? We can have the ceremony at the little church down the block; then we can go to New York or Washington, D.C. We can even go to a famous zoo and see some of these foreign animals you like looking at in these magazines. You can see them for yourself. How does that sound? You want to do that?"

"I want some pu–pu–pussy!"

"You always want pussy, Levi."

"Sh–Sh–Shirley, I–I love y–y–your p–p–pussy." He tried to pull me closer, but I leaned away from him. He reached for me again. "I–I–I–I w–w–want some p–p–p–pussy!" he said more forcefully.

"And I want a man who can take me out to eat and talk to me. Maybe get down on one knee and propose," I said with a sigh.

Levi looked at me with confusion, and I immediately felt bad for saying out loud what I had been thinking.

"Well, I guess one of us can get what we want."

A grin spread over Levi's face as I stood up and began undressing. He wasted no time taking off his clothes and pulling out the sofa bed. I glanced at the discarded magazine on the floor and thought about Chippy and all the places she and LC had gone in the past few years, and Nee Nee and Larry and their fancy new house in Atlanta. And now, here was Li'l Momma, who was headed to the Bahamas and planning her own future. I was starting to wonder if running a brothel and being the girlfriend of a man who didn't even have enough sense to understand marriage, let alone propose, would be all that life had in store for me.

23

"Thirteen! Can you beat thirteen?" Larry shouted, dropping his cards on the pile of money in front of us. Mr. Mahogany, his right-hand man James, and I threw our cards down in disgust. Major Gary Holmes from the Council, however, lifted his hand, causing us all to take pause as he counted the points on his cards.

"Damn." Holmes threw his cards down on the pile of money in defeat. "I had fifteen."

"Thank you for the donations, gentlemen." Larry leaned across the table to rake in his winnings. "Hey, Nee! We just might be getting that living room set you wanted."

"Do your thing, baby," Nee Nee shouted across the yard from over by the grill.

Since Larry and Nee Nee had gone and gotten married on a whim, I'd invited some family and friends over to the new house for a small barbecue reception. The guys had been sitting around a folding table near the pool, laughing, talking shit, and playing cards, while the women congregated around the grill and picnic table, drinking mimosas and watching the kids.

"Just deal the damn cards," Holmes said, lifting a beer to his lips. "I swear, LC, if this motherfucker wasn't your brother, I'd shoot his ass. 'Cause nobody's this damn lucky."

"That's because it's not luck; it's skill. I'm like that Wolverine dude in the comic books: the best there is at what I do." Larry laughed at his own joke.

"Speaking of what you do, Larry, how are things with your trucking company?" Mr. Mahogany's eyes never left Larry as he shuffled the cards methodically.

"Things are good. I think I've found my calling," Larry replied pridefully as Mr. Mahogany began to deal the cards.

"Good, good." Even as he passed the cards around, Mr. Mahogany's eyes never left Larry's face. I'd seen that look from him before, and that made me nervous. Larry wasn't the type to be tested. "Forgive me for being blunt, but do you have room for expansion, or are you going to remain a Mickey Mouse operation?"

"What the fuck is that supposed to mean?" Larry glanced over his cards, locking eyes with my new mentor.

I could see James fidgeting in his chair. He knew this whole thing could explode at any time too. Larry was so unpredictable. He could fly off the handle for the smallest of things. I shifted my chair just in case Larry decided to leap over the table and I had to intervene.

"It means exactly what I said. Do you plan on being a small-time black-owned car transporter, or are you ready to become a big-time trucking outfit? If you're trying to reach the big time, I can help you become the black king of trucking."

Larry took a moment before he spoke. "Unlike my brother, I'm not looking for any partners that don't have the last name Duncan."

Mr. Mahogany wasn't fazed by the brush-off. "I think I know how the Duncans operate," he said. "So what about you give me a five percent commission on any business I bring your way in lieu of any type of partnership?"

Again, Larry took some time to think before responding. "Okay, let's say I accept your help. How exactly are you going to help me expand my business?" He looked down at his cards and then dropped them.

Mahogany wrapped his arm around Holmes. "Major Holmes here is in need of transport of some very important cargo, and he needs a reliable shipper to get it up to the Northeast without a bill of lading."

As he always was when it came to Mr. Mahogany, Larry looked skeptical. He glanced over at me. "You know anything about this?"

"Know anything about it? It was his idea," Mr. Mahogany replied pridefully.

"I wasn't talking to you." Larry delivered his response forcefully. It wasn't disrespectful, but it wasn't exactly deferential either. Thankfully, Mr. Mahogany took it in stride, because although my brother was a true bad-ass, this was not Waycross, and he had no idea of the hierarchy up here in Atlanta.

"What's he talking about, little brother?" Larry asked me.

"Mr. Mahogany was telling me about the problem several of his associates were having transporting goods around the country. I mentioned how well you were doing with the trucking company and how you solved my shipping problem. The more we talked about it, the more we came to the conclusion that you were the type of person who would use discretion in moving their goods."

"It's very important to my people that they work with someone who can be discreet," Mahogany added.

"Discretion, discreet, that's all code for illegal, isn't it?" Larry chuckled, shaking his head.

Mr. Mahogany glanced in my direction. This was either going to be really good or really bad. I shot Larry a look, hoping he understood that I was telling him to cool out and treat this man with a little more respect.

"So, what's the cargo?" Larry asked.

"The beauty of my cargo is that you only have to make two trips a month," Major Holmes interjected.

"All I'm hearing is you beating around the bush. What's the cargo?" Larry studied him for a second then answered his own question. "You want me to move guns. Why else would a military man want something shipped?"

"Okay, let's say it is guns this first trip. Do you have problem with that?" Mr. Mahogany set down his cards.

Larry leaned forward and stared at Mr. Mahogany. "I guess that all depends on how much money we're talking about. Moving guns is risky business. The state police are searching box trucks and tractor trailers at weigh stations up and down the Interstates all the time."

"Yeah, bro, but are they searching the cars on car carriers?" I asked.

Larry thought about it, but only for a second. "They pretty much let us go right through once they check the make and model of the cars against the bill of lading."

Mr. Mahogany and I shared a knowing glance as I continued to explain my idea to my brother. "So, what if we load the guns in the trunks of high-mileage trade-ins headed to auction up in New York and Pennsylvania? Things should go through without a hitch, don't you think?"

I could tell from his expression that Larry was intrigued, but he wasn't ready to sign on just yet. "It sounds good, but what if me or one of my guys get pinched?" he asked.

We had anticipated this question, and Mr. Mahogany was ready with an answer.

"We supply you with the best lawyers money can buy, bail money, and a thousand dollars a day for every day you're incarcerated. It's in the client's best interests that you don't get pinched."

"We'd only do it two times a month. We're not trying to draw anyone's attention," Major Holmes added.

"Son of a bitch, you really thought this thing through, didn't you?" Larry grinned at me.

"Your brother is one of the smartest men I've ever met." Mr. Mahogany patted me on the back. "He's going to lead us all one day."

"Yeah, well, my momma always said he was the smart one."

"So, do we have a deal?" Holmes asked.

"Well, that kinda depends on how much money we're talking about. I've got a lot to lose shipping those heaters up Ninety-five, so you're going to have to make it worth my while."

"How's twelve grand a month sound?" Major Holmes asked.

Larry glanced at me then broke into a wide grin. "When do we start?"

Chippy

24

"Chippy, everything is so nice. This is wonderful." Mr. Mahogany's wife, Belinda, walked over to the table where I was sitting with Nee Nee, Shirley, and a couple of family members from Waycross. She'd just made a plate and was nibbling on a rib. I had to give her credit: she was one elegant older woman, even with a rib bone in her hand. I liked her because she had a presence about her that said, "Yes, I'm a lady, but I'm not to be fucked with. This is your last and final warning." Bad to the bone.

"This has to be the absolute best barbecue I've ever tasted, and the greens. You just have to give me the number of your caterer," she gushed.

"Why give you her number when I can introduce you?" I turned to Nee Nee and pointed. "Belinda, have you met my sister-in-law, Nee Nee? She made everything on your plate."

"You're kidding, right? You did all of this?" Belinda sat down next to Nee Nee. "Now, you are a woman I need to know. You have a rare talent."

"Thank you." Nee Nee beamed with pride. At the same time, I could see Shirley roll her eyes.

"If you think that's something, you've gotta try her peach cobbler and her banana pudding before you leave," I added, choosing to ignore Shirley.

"Lord, don't let my husband find that out. He absolutely loves banana pudding," she joked.

"She's the best cook in the world, that's for sure. Fool around with Nee Nee and you'll end up my size," Shirley announced. I guess she figured out that her bad attitude wasn't going over too well.

"All I know is that I'm not leaving here without your card."

Belinda stuck out her free hand, palm up.

"I'm sorry. I don't have a card. I just do this for fun." Nee Nee just kind of smiled at Belinda innocently.

"Have you ever thought about opening your own catering hall?" Belinda asked, finishing off the food on her plate. "With all the people me and my husband know, you could make an absolute fortune."

"Don't I know it," Shirley said under her breath.

"Um, well, thank you," Nee Nee said.

"No thanks necessary. Meeting you and tasting this food is thanks enough. You don't mind if I get your number from Chippy, do you? I could really use your help at the Ladies of Atlanta picnic next week. How's one thousand dollars sound?"

Nee Nee looked like she was about to fall out of her chair. Belinda was offering her more money than she could make in two months selling sandwiches at the gas station. She tried to play it off, but she couldn't hide her excitement when she broke out into a huge smile.

"That's just wonderful, Ms. Belinda. I'd be happy to help you. Get my number from Chippy and call me Monday."

"I will do that," Belinda answered. "Now, ladies, if you'll excuse me, I have to get some of that banana pudding for my husband." She stood and headed for the dessert table.

"Wow, she seems nice," Nee Nee said when Belinda was out of hearing range. "A little intense, but nice."

"Girl, please. She's what you call scary nice," I replied, watching as Belinda worked the crowd around the dessert table. "Not the type of woman you cross."

"Yeah, I'd hate to meet her in a dark alley," Shirley mumbled.

"The crazy thing is that lady has got it going on like nobody I've ever seen before. I wanna be like her when I grow up," I said, again brushing off Shirley's negative vibe.

"Does that mean you're going to pay me a thousand dollars to cater you next party?" Nee Nee asked with a laugh.

"Hell no!" I shoved her shoulder playfully then stood up from the table, looking into the nearby bassinet where Vegas was sleeping. "Nee, can you—"

"Yeah, yeah, go 'head. I got him," she answered before I could even ask.

"Thanks. I'll be back. I'm gonna go get into my bathing suit."

I made my way through the crowded backyard. Like LC had predicted, everyone was enjoying themselves as they ate, drank, played cards and dominoes, and danced. No one, however, was enjoying the beautiful swimming pool. I shook my head and wondered if it had been a waste of money.

I saw LC deep in conversation with Mr. Mahogany, Larry, and two other gentlemen. He nodded toward me, and I winked at him.

In the house, I found Levi sitting on the sofa by himself, watching cartoons and laughing. "Hey, Levi. Those good cartoons?"

"They fu–fu–funny," he said.

I was about to head up the stairs when I spotted the unthinkable in my driveway. Bursting out my front door like a bat out of hell, I barked, "What the fuck is she doing here?"

I don't know if it was the humidity or the heat of my anger, but I could feel beads of sweat forming on the back of my neck as I stood in front of my house, staring at Lou with bewilderment.

"Oh my God, Chippy," he said, lowering his head in shame.

When I saw them from inside the house, I had thought he was arguing with her to leave. But now that I was up close and personal and saw the guilty look on his face, it didn't seem like he was too surprised to see her there.

Fuck. This is not happening, I told myself as I marched angrily toward them.

I repeated my question, this time screaming at the top of my lungs. "What the fuck is she doing at my house? I know you didn't bring her to my house, Lou."

He looked back at her and frowned. "She followed me here."

"Followed you from where?" I was still screaming. There was now a crowd of folks gathering in the front yard to witness this.

"Lou, what the hell is going on?" LC yelled as he made his way through the crowd.

"I'll tell you what's going on!" I shouted loud enough for everyone within five miles to hear as I jumped in my husband's face. "Your brother brought your bitch to my house!" I pointed at Donna, and LC's jaw almost hit the ground.

"LC, I can explain." Lou stepped toward LC humbly, but the way Donna looked at him made me want to pluck her eyeballs out.

"Explain what? There's no explanation for this." My chest was heaving with every angry breath I took. I turned to my husband, taking his arm. "LC, I want this bitch off my property."

"Who you calling a bitch?" Donna finally spoke, stepping toward me. That was the wrong fucking move, because I snapped.

"You," I replied, reaching out and grabbing a handful of her hair. I tried my best to twist and rip it out, but LC pulled me off her, and Lou grabbed Donna. "Lou, you need to get her away from here," LC said.

At this point, my feet weren't even on the ground as I struggled to break loose and get to her.

"I ain't come here to start no trouble, LC," Donna huffed from behind Lou. Lucky for her, she had enough sense to take a step back. "Lou and I—"

"I don't give a damn about anything you and Lou got going on." LC was yelling now too. "Both of y'all need to leave my property."

Larry stepped up and stood on one side of LC, and Mr. Mahogany stood on the other. It reminded me of the old days, when the three brothers were together, only this time, one of them was on the other side. Not that I cared, but I could see Lou was hurt.

"Really? Y'all gonna do me like this?" Lou looked over at Larry.

"Naw, Lou. You did this to yourself. You dead-ass wrong for this one, bro." Larry shook his head.

"Y'all don't understand. I'm doing this for Momma." Lou's eyes traveled from one brother to the other. He was on the verge of tears. "Donna can help us find Momma."

"Lou, get the hell outta here. Don't you think you caused enough trouble for one day?" Larry moved forward, and he and Lou stood eye to eye.

"Come on, Lou." Donna pulled at his shirt. Lou didn't budge.

"She can help us, Larry," he pleaded.

"Let it go, Lou," Larry replied.

"I'm not going to tell you to leave again," LC said.

"Yes, I think it's best that you all go." Mr. Mahogany gave a slight nod. Within seconds, out of nowhere, the two big men who had been at the table with him were standing beside LC, flexing their muscles like they were itching for a fight.

I could see the anger and hurt in Lou's face. For a split second, I felt sorry for him. Then my eyes went to Donna, and any type of sympathy I had vanished.

"This is some bullshit," Lou said, glaring at Mr. Mahogany just before he turned and walked toward his car.

We all watched silently as Donna followed him. She got in the car, and they sped away.

"All right, folks. Show's over. Let's get back to partying," Mr. Mahogany announced like he was the host as he started to herd people back into the house.

LC reached for me, but I snatched my arm away. "Dammit, LC, am I ever going to get away from this bitch? Did you know he was bringing her here?"

"No, I swear I was just as surprised to see her as you were."

"I want one of those burglar alarms put on the house like you've got at the dealership." I folded my arms, staring down the street where Lou's car had traveled.

"No problem. I'll have them install it first thing in the morning." He leaned in, and I let him kiss me. "I'm sorry. I don't know what Lou's thinking these days."

"She'll be okay, LC. You run along with the rest of the men and let us girls talk." Belinda's words came out of nowhere. I had completely forgotten that she was there with us. I turned around and watched her walking toward me, looking calm and serene, standing with her perfectly coifed hair and baby blue lounging suit, belted at the waist. It was the strangest thing: my life felt like it was falling apart, and there she was looking flawless, giving me some level of comfort. She stared right in my eyes, and when we were face to face, she gave me the most confident smile I'd ever seen.

She spoke softly but with an air of authority. "I don't know who the hell that woman is, but you don't have to worry about her again. She means nothing, has nothing, and can do nothing to harm you or your family."

"But she—you—I . . ." The words wouldn't form correctly.

"She's nobody. You are the wife of LC Duncan. Your position and title are protected, right?"

I stared at Belinda. She was so regal and poised that I was almost enchanted. Then I realized what she was saying. I was the wife of LC Duncan, who held a seat on the Black Council. We were one of the most powerful couples in Atlanta, which meant that we were protected. The fact that LC and I would have eyes on us and wouldn't even know it was one of the things Belinda had taught me when she first told me about the Council. I thought about the two men who had immediately appeared when Lou refused to leave.

"Right," I said, feeling better already.

"No worries. Now, let's go and check on those precious boys of yours. You have a backyard full of guests, and I'm sure they're worried about their hostess." She brushed the hair from my face and affectionately pressed her forehead against mine. I gave her a smile, and we linked arms and headed back to the party.

Lou

25

"What the fuck did I tell you?" I yelled, pulling off so fast that the tires of my car burned rubber on the street and then screeched as I turned the corner.

Donna had a death grip on the handle of the car door, but I didn't care. She could have opened that bitch and jumped out and it wouldn't have mattered to me, because I was just that fucking mad at her ass.

"I give you one fucking instruction and you can't even do that."

"I'm sorry!" she yelled, her voice cracking.

"Sorry ain't good enough. You got my whole family against me when I need them the most. Now I'm never going to get them to believe my momma's alive. Fuck!" I slammed my hand against the steering wheel.

"I know I should have listened to you," she cried, "but I just wanted to see him so bad."

I shook my head angrily. "We had an agreement when I dropped you off downtown. I told you I'd bring him to the park."

"Lou, please, I thought you were lying about bringing him to the park." She reached out and touched my shoulder, but I shrugged her off. "I really didn't think things were going to go that far."

"How the fuck did you even know where to find me? What did you do, follow me?"

"I was taking a cab to the park like you told me," she answered. "We just happened to pass by the house. I saw you parking, so I told the driver to stop,"

"You didn't think showing up at that house would piss people off? What the fuck did you think Chippy was gonna do, invite you in and make you a plate?"

Donna sucked her teeth. "I didn't care what that bitch did. This wasn't about her."

"That's your fucking problem! You don't care about anybody but yourself. I should've known trusting you was gonna turn around and bite me in the ass. But that's okay. I'm done. I'm taking your ass to the bus station." I reached over and grabbed her shoulder so hard that she gasped. I wasn't going to hit her, but I needed her to understand how serious I was. I only released my grip when I noticed that she was on the verge of tears.

"I'm sorry," she said softly, wiping away a tear as she leaned against the window to put as much distance between us as possible.

"Look," I said, "I didn't mean to hurt you. But I care about my family, and now they're all pissed at me because of you. I need them to help me find my momma, and now they probably won't even talk to me."

We both sat in silence as I drove. My mind was filled with thoughts of LC and Larry. I couldn't believe my brothers had refused to listen to me and then allowed that bastard Mahogany to talk to me that way. I didn't know who this man thought he was, and I didn't care. He would definitely be handled—once I found my mother and got back to my old self.

"Lou." Donna called my name softly.

"Yeah."

"Please don't take me to the bus station. I can still help you find Miss Bettie." At the sound of my mother's name, an ache came across my chest. I missed her. Hell, she had only been home a couple of weeks, and then she was gone. People always talked about how she and LC had a close relationship, and they did, but I was close to her too, and I missed her so much.

"I know I'm not your family." She surprised me when she eased closer to me, taking my hand and placing it on top of hers. "But we can get her back if we work *together*."

I looked over at her, and she stared right into my eyes, I guess trying to let me know how much she cared. Shit, I knew she had another motive, but maybe she did care just a little. Besides, at the moment, she was all I had.

I patted her hand. "All right. I won't send you home yet, but just so you know, you still gotta figure out how to get some more information outta Eddie—and if that means fucking him, then that's what you're gonna do."

She sighed, but she didn't say she wouldn't do it. "Just remember your part of the deal too, Lou."

Shirley

26

"Sh—Sh—Shirley!"

Hearing Levi call my name, I slipped out the back door and didn't look back as I got into my car. I couldn't take it anymore. We'd only been back from Atlanta a few hours, and I had already given him some pussy thinking it would shut him up and give me some peace for the rest of the night, yet here he was asking me for more. Why the fuck couldn't he just leave me alone once in a while? Sometimes I felt like nothing more than a sperm receptacle for Levi.

You're just thinking this way because you're pregnant. It's just hormones, I tried telling myself. Hormones or not, I was sick of it. I reached under the seat of my car, pulled out a pack of cigarettes, and lit one. As I took a long drag and blew out a stream of smoke, I closed my eyes and allowed the nicotine to calm my nerves. By the time I got back from my drive, I had smoked another one and was thinking about smoking a third when I reached the bar.

"How was your trip to the big city?" Moe, the bartender, asked when I sat down in front of him. The Friday night crowd was in full swing, and I calculated the night's intake as I scanned the room. My girls were in high demand, and from the looks of things, I might need to hire a few more, especially with Li'l Momma away on her vacation.

"Better than an episode of *General Hospital*," I said with a laugh. "Luke and Laura ain't got shit on these damn Duncans. I ain't seen that much drama since I caught Big Sam getting head from that dude that did his bookkeeping."

"Get the fuck outta here!" He looked shocked. "It must've been something big to top that."

I lit a cigarette. "Honey, Lou brought LC's ex to the house, and Chippy tried to rip every last one of her hairs out her head. Kinda put a damper on that picture-perfect life LC and Chippy are living," I said bitterly. "Oh, and LC and Lou almost got into it too."

"You lying." Moe took a step back. "They don't ever fight. At least not in public."

"If I'm lying, I'm dying." I raised my hand. "Ask Lou next time you see him, but don't tell him I told you."

"No, no, I believe you."

"Where's Levi?" I asked, exhaling a smoke ring.

"He left about ten minutes ago. He was looking for you for a minute, and then he said he was going to walk over to the service station."

"Good. He won't be back for a while. Pour me a bourbon."

Moe gave me a strange look. I knew it was because news of my pregnancy had begun to circulate. I hadn't confirmed or denied the rumors. Still, what I did was none of his damn business whether I was pregnant or not. I gave him a daring look, reminding him that I was his damn boss and he'd better do what I said. As quickly as he fixed my drink, I swallowed it and immediately asked for another. This time, he didn't hesitate.

"Looks like you could use some company, Slingshot Shirley."

It had been years since I'd heard someone call me that name. I turned around to see if I was imagining things.

"Eric?" I said, now facing the tall, attractive, dark-skinned man standing in front of me.

"How are you, Shirley?" His smile brought back memories of my youth.

"I . . . I'm good. How are you?" I tried to catch my breath.

Back in the early days when Sam ran the place, Eric was his best friend and my best customer. He lived in Atlanta, but he'd come down every weekend up until a few years ago. Sam told me he stopped because he got married and his wife didn't like him hanging out with a pimp; however, they still hung out when Sam made his bi-monthly trips to Atlanta. I hadn't seen Eric in so long that he had become a memory in the back of my mind until now.

"I'm good. Been thinking about you ever since I saw you at Juan's wedding last month."

That surprised me. I had no idea he was there. But then again, there was a big crowd there, and I pretty much stayed by Levi's side all night. "You was at the wedding? Why didn't you say something?"

"I kept my distance because you was with some giant ass motherfucker who must have been seven foot tall."

I laughed. "Oh, that was just Levi. He might look scary, but he's a pussy cat."

"Well, anyway, I figured I'd stop by on my way to Jacksonville. Come see if the prettiest girl in South Georgia still worked here," he said as he took a seat beside me. "And now I'm glad I did."

"Prettiest girl in south Georgia? You always were a smooth talker, Eric," I said with a smile. "You make lies sound like the truth, and I appreciate it."

"It's not a lie. I do think you're the prettiest girl in south Georgia. That's why I'm here." He held up two fingers toward Moe, who poured us a round of drinks. "Seriously, you're looking good, Shirley. Fine as ever."

I turned away slightly, trying to hide the scar on my face, which I was sure was the first thing he'd noticed when he saw me. "Another lie. I've had a couple of rough run-ins, as I'm sure you can see."

"You're still looking like the same beautiful Shirley to me. Run-ins or not, that ain't changed." He touched my cheek, and a shiver went down my spine. It might sound like a funny thing to say about a paying customer, but he had always touched my spirit and brought out the woman in me.

"Can I take you upstairs?" he asked.

I let out a long exhale as I took this man in. He was well dressed, well spoken, and smelling good. I had often wondered why he always seemed to ask for me. Although I was good at my job, I wasn't naive to the fact that there were younger, prettier, skinnier girls than me. And when we would go upstairs, he never treated me like a whore. He would talk with me and make me laugh. I almost felt bad for charging him, because in addition to having some good-ass dick, Eric got off on pleasing me with his mouth, something men rarely did when they came to see me.

"Shirley, did you hear me?"

"Yes . . . Well, I . . . That's not what I . . . I don't really do that kinda work anymore, Eric," I said.

"I'm not just any customer. Money ain't an object." Eric reached for his pocket like he was going to pull out his cash, but I stopped his hand.

"No, that's what I'm trying to tell you. I'm no longer working."

"Well, what are you doing here then? I gotta have some time with you, Shirley. You know that's why I came here."

"Didn't you see the sign out front? I'm the boss now. This is Big Shirley's place. I run things," I said with pride.

He leaned back with a look of amused surprise on his face. "Well, I'll be damned! Congratulations, Shirley." The way he said it let me know that he really meant it, and I felt a surge of happiness that I hadn't felt in God knows how long.

"Thank you. So, that's why I said I don't really—"

"I get it," he said. "No need to explain."

We dropped that subject then sat together for a while, talking and laughing like old times. For a second, I thought about telling him I had a man in my life, but ultimately, I didn't divulge that information, nor did I mention the baby I was carrying. It felt good to have someone paying me compliments the way he was, and I knew if I told him about Levi, it would put a stop to it. I figured that as long as I didn't have any intention of acting on it, what was the harm in sitting there and soaking up his admiration for a while?

Then he decided to get serious again.

"Shirley, we really can't go upstairs? You don't even have special customers?"

"No, I don't have special customers. I'm sorry. I just don't. I can get another girl for you. I'll get someone real special. I know what you like. . . . Dana, come over here!" I yelled over the music and called one of my best girls, who was sitting across the room. She was a thick girl, like I was, with full breasts and wide hips.

"That's not what I was getting at, Shirley." Eric grabbed me by the arm and stared at me. "I just wanted to make sure before I ask you . . ."

"What?" I said. He was so close that I could feel his breath on my cheek.

"I don't see any rings on your finger, so how about we go out on a date?"

"A what?" I frowned.

"Can I take you out? We can go to dinner, maybe check out a movie if you'd like. When was the last time you went on a real date, Shirley?"

A date. A real date. I had never been on a real date. I had been fucking for money since the age of seventeen, and no one had ever asked me out. Hell, I'd been with Levi for almost four years, and we'd never gone on a date. Now, here was this tall, dark, and handsome man, asking to take me out. I didn't know what to say.

"I . . . uh . . ." I eased away from him, hoping that taking a step back and not having him touch me would help me think clearer. My heart continued racing, and my nerves caused my stomach to flip.

That's not your nerves, fool. That's your baby. Levi's baby. Levi Duncan's baby. And if Levi or any other Duncan finds out you went on a date with another man, you're gonna end up just as dead as their momma.

Eric pressed on as I fought internally with my conscience. "Come on, Shirley. I can pick you up tomorrow night at seven." He flashed a sexy smile. "I been wanting to take you on a date for a long time."

I thought about a proper answer; how I needed to tell him that I couldn't go because I had a man and a baby on the way; how as much as I would love going to dinner and a movie, I just couldn't. It wouldn't be the right thing to do. I stared at all six feet three inches of him, with his smooth chocolate skin and perfect teeth, dressed like he had stepped out of the *Ebony* magazines I read when I was in my office sometimes. This was a dream come true and a nightmare all at the same time. I had to say no.

I closed my eyes and told myself to respectfully decline his offer, but as I opened my mouth, the words came tumbling out before I could stop them. "Sure. Why not? I'd love to."

Bettie

27

"Are you hungry?" I asked Lisa. We had been in the same room for a week now, and I had been trying to nurse her as best I could. The physical bruises were healing, but the ones I was most concerned about were the ones on the inside. I knew the young girl had been beaten and raped repeatedly to the point that she wanted to die. I had only been in this hell for a few weeks. To know that she had survived for a year showed me that she was a much stronger young woman than she thought she was. Until she could believe in herself again, I was determined to fight for both of our lives.

Lisa mumbled something in response to my question and shook her head, then lay back down in the corner of the room. She had barely eaten anything in the past few days.

"Hey." I crawled over to her and held out a slice of cheese that had been tossed into the room along with a few slices of bread a little while earlier. "You've gotta at least eat a little bit. We gotta get your strength up and get you well."

She looked at me with her eyes full of sadness. "Why? So I can be full of energy the next time he rapes me? No, thank you, I'd rather be dead."

"I'm not gonna let that happen again. I'm gonna protect you," I assured her, pulling her to sit up. "You can't protect me. You can't even protect yourself. They beat you too."

"You're right, they do beat on me." I sighed. "But you're in here with me now. You ain't alone."

For a split second, Lisa looked over at me with a glimmer of hope in her eyes. I smiled at her, and she took the cheese from my hand. She winced as she bit it and chewed.

"Thank you."

"You're welcome, sweetie." I watched her take another bite as I asked, "So why are you here? Why have they been holding you for so long?" I passed her the cup of water that I had saved for her, and she drank from the metal cup.

"Have you ever heard of J. Michael Miller?" she asked.

I nodded. I used to know the crooked son of a bitch. "Yeah, every black person in Georgia knows who J. Michael Miller is. He's big time."

"Well, he's my father, and he's not quite as big time as you think."

This information shocked the hell out of me. The J. Michael Miller I knew would have tore up the state to find his daughter.

"Not big time? Doesn't he own Georgia Star?" I asked.

"On paper, maybe, but he was in so much debt to the Georgia underworld that he gave me to them as collateral."

My stomach dropped. That was about the worst thing I had ever heard. "Get the fuck outta here. What kind of a father does that?"

"Well, I can't blame it all on him," she said with a sigh. "When those men came to the house with guns to kill my daddy, I told them to take me until he could pay them back."

I straightened up. "That's admirable." *And a little crazy*, I wanted to say.

"No, it wasn't. It was stupid. I should have let them kill him after what he's let them put me through." She was starting to cry, and this time it was because of even deeper wounds. "For the first few months, they had me living in a condo over in Buckhead. They let me go shopping, took me out to a couple of clubs. They treated me good. That is until dear old Dad decided to play games with their payments."

"Oh, no he didn't!"

She nodded. "Oh, yes he did, and that's when they threw me down here. But that's not the worst of it. He really must have pissed them off about three months ago, because that's when the rapes started."

"Does he know what they're doing to you?" My own eyes were welling up with tears after hearing this story.

"They take Polaroid pictures of me once a month and send them to him and my mom to remind them to make their payments. I should have been out of here after a year, but he's screwed up the payments so bad that the guy who takes the pictures said it's going to be at least another nine, ten months."

"Damn, that's fucked up. I'm sorry." My words were inadequate, but I had no idea what else to say to someone whose family had betrayed her so badly.

"It's okay. I just try not to think about it." She took one last sip of water and laid her head down. "I probably won't be alive in nine or ten months."

Donna

28

"Donna?"

"Yeah?" I looked up and saw Eddie frowning as if he could read my mind. Thank God he couldn't, or else he'd probably want to kill me. I was thinking about Lou. As big of a pain in my ass as he was, he was starting to grow on me. Not that I even understood what that meant. I just knew I was thinking and worrying about him a lot.

"Pay attention. You're the one who said you wanted to understand my world."

"You're right. I'm sorry." I gave him a fake smile then turned my gaze to the big house we were parked diagonally across from. Eddie had decided to take me out with him to show me what he did for a living. Believe it or not, he'd shocked the hell out of me by proposing with a big-ass ring the night before. I hadn't even done more than let him kiss me a few times, yet he actually got down on one knee and said he wanted to marry me. Of course, you know I said no, coming up with the excuse that I couldn't marry a man if I didn't know everything about him and how he was going to provide for me. Well, that prompted him to pick me up from work and drive over here. "But we've been out here two hours just staring at an empty house."

"It's not empty." He pointed at the side door, where a woman in what looked like a maid's uniform was placing a bag in a garbage can. She began dragging it down the driveway. "In my line of work, you have to be patient."

We watched the woman place the garbage can at the curb and walk back up the driveway and into the house. The second the door closed, Eddie hit the gas, pulling up next to the trash can. He hopped out of the car, popped open the trunk, and placed the entire garbage can in it. Five seconds later, he was back in the car and we'd sped off.

"Mission accomplished," he hollered.

"So you steal garbage cans for a living?" I asked sarcastically.

"Well, no . . . but yes. Well, sometimes," he replied, sounding crazy as hell. "Stealing garbage can be part of the job in my line of work."

I was starting to think Eddie really was nuts. "What exactly is your line of work, Eddie?"

"Information." He said it proudly. "People will pay a lot of money for information, Donna. Now, take that house I just took that garbage can from. That's the house of Dwayne McCarty, an influential man looking to run for congress. His opponents are a little afraid of him because he comes from money and his father used to hold the seat, so they've hired me to find out as much as I can about him."

"What's his garbage got to do with it?" I asked, and Eddie laughed.

"You ever think about the things people throw away in their garbage?"

"Yeah, and they are disgusting." The things I put in my own garbage can made me cringe, so thinking about going through someone else's made me want to hurl.

"Some of them are nasty, but what about the other things, like credit card bills, phone bills, medication bottles, letters, notes? You can find out a whole lot about people by looking through their trash. Trust me."

I considered what he'd said for a minute. It actually made a lot of sense. It also was a good opening for me to try to pry more useful information out of him. After all, that's why I was spending so much time with this cretin: to get information for Lou.

"So, is that why you've been avoiding Lou Duncan? Did you go through his trash?" I laughed, hoping to make it sound humorous and not like I was prying.

"No, Lou wanted information about his momma. He paid good money for it, too, only the people who are involved in her abduction aren't the type I wanted to cross." Whoever these people were, they were clearly no joke. I could hear the fear in Eddie's voice. "So, at their suggestion, I returned his money. I'm sure he wants to kill me, but there are worse things than death."

"These sound like some scary folks."

"They are about as scary as they come in this part of the country. But I been getting a lot of work from them since. They're the ones paying me to get the information on Dwayne McCarty and a whole slew of others."

"My God! Who are these people?" For a second I thought I was close to getting some truly valuable information for Lou, but Eddie dashed those hopes real quick.

He shook his head. "Nobody. Forget I even said anything about them. I forgot you had history with the Duncan boys. Running my mouth like this could get us both killed."

I knew I had to be very careful about how I handled this moment, but I still felt like I was on the verge of getting what I needed as long as I didn't blow it. Eddie may have had the manners of a barbarian, but he wasn't a dummy. I had to play it cool.

"I don't give a fuck about them. I'm more concerned about you and your safety," I said, appealing to his ego.

I reached for the radio and turned the volume down then grabbed Eddie's hand. He seemed surprised by my actions, because I never initiated any type of physical contact with him. When he looked over at me, I stared at him intensely and licked my lips slightly before speaking.

"Listen, Eddie, you know that I am starting to have feelings for you. But it's moments like this that show me that maybe you don't feel the same way."

"What the hell does that mean? You know I have feelings for you. I take you out every week. I buy you whatever you want, take you to the nicest restaurants . . . Shit, I gave you a ring. Doesn't that prove how I feel?"

I shook my head. "You did that because you wanna fuck me, Eddie. Come on now. That doesn't have shit to do with how you feel about me. Here I am asking you about what's going on with you, and you're acting as if you can't trust me. If you were digging me like you say you do, you would be able to tell me." I gave his hand a gentle squeeze. "Shoot, I was almost ready to give myself to you, but if you don't even trust me, then I don't know."

Eddie sat back and stared at me. "You really digging me, Donna?"

I nodded.

"Does this mean you're ready to give me some of that sweet thang you been holding on to?" His expression was serious.

"When you show me that I can trust you and you trust me, you can have all the sweetness you can handle. But I don't think we're at that point yet, Eddie. I thought we were, but—"

"I trust you, Donna." Eddie inhaled deeply and remained quiet for a few seconds, his eyes focused on the road.

"Then tell me what's going on. LC used to tell me everything." I was hoping that would get in his craw and his ego would force him to tell me what I needed to know, but something else seemed to be more important than what I had to say.

"Shit!" He kept looking to the rearview mirror.

"Oh my God, is someone following us?" I glanced back and saw that there was someone close behind us with their high beams on.

"Just stay calm and let me handle this." He opened the glove box and retrieved a pistol, tucking it into his pants.

"What are you going to do?"

Eddie didn't answer the question. He turned into the parking lot of a corner store and parked. The car that had been behind us, an older model green Cadillac, parked right beside us. Inside was a scary-looking man, smoking a cigarette and looking anxious.

"Stay in the car and lock the door. I'll be right back." Eddie sounded scared. "I gotta go handle some business right quick."

We weren't in the safest part of town, and although I had been in worse places in my darker days, I still didn't want to be left alone, especially with that scary-looking motherfucker staring at me.

"Do you know him? Who is it?" I asked, staring at the man who was now leaning against his car.

"Just wait here for a second." Eddie climbed out of the car and walked over to the stranger.

I cracked open my window, wide enough to hear their conversation, but not enough for someone to reach an arm or even a gun—through.

"Hey, man, what are you doing here?"

"I came to see you. We got a problem," the guy said, puffing away at his cigarette. "The boss wants to up the timetable on Dwayne McCarty."

"I don't got that much. I just started working on it." Eddie looked pretty shook up.

"Well, he's got something to do with that old broad Bettie, and they want to find out what it is before they move her."

The guy began talking low, and I couldn't make out the rest of what he was saying. All I could understand were the words "old woman" and "Homerville." They had to be talking about Bettie Duncan. I could feel it in my gut.

Desperate to hear more, I cracked the window open an inch more and leaned toward it.

"I can't go right now. I got plans with my girl," Eddie said.

"Fuck your girl and cancel them plans," the man said, snatching him up by the collar. "Now hurry up and get rid o' the broad. I'm driving."

"Okay, okay." Eddie looked over at me, and I quickly pretended to be checking my reflection in the rearview mirror. "Lemme get her home safe, and I'll get there as soon as I can."

"What part of 'I'm driving' don't you understand?" the guy asked him just before lighting another cigarette and climbing into his car. "Do you want to ride there in the trunk?"

"A'ight, just give me a second," Eddie said, sounding defeated. He walked over to the car.

"Who the fuck was that?" I asked as soon as he got in.

"Nobody important. But listen, you take my car and head on home. I got some business to handle."

"What about dinner? And the movie we were supposed to go see?" I folded my arms across my chest, pretending to be disappointed.

"I'll make it up to you. I gotta head up the road right quick."

"Let me go with you," I suggested. I was nervous, but still halfway hoping he would say yes and I would be able to find out exactly where Bettie Duncan was.

"Naw, I can't do that." He leaned over and kissed me on his way out of the car . "I'll see you back at your place in a couple of hours."

I watched them leave and rushed to get into the driver's seat to follow. Thanks to a tractor trailer blocking my exit, by the time I got out of the parking lot, they were long gone.

From the corner of my eye, I spotted a pay phone and I got an idea. I jumped out of the car and rushed over to the phone. I dropped a dime into the slot and quickly dialed Lou's number, praying that he would pick up. It rang twice, and as soon as he answered, I blurted out, "She's alive, Lou!"

"What? Are you sure?" His voice was shaking.

"Yes, I'm sure."

I told him everything that Eddie had said in the car, and then about the guy he'd just left with. "They're in a green Cadillac, and I think they're headed to Homerville."

Shirley

29

"That movie was so funny. I haven't laughed like that in a long time. Thank you," I said to Eric as he passed me some of the best reefer I'd ever smoked. We were sitting in his car by Ware County Reservoir, about twenty minutes south of Waycross.

"Me either. I can't wait for us to come back and see the one with Richard Pryor."

I stopped mid-inhale. "Us?"

"Yeah, unless you don't wanna come see it with me?" Eric turned to me with a questioning look.

I didn't know what to say, so I put the joint back in my mouth. When we were watching the preview for the Richard Pryor movie, I knew I wanted to see it, but I never thought there would be a possibility of it happening.

"I'd like that," I said softly.

"Good. 'Cause now that I'll be working down here, I'm gonna do just that. You've always been special to me, Shirley." Eric reached over and took my hand. The smile on his face and the look in his eyes made me feel as if I were the most beautiful woman in the world. It was something I hadn't felt since the early days with Levi.

"You're going to be working here?"

"Yep." He nodded. "We're expanding our business into south Georgia. I'm going to be spearheading that expansion."

I held my breath for a second. I loved the idea of him being around, but I was afraid of him running into Levi or the rest of the Duncans. "Eric, there's something I need to tell you."

He chuckled. "I already know all about Levi Duncan, Shirley. He's the big guy you were at the wedding with, right?"

"Yes." I swallowed hard. "How did you know?"

"It's not important. What I need to know is, do you love him?"

I released a big sigh. "I don't know. . . . Sometimes I think I do."

Eric slowly nodded his head. "Sounds like you have one foot in the door and one foot out."

I raised my eyebrows and laughed. "That about sums it up." I passed him the joint as I steered the conversation away from me and Levi. "And what about you? You still married?"

"Divorced. I'm the kind of man who needs a queen, not a princess. I'm trying to build something, and I don't need some weak woman standing in my way."

"I hear that. Most men want a puppet or a Barbie doll." I was flattered that he seemed to be telling me I wasn't in that category.

"So, let me ask you a question, Shirley." He toked on the joint.

"Mm-hmm?"

"I know your name is on the sign out front, but do you really own Big Shirley's?"

I tensed up for a second, wondering if I should tell the truth. I hadn't lied when I told Eric I was now running the place, but I wasn't exactly honest either. I took a deep breath and said, "No, I don't."

He frowned. "So, my people were right, the Duncans do own it, huh?"

"They pay me ten percent of the intake," I said, a little defensively.

"Ten percent? Shit, Shirley, that's all?"

I turned my head away in embarrassment. "Yep, that's it."

He reached out, taking hold of my face and turning it back to him. "You're worth more than that. Have you ever thought about owning your own place?"

"What do you mean?"

"Leave the Duncans and open your own spot. Hell, you obviously got the knowledge and experience or they wouldn't be having you running it. So, why not do it?" Eric nuzzled his chin against my forehead. "I've got some money. I can be your partner."

It was like déjà vu. He was giving me the same speech I had given Nee Nee. I had been so consumed with convincing her to open the Soul Cafe that opening my own place had never crossed my mind.

"I can't do that," I told him.

"Why not? Listen, I told you my family is expanding their business, and now would be the perfect time for us to partner and make shit happen. We could open up down in Brunswick off the interstate and get some of that I-95 traffic."

"It's not that simple, Eric," I said sadly.

He pulled me closer into his arms, and I leaned back into his chest. I inhaled the scent, a combination of Old Spice after shave and Irish Spring soap. "I have Levi."

"Be for real, Shirley. Is he gonna marry you? Do you even wanna marry him?"

I thought about what Eric was suggesting. He was presenting me with what seemed like the opportunity of a lifetime. I could be my own boss and not have to work for pennies on the damn dollar. Eric and I could be partners, lovers.

"I don't know." I shrugged.

"Well, then let me convince you."

Eric slid his hand under my dress. I felt his fingers sliding along my thighs until they reached my panties. Heat began to rise between my legs as he eased the satin garment to the side and found the exact spot that he was looking for.

"Shit," I moaned. Maybe it was the effect of the marijuana, combined with the fact that I was pregnant—hell, it may have been because I was being fingered by a man who clearly knew what he was doing for a change—but I was hornier than I had ever been in my life.

"Eric, wait," I said, trying to push him away.

"Come on, Shirley, you know you want it." His fingers entered my wetness, causing me to gasp. It had been so long since I'd had a man touch me that way that I instantly melted. With Levi, it was pretty much straight fucking. Now, here with Eric, it was hot, inviting, and intimate. I closed my eyes, arched my back, and spread my legs wider. Then, I felt it—I was no longer being pleased by Eric's fingers, but instead, I felt another sensation and realized he'd lowered his head between my legs. His arms brushed my hands away, and he tasted me with his tongue. The sensation was driving me insane, and I didn't want it to ever end. All thoughts of Levi, the Duncans, and the baby I was carrying left my mind, and I allowed my body to enjoy this pleasure, even though I knew I may have been losing my soul in the process.

Bettie

30

The sound of someone coming down the stairs was loud enough to wake Lisa and me. As they came closer, she became more and more fidgety. We knew it was the monster; his heavy footsteps were unmistakable. It had been a few days since we'd seen him. Another guy had been bringing us scraps of food and water. He was at least a little nicer and he wasn't abusive. I had hoped that the monster was gone forever, but that would have been too good to be true.

"No, God, please no," Lisa whimpered, trembling as she scrambled to the far corner of the room.

I felt so bad for the young girl, because I knew just as well as she did what was about to happen. I didn't have much time to talk. I just had to hope that she would do what I told her. I rushed beside her and gently placed my hands on her shoulders. "Lisa, I need you to listen to me."

Lisa's eyes were shut, and she shook her head from side to side in a frenzy. "No, no, no."

"Lisa, look at me. I need you to look at me right now!" I grabbed her tighter and shook her a bit. It was enough to get her attention. Tears streamed down her face, but she stared at me as I whispered, "We know what he wants, and I know this is gonna go against everything you believe, but baby girl, listen. You're gonna have to just give it to him—willfully."

"What?" She looked terrified.

"Yes, you're going to have to. If you give it to him, he can't take it by force, and he loses his power. When he comes to get you and takes you into that room, I need for you to act like you want it. Act like you've been missing it. When you do, you take back all the power he thinks he has over you."

Lisa looked at me like I had lost my damn mind. I knew my telling her to willingly fuck the man who had been raping her sounded sick, but I also knew that it would work. I had seen it work. In prison, once an inmate began to act like she enjoyed being fucked by an officer who had raped her, he stopped, as if he lost all desire to be with her. The thrill of forcefully fucking a woman was gone.

"I can't."

"You can. You have to if you want him to stop."

The lock on the door clicked, and he stepped inside. He didn't see us at first, and then, his eyes spotted us in the corner, Lisa hovering and me comforting her.

"There you are." He stomped over to us. "You trying to hide from me?"

"No," Lisa cried and cowered behind me.

"Leave her the fuck alone." I stood up, but he smacked me across the face so hard that I stumbled and fell on top of her.

"Get your old ass out the damn way. You better be glad you old as fuck, or I would be taking that pussy from you too, but I don't do cobwebs." His sinister laughter caused me to cringe in spite of the strength I wanted to portray.

I pulled myself together and spat, "Your little-ass dick wouldn't be able to handle it anyway, you non-fucking prick. The only time you probably get pussy is when you take it from her, and she's already told me you're a lousy fuck." I laughed right back at him.

His face contorted into a look of pure hatred, and he kicked me on my side. The pain was excruciating, but I refused to cry out. I had to take my own advice, and I knew that seeing my pain would only bring him more pleasure. Just as I prepared myself for another kick, I felt Lisa moving beside me.

"Leave her alone," she said softly as she stood up. "You didn't come for her. You came for me." The look of confusion on his face was priceless as she cupped his junk then brushed past him on her way to the door. "You coming?"

As he followed her out of the room, her eyes met mine, and she gave me the slightest nod. It was time for her to take back her power. I closed my eyes and began to pray as the door slammed behind them. I waited for the sound of the lock, but it didn't happen.

Shit, this is my chance.

My heart was beating out of my chest as I eased the door open enough to peek out. I eased out into the corridor as soon as I confirmed the coast was clear. I was just about to ascend the stairs when I heard Lisa's whimpers.

Forget that little girl, Bettie. Save yourself, I told myself, picking up a ten-inch wrench that was sitting on the desk outside my room. *You can always come back and rescue her once you're with the boys. Smartest thing you can do right now is run like the wind.*

Of course, you know I didn't take my own advice. I turned around and headed for the room the noise was coming out of, brandishing the wrench like a club. The door was already half open, and I slipped in unnoticed. The monster was on top of Lisa with his back turned to me. I took a deep breath, moving as quickly and as silently as I could toward him. He turned briefly, but before he could react, I slammed the wrench upside his big-ass head.

"Bettie, stop!" Lisa yelled from underneath him about ten blows in. I did as she asked, mainly because he wasn't moving anymore.

"Come on! We gotta get outta here." I rolled his fat ass off her. He landed on the floor in one big thump. I grabbed her arm, tugging at it to make her follow me. She took one more angry glance at the monster. I'm sure she wanted to kick him or something, despite the fact he was lying there motionless.

"I think he's dead," she said.

"Yeah." I smirked, waving her on. "That was the idea when I hit him with the wrench. Come on. Let's get outta here."

I grabbed Lisa by the arm and we rushed out of the room, both in a panic. We took off down the hall to the stairs. Lisa was heaving and crying. I commanded her to hush as we tried to figure our way out. I didn't know if he was the only one there, and I didn't want to take a chance of anyone hearing us.

"Be quiet," I whispered and tried to listen for footsteps. When I didn't hear anyone, I eased up the steps one at a time with Lisa right on my heels.

We made it to the top, and thankfully the door was already cracked open. I held my breath, pushing it open just enough to stick my head out. It was a kitchen, but I couldn't see beyond that point. I listened for a minute then moved slowly. Based on the rusted sink and filth on the floor, I could tell that wherever we were, it was abandoned and had been for a while. I spotted a rusted butcher knife on the worn countertop and grabbed it for protection to go with the wrench, just in case. I cursed myself for not thinking about taking that fool's gun when I had the chance. I spotted what I hoped was a back door.

BAM! We heard the loud noise coming from the basement and then loud footsteps.

"Son of a bitch, he was still alive," I said. Lisa had already bolted toward the back door.

She pulled at the doorknob, but it wouldn't budge. She tried to turn the knob again and shook the door. It still wouldn't move. Lisa began whimpering in frustration. I knew that as soon as he made it to the top of the stairs, because of the beating I'd put on him, our lives would be over.

I pushed her out of the way and fumbled.

Click.

Surprisingly, the knob turned for me, and I yanked the door open. We fled out into the darkness, stumbling over the uneven ground. We scrambled over rocks and trees, huffing and puffing to escape the demon behind us. Into the woods, through the bushes, and around the tall, thick trees, we continued running until Lisa's foot got caught on something and she tumbled. I tried to help her up, but she couldn't move.

She shook her head and pushed me away. "Go ahead. You go."

"I'm not leaving you here by yourself. Come on." I reached down, and after a brief hesitation, she put her arm around me and we continued our journey, much slower this time.

"I have to stop," Lisa said after a while as she released her arm from around my neck and fell to the ground.

I didn't know how long we ran or how far we had gotten, but I no longer heard the monster. I fell beside her, and we sat in silence, me with my fingers wrapped tightly around the knife. I hadn't even realized how cold it was until I felt Lisa shivering. We were both still naked, and now in the middle of nowhere in the cold. I had to wonder if our escape had only led us to find death another way. I closed my eyes and began to pray.

God, please don't let us die now.

When I opened them, it was as if God had actually heard me and felt sorry for us. The moon peeked from behind the clouds in the sky and provided enough light for me to see something through the trees. I stood up slowly.

"Come on." I helped her off the ground.

"Where are we going?" she moaned.

"Somewhere safe, I hope," I said. We tumbled our way back to the building I had spotted in the moonlight.

I wanted first of all to make sure I wasn't seeing things, and I also wanted to make sure whatever I was seeing wouldn't put us in any more danger than we were already in. I walked closer and found that what I thought was a cabin turned out to be a wooden shack. I peeked through the small window and saw that no one was inside. Using the blade of the knife, I pried open the door, crept inside, and looked around the one-room building. It held nothing more than a cot, a wooden chair, a box of old clothes, and a small table. There was also a small fireplace.

Thank you, God.

"What if he knows about this place? What if they come here and find us?"

"Let's just pray that he doesn't. We're only gonna be here for the night. As soon as it's light enough to see, we'll leave," I told her. I reached into the box of old clothes, pulled out a thick shirt, and tossed it to her. "Put this on."

As she obeyed, I found one for myself, along with a pair of pants. The clothes were way too big for us, but after being naked for God knows how long, we were grateful for anything, especially in the cold.

"Bettie, thank you."

"For what?"

"For saving my life."

"We ain't saved yet," I told her. "Now, you just lay down and get some rest as best you can. Come morning, we're going to find our way home."

"Aren't you gonna rest?"

"I will, but I'm gonna stay up a while just in case someone shows up." I held the knife up to the small window so she could see it in the moonlight.

LC

31

I was curious as to why Mr. Mahogany had requested an emergency meeting of the Council. We'd just had our weekly meeting three days before, and all our usual business seemed to be up-to-date. As I sat in the room among the other members, waiting for Mr. Mahogany to appear, I suddenly went from curious to concerned. I noticed a few other members shooting each other uneasy glances, some shifting in their seats. I hadn't been a member of the Council for nearly as long as the others, but from the looks on their faces, it was clear this wasn't a normal thing for Mr. Mahogany to do.

"I want to thank you all for managing to meet on such short notice," Mr. Mahogany said when he entered the room and took his seat. It was clear from his demeanor that whatever he was about to speak about had him seriously concerned. "I try to adhere to the bylaws when it comes to notifying members of mandatory meetings, but this was an emergency indeed." He made eye contact with several members, and when he was sure he had everyone's attention, he explained the reason for the meeting.

"Here in Atlanta, as of late, it seems as though we've had to deal with a thorn in our side," Mr. Mahogany said. "I'm referring to no other than a group called the Young Bloods. The last time we discussed the matter, we decided to give things some time. Unfortunately, they don't know—or perhaps don't care—about the rules of the streets. For some reason, they seem to think that people who look like them, have the same skin color as them, are the enemy."

"Humph, those hooligans not only don't know the rules of the streets," Cat said, "but they don't have any rules. They're down in Memphis, too, robbing my guys."

"Yeah, and I've seen them in Charlotte, also," Tommy Rawls said.

"And that is, quite frankly, the problem," Mr. Mahogany said. "Before you know it, it will be martial law in this city, and we definitely can't have that."

"So, what do you suggest we do?" Rawls asked.

Mr. Mahogany didn't even hesitate long enough to blink. "We take them out," he said bluntly. "They need to be eradicated ASAP. And who better to get the ball rolling than us? I feel, and I'm sure you all will agree, that we've given this thing enough time. Now the situation needs to be taken care of before things get too far, making it an even harder problem to fix."

"Like roaches," another member chimed in. "I haven't always eaten my sorbet with a silver spoon. I know how hard it is to get rid of roaches once they've infested a place. And it seems like they just keep growing in numbers."

Mr. Mahogany looked around the room. "So, do we all agree?"

There were nods from a couple members. Some exchanged approving looks, while others verbally expressed their agreement.

"Then let's make it official with a vote," Mr. Mahogany said. He looked toward the secretary. "Please prepare to take a count."

"Before we vote, can I say something?" I asked. I never said too much during the meetings. I felt like a member-in-training at times, and I had never been one to do a whole lot of talking anyway. That way, whenever I did have something to say, chances were better that others would listen. People have a way of tuning out the person who loves talking more than listening. I had figured out a long time ago that I learned far more by staying quiet.

"LC, you're welcome to say anything you want." Mr. Mahogany appeared to be happy that I was finally taking the opportunity to contribute to the dealings of the Council.

"When you say *take them out*, can you clarify?"

Mr. Mahogany looked around at the members with a kind of grimace on his face, as if he was embarrassed by my words and regretted granting me permission to provide input. "Now, LC, surely you wouldn't want that answer on the books, would you?"

There were chuckles in the room.

"I think you know exactly what I mean, and if you don't, I can almost guarantee your brothers do."

Again, there was laughter.

Okay, I got the point. Rather than respond to Mr. Mahogany's slight sarcasm, I decided to just say what I had to say. "Why take out an army that we can use to our benefit?"

One would have thought I'd just spoken a foreign language from the quizzical looks on each face. I proceeded to explain myself. "What do animal tamers do with wild animals? They train them, but they train them to be obedient to them and only them. Everyone else they will eat alive given the opportunity, but the animal respects and shows loyalty to the trainer."

I could tell from the shift of energy in the room that some of them were starting to understand what I was trying to say. Still, I felt the need to continue for those who remained confused.

"We may look at them as thugs, but in all actuality, they're just out there doing what young cats with no direction do. Have you ever thought about what they might do if they were given opportunities with a little direction? Instead of being a thorn in our side, they could possibly be . . . well . . . on our side."

Mr. Mahogany raised an eyebrow. "So, are you suggesting we invite the hoodlums to one of our meetings and sit down and try to actually talk with them?" He let out a slight chuckle under his breath.

"That's exactly what I'm saying," I replied. "I mean, not invite them to one of our actual Council meetings, but just sit down with them and talk this out, explain the rules to them."

"No offense to you, LC," Mr. Mahogany said. "I know you're from a small town and perhaps not quite familiar with how things are done in the big city, but talking is not what those kinds of fellas do."

There were mumbles of agreement in support of Mr. Mahogany's statement, which produced a sudden boost of confidence in his original decision.

"How do we really know that for sure? Has anyone ever tried to talk with them?" I asked.

From the silence that followed my inquiry, it was safe to assume the answer was no.

I continued, "The simple solution may be a matter of putting some money in their pockets. I bet you they could move a lot of product."

"LC, I hear you loud and clear, but—"

"Please, Mr. Mahogany, let me finish," I said, waiting for a sign that his permission was granted. After he nodded slightly, I continued. "I know I'm the young buck in the room, but perhaps that's where my input is most beneficial in this matter. You older folks simply don't understand what the younger generation goes through." I turned to Cat, who had spoken earlier about the "hooligans" Mr. Mahogany wanted to get rid of. "Yes, you have some hooligans and wannabe gangsters in Memphis where you're from, but can you imagine if we take all that energy in them and bring organization to it? Add a method to the madness? Let's put them to work for us instead of killing them. These kids are people's sons and daughters— black families. You ever think how many we're gonna have to kill before they get the message?" I looked to Mr. Mahogany, who cast his eyes downward.

In a way, I suppose I'd just made him eat his own words. My intent was in no way to embarrass him, but I'd never been one to bite my tongue when I finally chose to speak up, and he'd be being a hypocrite if he made the gang members—young dudes with the same color skin as ours—the enemy.

I looked around the room to get a feel for whether I'd influenced the members' votes in any way. From some of the nods and why-not-give-it-a-try shoulder shrugs, I think what I'd said was starting to sink in and that they might consider my suggestion.

"Well, the Council truly appreciates your input, LC," Mr. Mahogany said. He then looked to Reverend Hawkins, who was the secretary. "Now, how about we go ahead and vote?"

"Sure," a couple members said.

"I vote for the sit-down with the hooligans," Cat said, surprising me. "If he can somehow get these kids to work, I could sure use the man power now that you've hooked us up with New York."

"I second it," another said.

A quick discussion ensued, followed by a vote, and before I knew it, the Reverend Hawkins said, "The ayes have it. A talk with the gang members it is."

The Council members gave me smiles and shoulder pats—all but one, anyway.

"This meeting is adjourned," Mr. Mahogany said. "I've got work to do." He exited with not so much as a glance in my direction.

Lou

32

"No, I'm here, but I haven't seen them yet," I said into the receiver.

I was on a pay phone at a truck stop about five miles outside of Homerville, watching Route 84 like a hawk. It was the only road that made any sense if Eddie and his flunky were truly traveling to Homerville. Luckily for us, I had been in Waycross, which was halfway between Homerville and Brunswick, when Donna called.

"Well, they should be there any minute," Donna replied. "It only takes about an hour to get from Brunswick to Homerville."

"Hold on, Donna." I'd just seen an El Dorado pass by me, and although it was dark out, I was damn sure it was green. "I gotta call you later. I think that's them."

As I hung up the phone, the last thing I heard Donna say was, "Lou . . . please be careful."

I had to chuckle as I ran to my car. I never thought I'd hear those words come out of her mouth.

I already had my car running and pointed in the direction of the road, so when I jumped in, I was balls to the wall. It took me about a mile to catch up to them, but when I did, my headlights illuminated the lime green paint, and I was sure it was them. I eased back, following the car from a safe distance, until I saw it turn into the parking lot of an abandoned feed mill and pull around back. I passed by without stopping, drove a little farther down the road, then made a U-turn, cutting my headlights off as I returned. Instead of parking around back, I parked on the side then quietly got out of my car.

I pulled out my .44 Magnum. The sound of my feet on the gravel parking lot seemed as amplified as the beating of my heart. I found the Caddie abandoned in the back of the building. I took a minute to let the air out of all four tires. These motherfuckers weren't going anywhere. Once that was done, I found a door and eased inside, pausing to listen to the shouting coming from another room.

"Your usefulness has come to an end!" a man shouted. My heart rate raced because I thought he could be talking about my momma. "I was told to shoot you right between the eyes, no questions asked, but I'm trying to give your dumb ass a chance."

"Hey, if this is about Dwayne McCarty, I just need a little more time."

I was glad I hadn't burst into the room, because the voice belonged to Eddie, who, surprisingly, didn't sound like his nervous, skittish self. "Y'all only gave me the case two days ago!"

"What's his connection to Bettie Duncan?" the man asked. "She visited him twice since she came home from jail."

His mention of my momma had me on high alert. I crept closer to make sure I didn't miss a word.

"Ain't nobody said nothing about Bettie Duncan," I heard Eddie say,

"Yeah, well, we were hoping you'd stumble onto that yourself. Now, tell me about McCarty's old man."

"I don't know. He was a civil rights lawyer. Marched with King down in Selma. Came into a good chunk of change about ten or eleven years ago then ran for Congress. He held a seat in Congress until he died back in seventy-three. That's all I know. But I can find out more."

Arriving at the doorway of the room where the voices were coming from, I peeked inside and saw Eddie standing in front of a tall shadow of a man. Dude was pointing some very distinct heat directly at his head.

"That's going to be a little hard, Eddie, considering you're going to be dead."

"Why kill a man who can help you?" Eddie said nonchalantly. This dude was a bucket of nerves any other time, but he was calm as hell under pressure. "I'm worth more to you alive than dead."

"I wouldn't bet my life on that if I were you," the man growled. "We just found out that your bitch has been hanging out with Lou Duncan. Not only that, but she had the nerve to show up at LC Duncan's house this weekend. We can't have that. It's not in our plans."

"Man, my girl wouldn't do that. She had a stomach virus this weekend."

"You sure about that?" The man let out a sarcastic laugh. "Yeah, I can tell from the look on your face that you're not."

"Fuck! I trusted her," Eddie screeched.

I hear the anguish in his tone. Damn, he really liked Donna's ass.

"Eddie, Eddie, Eddie. That bitch is so tied into the Duncans. You should have known better."

"That fucking bitch!" Eddie huffed angrily.

"I been there. That pussy can blind you, but I need to know what you told her about us." The shadow pushed the gun closer to Eddie's head.

"I would never tell anyone about y'all. I'm not afraid of dying, but I don't have a death wish."

"What about Bettie? Did you tell her she's alive?" the man asked, and I swear my heart skipped a few beats.

Eddie got quiet, which I guess was enough for the man to know the answer was yes.

"Well, she's been moved since you seen her," the shadow said. "You ready to die, Eddie?"

"Man, don't play no games with me. Just pull the fucking trigger," Eddie demanded. "I'm not afraid to die."

There was a slight click as he cocked the gun. A shot rang out, and I watched as Eddie's body hit the ground with a thump.

Fuck! This was bad, really bad. The shadow stepped over Eddie's body as if it were a discarded piece of paper. I eased back into the darkness and calculated the precise moment that he walked out into the hallway where I stood. As soon as he turned the corner, I took a step toward him and cocked the barrel of my .44, pointing it directly at his head.

"You got three seconds to tell me where the fuck y'all got my momma, or I'm gonna I blow your fucking head off."

Shirley

33

"Where the hell you going?" Li'l Momma asked loud enough for half the damn joint to hear. I made my way down the steps to the bar where she was sitting, making sure to put a little extra sway in my hips. I felt good. For the first time in a while, I wasn't dressed like a whore or madam; I was dressed like a lady going out on a date.

I sat down at the bar.

"I asked you a question, Shirley. Where you going?"

"To mind my business and leave yours alone." I kinda posed as I said it to her. "Then again, you are my business, aren't you? And why you dressed like that?'

She was wearing a simple yellow dress with matching sandals instead of her usual kimono with lingerie underneath and heels. Damn girl had gone on one vacation and now she was acting like she forgot how to do her job.

"Well, I've been waiting to talk to you," she said.

Moe brought me over a bourbon with Coke chaser. "If this is about another vacation, you might as well hang it up," I told Li'l Momma.

"No, it's a little bigger than that." She got quiet, and I got impatient, which I'd been doing a lot of lately.

"Damn, girl, just spit it out already!" I snapped.

My attitude didn't darken her mood at all. She turned to me with a smile, holding up her hand with the back facing me. "David and I are getting married," she announced gleefully.

I stared silently at the small diamond on her finger.

"Shirley, aren't you gonna say something?"

I patted her thigh. "Good for you."

She looked skeptical. "Do you really mean that?"

"I do." I nodded. "I'm glad you got sense enough to get out and make a life for yourself while you still got a chance. Secure you a plan for your future. We all need to do that. Have you told Lou yet?"

She shook her head. "No. I wanted to tell you first."

"Well, you need to go ahead and let him know. He ain't gonna like it, but you gotta do what's right for your own life," I said, thinking of myself as much as of her. "You at least gonna finish out the week, right?"

"Yeah, probably until the end of the month. I wanna make some money before I go."

We sat in silence for a minute, sipping on our drinks.

Finally, Li'l Momma shook her head like she was confused and said, "You know what, Shirley?"

"What?"

"This just wasn't how I thought you'd act when I told you. I thought you were gonna flip out on me."

"I got a few things I gotta tell Lou myself that he ain't gonna like, so why should I give you grief?" I picked up my drink and finished it.

"Someone is waving at you," she said, pointing across the room.

I saw Eric walking into the room, headed toward me. As he stopped and talked to a couple of guys sitting at a table playing cards, he waved again to make sure that I knew he was there.

"Oh, that's just Eric," I said, trying to conceal my happiness at seeing him there.

"Eric. How come I've never seen him before?" Li'l Momma was breaking her neck trying to get a better look.

"'Cause he's an old friend. Me and him go back to when Sam first opened this place."

"Well, your old friend is just my type: tall, dark, and handsome. When he comes over, you should introduce us so I can take his fine ass upstairs."

I placed a stop sign up for that shit. "Oh, no you're not. He's not that type of customer. He's already taken."

Li'l Momma glanced over at Eric then looked back to me with a crazy-ass expression. "Oooh, Shirley. I didn't know you started working again. Is he one of your special clients?

"He's special all right, but he ain't no client."

Li'l Momma was now staring at me like I was a movie and all she needed was popcorn. "What?" I asked, as if that would be enough to get her to drop the subject.

She began nodding her head. "I can see it. You glowing, and it ain't the baby. What that man do to you?"

"He talked to me, then he listened to me, and most of all . . ."

She finished my sentence for me. "He fucks the hell outta you."

"Yes, he does that too, but most of all, he makes me feel safe." I stared over at him, understanding exactly what she meant when she said I was glowing. Just knowing he was around added a pep to my step.

"But Shirley . . . what about Levi?"

"What about him?" I snapped. "Lou made it very clear if all the brothers move to Atlanta, Levi's moving too, with or without me."

"Shirley, you know Levi loves you and he would never leave you, whether his brothers say so or not. I know that for a fact."

"I love Levi too, but there's no future in him," I told her, feeling the warmth from Eric's body as he came and stood behind me. "You of all people should understand that a woman has to secure her future. I gotta do what's best for me and mine. Ain't that right, Eric?"

"That's right, baby, and me and Shirley got big plans." He winked at Li'l Momma and put his hand around my waist. I quickly scanned the room to make sure Levi wasn't nearby. Lord knows I enjoyed the feel of Eric touching me, but if Levi saw it, he would've lost his mind, and that was the last thing I needed to happen.

Eric leaned down and whispered into my ear, "I gotta go holler at these cats over here about that house across town. I think it would be perfect for us. I'll be right back."

"I'll be right here when you return," I told him. He had told me about the house, and the fact that he meant it to be for us made me so happy.

"You've got a fucking death wish, don't you?" Li'l Momma said when he was gone.

"What the hell are you talking about?"

"I'm talking about Levi Duncan. You are carrying his baby, Shirley. And have you even told this guy you're pregnant?"

"Mind your business, Li'l Momma. Let me worry about what Levi deserves and what Eric knows," I scolded.

Calm down, Shirley. You're starting to sound really bitter, I told myself when I saw how wounded Li'l Momma was by my words. Once upon a time I would have told her everything, and now here I was telling her to butt out of my private life like she was a stranger.

"We'll see if you talking all that shit when Lou and Larry find out." Li'l Momma jumped off the barstool to signal she was done with the conversation. "I bet you that."

"I'm not worried, because Lou and Larry aren't going to find out." I grabbed her arm and squeezed so tight that she cried out. "Especially since you gonna keep that mouth of yours shut, or else David won't be planning no fancy wedding at the end of the month. He'll be planning your damn funeral. You got that?"

Tears began forming in Li'l Momma's eyes, either from the pain of my grasp or the fear of my threat. I could, however, see that she understood I meant what I said.

"Yeah, I got it," she sniffed. "But it's still fucked up, and karma is a motherfucker."

When I finally let her go, she hurried to the other side of the room. I turned back around and looked at Eric, who smiled at me and blew me a kiss. Li'l Momma was right; sooner or later I was going to have to tell Eric I was pregnant. Damn, maybe I did have a death wish.

Bettie

34

The sudden jerk of my head caused my eyes to snap open. I felt like I was waking up from a nightmare . . . and I was. Even though I was in some old, rickety shack in the middle of God-knows-where, it was like a dream come true. I was no longer being held prisoner.

"Lisa!" I frantically said her name out loud, my eyes darting around the room in search of my fellow escapee. She was nowhere to be found.

Shit! I pushed myself up from the floor. Before I was on my feet, the doorknob to the little shack began jiggling. *Shit! Shit! Shit!*

I'd looked around that little place enough to know that there was nowhere to run and nowhere to hide, which meant I had to do what I'd done practically all of my life: fight. I gripped the knife in one hand and the wrench in the other. The second that door opened, I sprang into action, charging for the door with the knife out in front of me.

"Jesus! Bettie, no!"

I swear on my boys' life, one more second and she would have been dead, or at least mortally wounded.

"Girl, what the hell are you doing?" I lowered my weapons.

"Me? What the hell are you doing? You could have . . ." She couldn't even find the words as her eyes went from the knife to me. "You could have killed me."

"I'm sorry." I exhaled, relieved that I'd been able to snap out of the killer daze I'd been in as I charged for the door. "I thought you were in here with me. I mean—" I didn't know what I meant. I was just as freaked out as Lisa at this point.

All of a sudden, my confusion turned to anger. "What the hell were you doing out there anyway? You could have been caught."

"It was cold in here, and I found some matches by the fireplace," Lisa said. "Which is why I went out there to get this." She bent down and began picking up the wood she'd dropped upon seeing a crazy old woman charging after her with a rusty knife. Hell, the thing may not have been sharp enough to kill her, but she damn sure would have caught tetanus. "Mind helping me out here?" Lisa looked up at me.

I placed the knife on the window sill and helped her gather the wood, which we then deposited into the fireplace. I headed back over to the window to keep a lookout again.

Lisa got the fire going. I turned my attention to her momentarily as she headed toward a large wooden door with a broken latch. She pulled the door open and stood there staring at whatever was behind the door.

"Looks like we got us a pantry." Lisa disappeared for a few seconds then reappeared with two cans in her hands. "Not much, but it will have to do. Thank God." Her face spread into a grateful smile, but it faded quickly.

"What?" I asked.

"We ain't got no can opener."

"Yes, we do." I waved the rusty knife and laughed. "But we're gonna have to sanitize this in that fire."

Lisa and I worked together to get those cans opened, and then we set them close to the flame to heat.

"So, what's next?" Lisa asked.

I thought for a moment before replying. "I figure we need to stay here at least until night. They'll be tired of looking for us by then and hopefully they'll figure we're long on our way somewhere."

"Where are we anyway?" She looked out the window.

"I have no idea," I replied. "But I know where we're not, and that's all that matters in this moment."

"How do we know which way is east if we don't even know where we're at or which direction we came?"

"We'll follow the moon. It rises in the east just like the sun," I said. "We'll find a house and call my boys."

Lisa nodded. "So, what do we do until then?"

I looked over at the cans. The content appeared to be boiling. "We're going to eat this here soup and get some rest. No telling how long of a journey we have ahead of us come morning."

"Sounds like a plan." Lisa smiled. Behind her smile were unspoken words of thanks.

"Miss Bettie? Miss Bettie, are you asleep?"

My eyes fluttered open, and I glanced around the room. For a second, I had forgotten where I was, until I saw Lisa lying on the cot across the room.

"Well, if I was, I ain't now." I leaned back against the wall and stared out the small window. My fingers remained wrapped around the knife, just in case I needed it. I had told myself I would just rest my eyes for a second, but I was pretty sure I'd been asleep a good half hour or more. "What's wrong? You hear something?"

"No, but I'm scared. You think he's gonna find us?" Her voice quivered.

"I hope not," I told her, "but we gotta get up outta here as soon as it gets dark, just to be safe. Now, you need to get some rest."

"I'm trying," she said. "Can I ask you a question, Bettie?"

"Yeah, what is it?"

"What makes you so sure they won't kill you? How do you know?"

I inhaled deeply. I hadn't realized that she had picked up on that statement. I was beginning to see that she was a little wiser than I had given her credit for. She had shared her story about her daddy and why she was being held, so I decided it was time that I shed some light on why I was in this predicament.

"Because I know too much about who they are and what they've done," I stated. "I know their secret."

"Isn't that even more of a reason for them to kill you?"

"Maybe, but I'm holding proof of the Council's deepest, darkest secret, along with something they'd probably kill each other to get their hands on if I'd let them," I said.

"The Council? Is that like a lawyer or a judge?"

"No, child. The Council, as they call themselves, are way more powerful than any lawyer or judge. These people manipulate governors and senators. They are the group of black men and women who control any and everything that happens in the South."

Lisa let out a small laugh. "Miss Bettie, ain't no way no black folks got control of anything in the South."

I laughed right back at her. "That's what they want you to think. Did you ever think about how a man as powerful as your father got himself in the mess he did?" She sat there in silence. "Had to be some mighty powerful folks to persuade him to let his little princess be held captive, don't you think?"

Poor girl looked like she wanted to cry as she nodded her head. "How do you know all this?"

I was embarrassed to say why, but in the spirit of fairness, I opened up. "I used to be part of the Council—or at least my husband was, until he quit and stole five years of their records."

"Is that why you were in the basement, because you have the records your husband stole?"

"Now you're catching on. But it wasn't just the records that they were upset about. Most of that could have been explained away as business deals. It was the evidence that they were involved with something that was so . . ." I paused.

"That was so what? What were they involved with?"

"You have to understand things were much different back then. It was the Sixties, and the country was changing. The Council felt like those changes were going to rob them of their power."

"What changes? And who was robbing them of their power?"

I hesitated to say the words. "The Civil Rights Movement."

She looked like she wanted to curse me out for stupidity, "What are you talking about? How could the Civil Rights Movement hurt black people? It freed us from all that Jim Crow bullshit."

"Yeah, maybe. That's one way to look at it."

"What other way is there to look at it?"

"The Council believed that the success of the Civil Rights Movement would jeopardize everything they had worked years to build. That once black folks were given the opportunity to spend their money in white businesses, they'd abandon black businesses and neighborhoods in search of white acceptance. Hell, there was talk about black folks going to white churches, and you know how much black folks love the Lord. All that money that they was giving in the offering plates was gonna be going to the white pastors eventually. They called it black flight."

"That is so short-sighted."

"I used to think so. But I'm not so sure anymore."

"You were in jail for the last ten years, Miss Bettie, but trust me, the world is a better place without Jim Crow, for me, you, and them."

"Let me ask you a question," I said. "When you were home with your family, when was the last time you purchased something from a black business other than your hairdresser?" She stayed silent. "They weren't wrong. They just went about shit wrong because they were scared and greedy."

"What do you mean? What did they do?"

"The Council was led by a man named Paul Wilson, who decided to take action and put a stop to the Movement."

She lifted an eyebrow. "How?"

"They met with the leaders of other powerful groups who wanted to keep the Southern way of life."

"You mean like the KKK?" She sounded appalled, and she should have been.

"Among others," I answered.

"You mean to tell me a group of rich black people met with the KKK and decided to sabotage the Civil Rights Movement?"

I said, "Sabotage doesn't even come close to the chaos and destruction they tried to orchestrate. They called for the killing of some good folks, some real good folks."

Lisa was now sitting up on the cot, her eyes were so wide that I could see the whites, even in the dimly lit room. "Folks like who?"

"Think about it," I said. "I'm sure you'll come up with something. I told you, these are some very powerful people."

"How do you know all of this?" she asked, sounding almost like she didn't believe me—or at least like she didn't want to believe me.

"I told you my husband was one of the founding members," I explained.

"Oh my God. Your husband helped them?"

"No, my husband was the only Council member who voted against it, and it cost him his life."

"Who killed him?" she asked, sounding horrified.

"Paul Wilson owned a string of pharmacies and soda shops and was expected to lose the most because of the Movement. He came to my husband and made what he thought was an offer he couldn't refuse to return the records and rejoin the Council. My husband took him up on the offer but then refused to return the records or rejoin the Council. Paul's response to my husband's rejection was to shoot. I'm the only person who knows what my husband did with the records and the bounty of his offer, and that's why they can't kill me," I explained.

"The bounty must be worth a lot if they're still trying to find it after all this time."

"Back then, it was worth ten million dollars," I told her. "Who knows what it's worth now."

Chippy

35

I don't know what pissed me off more: the fact that Donna had the audacity to show up at my fucking house, or the fact that Lou had brought her there. I had never felt so betrayed in my life, nor had I ever felt so afraid. My entire world was in jeopardy of spiraling out of control, but I wasn't about to lose my family or our way of life because of a woman who just couldn't get the message.

As soon as NeeNee got home from her and Larry's brief two-day honeymoon in Myrtle Beach, I dropped the kids off at her place, convincing her to watch them while I headed down to Waycross. I didn't know where I could find Donna, but I was pretty sure I knew who did.

I was happily greeted by several of the girls who rushed over and hugged me as I walked into Big Shirley's. Some were old friends who'd been around ever since the days I had worked for Big Sam, and some just knew me as the wife of one of the bosses.

"Hey, ladies. Looking good." I tried to smile and sound polite, but this wasn't a friendly visit, and I wasn't interested in small talk. I was on a mission.

I scanned the crowded room, hoping to find Lou, confront him, and get the hell out of there as soon as possible. I had to be back in Atlanta before LC got home, so I was pressed for time. I had already been to the farm and the service station in search of Lou, and he wasn't at either of those places, so I figured he was indulging in his favorite pastime.

I was surprised when I didn't see him or Shirley, so I walked over to the bar where Li'l Momma, one of Shirley's tenured girls and a good friend, was sitting.

"Hey, girl, it's good to see you." Li'l Momma smiled at me softly as she stood to give me a hug. She was a pretty girl who had a good head on her shoulders. She had started working for Big Sam about a year before I had, and although we had bumped heads a time or two, eventually we had grown to be friends.

"It's good to see you too." I returned her smile then asked, "Where's Shirley?"

"I don't know. She's probably gone for the night." Li'l Momma made a face that I couldn't interpret and then took a sip of her drink.

"Gone where?" I asked.

"Look, I don't know." She shrugged. "I'm not trying to get into Shirley's drama. I'm just trying to sit here and finish up my last day."

"Your last day? Where you going?"

"I'm getting married." She flashed her hand at me, beaming at the diamond ring on her finger.

"That's wonderful! Congratulations." I hugged her again.

"Thank you." Li'l Momma nodded.

I easily recognized the look of love in her eyes. It was the same look I'd had when I fell in love with LC. We were young and we had so many dreams. It seemed like it was so long ago and we had come so far, and were now reaching those things that we had imagined and talked about. I wasn't about to let anyone ruin what we had. I had to find Lou.

"I hate to change the subject, but if Shirley ain't around, where's Lou?"

"He ain't here either."

"Are they together?"

"I seriously doubt it. I ain't seen Lou all week. He ain't even been here to pick up the deposit for the week or get some pussy."

I frowned. Shirley not being here was strange enough, but for Lou not to have picked up the week's money was even more outrageous. It was as if he had lost his damn mind completely. Not only was he out running the fucking streets with Donna, but he wasn't even taking care of his responsibilities for the family businesses. LC was not going to be happy about this when I told him.

"And you don't know where Shirley or Lou could be?" I sighed.

"Not exactly." Li'l Momma became serious and dropped her voice practically to a whisper. "But I've got an idea where Shirley is."

"Okay, where?"

"I hate to throw her under the bus, and she might kill me for telling it, but right is right and wrong is wrong," Li'l Momma said.

"Shirley ain't gonna kill nobody."

"She might." Li'l Momma lifted up her arm and displayed a large purple bruise that was clearly caused by someone's hand. "This is what she did when I tried talking to her about what I'm about to tell you."

"Shirley did that? Why? What the hell is going on?" I demanded to know. Although Big Shirley ran the place, she didn't have a right to put her hands on anybody. I didn't like that.

"Shirley has a new beau."

"A new beau? Like in a new man?" I asked, and she nodded. "Who is this man?"

Li'l Momma pointed to the bruise on her arm. "I don't know, but she said it was none of my business."

My mind was racing, and I didn't know who I was going to fuck up first when I found them: Donna, Lou, or now, Shirley.

"Poor Levi's going to be devastated," I said.

"That's what I said, but Shirley didn't seem to care."

"Where is Levi?" I stood up.

"He's with them damn dogs." Li'l Momma nodded toward the back of the building. "He's come out here looking for Shirley about ten times already."

I didn't even say good-bye as I exited the bar area, speed-walked down the hallway, and out the back door. Larry and Lou had built a dog pen in the back of Big Shirley's so that Levi could be occupied while Shirley was working. I called his name, and a few minutes later, he came trudging toward me, carrying a small puppy.

"Ch–Ch–Chippy." Like always, he was grinning.

"Hey, Levi." I tried to muster a smile.

"P–p–puppy fo–fo–for J–J–Junior." He held the small animal up for me to see.

"Aw, that's so sweet, Levi. Junior's going to love him."

I looked at my brother-in-law. Dressed in dusty jeans and a plaid shirt, he was a good-looking man, just like his brothers. He was as big as an ox and had the heart of an angel despite his mental shortcomings. He didn't deserve this. He was worthy of real love the same way I was, and Li'l Momma, or even Shirley, for that matter.

"Levi, you're coming home with me to Atlanta, okay? To see Junior."

"W–w–with you?" He seemed confused. "Wh–what about Sh–Sh–Shirley? Sh–she with tha–that m–m–man." Levi looked so sad. People could call him simple, but he wasn't stupid.

"Yeah, I know. LC will take care of that, okay? Now, come on." I reached for his arm, but he pulled away.

"P–p–puppy." He looked down at the animal then up at me.

I realized that he wasn't going anywhere without that damn dog. I gave him a nod of approval and said, "Yes, Levi, the puppy can come too. But we've gotta go now."

Fifteen minutes later, after much coaxing, I was headed back home to Atlanta with Levi in the passenger's seat, holding the puppy, and ten more dogs in the back seat. I hadn't talked to Lou or found Donna, but what I was returning with was just as important. I just had to figure out a way to explain to my husband why I had taken a trip to Waycross and hadn't mentioned a word to him about it.

Nee Nee

36

"Momma! Momma! Momma!" Curtis called my name for what seemed like the hundredth time. I had put him and Junior to bed almost an hour ago and had just given Vegas a bottle and laid him down, but he still hadn't gone to sleep. The boy's energy was nonstop. I had taken them to the park twice, gave them a heavy meal and a hot bath, but unlike his cousins, my boy was still wide awake. I was more exhausted than he was at this point.

"Yes, Curtis," I yelled from the living room.

"I'm thirsty. Can I have some water?"

"No, Curtis. It's too late for something to drink. You'll pee the bed."

"No, I won't, Momma. I promise," he pleaded.

"Curtis, I swear if you wake up Junior or Vegas I'm gonna whip your tail good. Now go to sleep."

I looked at the clock and checked the time. It was almost ten, and Larry had said he would be home by ten. I needed Curtis to hurry up and go to sleep, because I had an itch that needed scratching, and I planned on taking care of it the second my husband walked in the door. *My husband.* Just being able to say those words made me smile. I had waited so long for the set of rings that now adorned my right finger. It even made the fact that Larry was on the road working four or five days out of the week worth it. I made sure to show him how much I missed him every time he came home, but tonight, my son seemed like he was trying to put a damper on my plans.

I waited a few moments for Curtis to respond, and when he didn't, I relaxed a bit, hoping that he had finally gone to sleep. I got up from the sofa. I needed to hurry and get ready.

Before I had even gotten to the hallway, I heard the sound of Larry's key in the lock of the front door. The fact that I hadn't had time to change into my new lingerie set overshadowed the happy news that he was actually a few minutes early.

"Hey, Nee," Larry said when he walked in.

I ran over and planted a big kiss on his lips and threw my arms around his neck, causing him to drop the two duffle bags he was carrying. "I missed you."

"Missed you, too." The way he was looking at me told me I didn't need to be bothered with any lingerie.

"Daddy!" Curtis came running down the hallway and leaped into Larry's arms. Larry lifted him off the ground and swung him into the air, both of them laughing.

Dammit, I loved my big-head son, but his refusal to go to sleep at a decent hour was frustrating as hell and putting a damper on my love life. I knew once he got out of bed and laid eyes on his daddy, it would be another hour before he would settle down enough to even get him back into his room. I couldn't help but smile, though. I loved to see the two most important men in my life interacting.

"Curtis, tell your daddy good night and go back to bed," I said sternly.

"But, Momma . . ." Curtis whined.

"Nee, let the boy stay up for a little while with his pops," Larry said to me.

I leaned over and whispered into his ear seductively, "Who would you rather stay up with, him or me?"

Larry raised an eyebrow. "Get in the room and get naked. I'll be in there in five minutes." He then looked down at Curtis and told him, "Come on, son. Let Daddy read you a story right quick and tuck you in."

Curtis frowned, but it was only for a moment, because before he could whine again, Larry had turned him upside down, and they were headed into Curtis's room. I rushed into our bedroom and quickly took off my clothes. Catching a glimpse of myself in the mirror, I paused to stare. Just like the Commodores said in their song, I was a brick house. Even after carrying a baby weighing nearly eight pounds, my waist was still small, my breasts full, and my hips and butt firm. I could see why Larry couldn't keep his hands off me when he was home.

"I love when you do what I tell you to do." Larry came and stood behind me while I was admiring myself in the mirror. My eyes met his as his hands began making their way to my breasts. My nipples instantly hardened from his touch, and I leaned my head to the side as he began kissing my neck and shoulders.

"Really? You like to tell me what to do?"

"I was born to tell you what to do." He slapped my ass, softly at first, then harder. I moaned, and when I went to turn around to kiss him, he nudged me. "Now, get your ass on the bed."

This was exactly what I had been waiting for. Larry was a man who enjoyed taking charge in the bedroom. There were the occasional times that we did the whole romantic lovemaking thing, but for the most part, my husband liked it rough, and so did I. Just hearing the force of his tone and the way he grabbed me let me know that tonight was going to be one of those nights.

"Wait, what about Curtis? He's probably not asleep yet."

"His ass ain't gonna bother us." He quickly walked over to lock the bedroom door. "Now spread open them legs and play with it while I'm getting undressed."

I lay on top of the comforter with my legs spread apart and began touching myself. His eyes stayed on me as he slowly took off his shirt. The sight of his chiseled shoulders and chest made the heat that was already between my legs even more intense.

"Yeah, keep doing that," he said as he removed his shoes and unbuttoned his pants.

My fingers plunged deeper, and I whimpered slightly as I played with myself. Between the impromptu strip tease Larry was giving me and the anticipation of what he was going to do to me, I was damn near ready to cum already. By the time he slipped off his boxers and I saw his bulging dick, I was more than ready for him to do whatever he wanted to do.

Larry climbed on top of me, kissing me forcefully while biting my bottom lip. His fingers replaced mine and found my waiting clit. My back arched, and my legs opened wider.

"Put it in, Larry," I begged. "I wanna feel you inside me."

"Shut up. You feel what I tell you to feel," he said, flipping me over onto my stomach. "Get on your knees."

He maneuvered to give me just enough room to get on my knees, and just as I did, he smacked me hard on my ass, turning me on even more; then he plunged into me from behind. He gripped my hips and pulled and pushed me alternately until he found the rhythm he wanted. The feel of his dick was mesmerizing, and I closed my eyes and savored the moment.

"Yessss, Larry. Harder," I moaned as he gripped my hair.

"What you say?" He panted.

"Harder, baby," I repeated.

"You want it harder?"

"Yesssssss."

Larry began stroking me more intensely until a wave of pleasure overtook me. I went to fall onto the bed, but he yanked me up and turned me over.

I reached between his legs, massaging his still hard dick, now sticky from my juices. I leaned up and took it into my mouth, glancing up and enjoying the smile on his face as he closed his eyes and enjoyed my skills.

"Suck it, Nee," he whispered, again grabbing my hair. I licked and sucked the way I knew he liked it. His grip became tighter, and I became aroused all over again.

His body tensed. I knew he was on the brink of climaxing, and then, he pushed me away.

"What?" I asked, confused for a moment.

"Lay on your back," he panted.

Before I could even get comfortable, he was on top, thrusting into me. I gasped with pleasure and clawed at his chest. I looked up and stared into his eyes, which were full of intensity. His strong arms held me down, and I reached for one of his hands, guiding it to my throat. He was hesitant at first, and then he wrapped his fingers around my neck.

"Tighter," I whispered.

He shook his head.

"Yes," I told him. "Tighter!"

He tightened them a little, but I wanted more. Larry knew I enjoyed being choked. My desire to do so to the point of passing out sometimes frightened him, but I didn't care. People called him Crazy Larry, and he had a reputation of being somewhat psychotic, but I knew he knew my limitations and would never do anything to harm me. I was just as freaky in the bedroom as he was.

"What the fuck is that?" He suddenly loosened his grip.

"Oh my God, is it Curtis?" I asked, thinking that our son may have somehow unlocked the door and walked in.

"Shhhhhhh . . . Shut up." The way he said it, I knew that he was serious and this wasn't part of our sexual playtime.

Then I heard the sound that he was referring to. Someone was knocking on our door, loudly.

"Who the hell is that?" I asked as if he had magical X-ray vision and could see who was on the other side. I couldn't imagine who could be knocking on our door this late at night. We'd only been in our home a couple of weeks, and the only people who ever came over were LC and Chippy, and they would have called first.

Whoever was on the other side began knocking even louder.

"Stay here," Larry said, getting up out of the bed and grabbing his boxers off the floor.

"What the hell are you doing? Larry, wait." I began scrambling to get up as well.

"No, stay here," he said.

I sat on the edge of the bed and folded my arms, but I stayed put. Fear began to creep into my body as he walked out of the room. Something told me that whoever was on the other side of the door wasn't there for a good reason.

Lou

37

I pulled into the driveway of Larry's house, jumped out of my car, and ran to the porch, where I started banging on the door. It was almost midnight, and I knew he wasn't going to like me showing up unannounced, but he was gonna have to get his ass up.

After a while I heard Nee Nee's voice, and a light came on upstairs. I continued pounding on the door. A minute later, Larry pulled back the curtain slightly.

"Who is it?"

"It's me. Open the door," I shouted.

There was a slight pause, but finally, the door opened and Larry stood in the doorway, looking from left to right.

"Dammit, Lou. What the fuck are you doing here?" He was dressed in his drawers and a wife beater, and he definitely didn't look pleased to see me. "You know what time it is?"

I wasted no time getting to the point. "I got some information about Momma."

"Momma?" He looked like he was about to close the door. "Man, get the fuck outta here with that bullshit. You come back to my house talking this shit again and I'm gonna have them lock your ass up in Central State."

"Well, go ahead and call 'em, 'cause I ain't leaving. Not when I finally got proof." My voice cracked with emotion, and I was breathing so hard that I could feel the rise and fall of my chest as I talked.

"Proof of what, Lou?" He sounded annoyed, but he wouldn't be for long after I showed him what I had.

"Come to my car with me." I went to step off the porch, but he still hadn't moved.

"Man, I ain't going out there. Whatever you got, bring it over here."

"Larry, God dammit, if you want to see proof come with me."

He finally stepped outside and followed me, grumbling all the way. I took the keys out of my pocket and unlocked the trunk so he could look inside.

"What the fuck? Who's that?" He stared into the eyes of a guy, bound and gagged, lying in the trunk of the car.

"He's your proof." I beamed proudly.

"Who the hell is this?" The man's face was bruised and swollen, and he looked scared for his life, and for good reason. I'd beaten the shit out of him. "What the hell is going on, Lou? How is he proof?"

"This motherfucker knows that Momma is alive. He's gonna help us find where she is. I just need some of that torture shit you learned in the Army to get it out of him."

"Is what he's saying true?" Larry asked the guy. He stepped back, his arms folded across his chest, and waited for an answer. Would you believe this fuckin' guy had the nerve to shake his head no?

"Motherfucker, stop lying!" I punched him three times before Larry stopped me. "This motherfucker's lying, Larry."

Larry waved his hand at me. "Man, you got me out here in my drawers looking like a fool."

"He knows about Momma. I swear to God, I can prove it. I can prove it," I insisted. Don't ask me where the tears came from, but they were rolling down my face. I stomped around to the passenger's side of my car and reached inside. I pulled out the gun I'd taken from this fuck at the warehouse and presented it to my brother.

"Here, recognize this?"

"Where the fuck did you get this?" he barked.

"From him." I pointed to the guy in the car with satisfaction. "Now maybe somebody will listen to me around here."

Larry looked down at Momma's gun. The expression on his face was one of pure devastation. I think he was freaked out by the reality in front of him.

"Pull this fucking car into the garage." Larry slammed the trunk down and stomped toward his two-car detached garage while I slid behind the wheel. I pulled the car into the spacious garage once he opened it. I had barely gotten out when he stuck out his hand, demanding the key.

"Is it true? Is my momma alive?" Larry asked my captive the second he opened that trunk. The man didn't answer; he just looked down. Larry pulled his tall afro hard, forcing him to look up, wincing in pain.

"She's alive, and he knows where the fuck she is, Larry." I grabbed a cigarette from a pack on a small table in the garage, along with Larry's favorite lighter. I lit it and took a long drag as I watched my brother handle the guy, who could barely stand when Larry yanked him up.

Larry pulled the dude's hair tighter and put his face so close that I was sure the guy could feel the heat from the sweat on Larry's forehead. "Now, when I take this fucking gag off, the only words that better come out of your fucking mouth are the ones telling me where the fuck my mother is."

He untied the bandana, and the guy began moving his jaw up and down, but he wasn't talking.

"Is my momma alive?" Larry asked again, this time reaching for a pair of vise grips.

"I heard you tell Eddie that your boss had you do it!" I yelled.

Larry clamped the vise grips down on the guy's nuts. The man screamed. He went to kneel to the floor, but Larry's hands caught him by the hair again and pulled him up.

"Where the fuck is my momma?" Larry clamped down again, but the man still refused to answer. He shook his head and groaned in excruciating pain.

"He's a tough fuck, Larry," I said.

"He ain't that fucking tough." Larry's fingers moved from his head to his neck, and he began to squeeze. The guy's eyes widened, and I could see pure terror in his face.

"Where is she? Tell me where she is!" Larry demanded over and over again.

"Fuck you," the man finally said. "I'm not telling you shit. You just gonna have to kill me." The man spit in Larry's face, and my brother went berserk, dropping the vise grips and using both hands to squeeze his neck. The guy began shaking his head back and forth, and Larry tightened his grip. I could see Larry's arms shaking, and beads of sweat began pouring down his face. The more the guy's head shook, the tighter Larry squeezed, until finally, his head stopped.

"Shit," I said, my voice barely above a whisper.

Larry dropped the man to the floor. He closed his eyes and shook his head slowly. "What the fuck did I do?"

"You just killed the only guy who coulda told us where Momma is."

Bettie

38

The sun was just about down when I walked over to Lisa's cot and gently shook her. "Come on, baby, it's time to go." She blinked open her eyes, smiling as she started to stretch.

"If I haven't said it, Bettie, thank you for saving my life."

Bam!

Unfortunately, Lisa had thanked me just a moment too soon. The door of the little shack was hanging by a hinge and the monster stood in the doorway, holding a shotgun. He had a huge bandage on his head, and he looked madder than a motherfucker.

Fuck! Fuck! Fuck! I stood there in disbelief. Lisa was paralyzed, as if she'd seen Satan himself. And for her, I suppose she had. Just then, another man dressed in military camouflage entered behind the first one. The rusty knife was within my reach, but the opportunity to use it was slim to none from my current standpoint. Both men were armed with military-style guns.

A third person approached to stand between them and said mockingly, "Oh, it looks like you ladies were about to leave. Did we come at a bad time?"

"Okay, so you found us." My voice was filled with hate.

"Of course I found you. You didn't really think I was going to let you run off without having another chat with an old friend, did you?"

I put up my middle finger. "You're no friend of mine."

"You never did have a sense of humor, Bettie. Let's see if you think this is funny." She turned to the monster then pointed at Lisa. "Get this little bitch outta here and teach her a lesson for running."

The monster's angry stare turned into a grin. Before he was upon her, Lisa was already screaming. He grabbed her, throwing her over his shoulder. Lisa kicked and flailed to the point that he almost dropped her. At that point, I decided to take a chance. I reached for the rusty knife.

"Oh, no you don't." The military guy had his gun pointed at my head in a flash.

"Do you have any idea what he's going to do to her?" I asked Belinda, watching helplessly as the monster carried Lisa out the door. "You're a woman, for Christ's sake."

"I don't give a shit about that little bitch. My concern isn't her. It's you." She folded her arms and stared at me as the military guy held me in place.

"I thought your daddy was bad, but you're one cold-hearted bitch. You make him look like—"

"Thanks for the compliment," Belinda said. "Now, let's have a little chat here, woman to woman. You have something that belongs to me, and I want it."

"Same ol' Belinda. Still trying to run shit."

"Trying?" She laughed wickedly. "Looks like I'm doing a damn good job of it. I managed to track your ass down, didn't I?" She shook her head. "Bettie, Bettie, Bettie. Did you really think you were gonna escape from me?"

"Whatever, Belinda. You know you can't keep me prisoner forever."

"I'm not trying to keep you forever. Just until I get that information and whatever it is that was so valuable that my father said you had."

"Well, I'll be damned. You don't have a clue, do you? You don't know what we've been hiding all these years?"

Her light face was becoming red. "I know I want it. I know my father killed that piece of shit husband of yours to get it."

"That's right, and I killed his half-white ass for killing my husband," I shot back.

"Yes, and every time I think about it, you're going to get one of these." She smacked me hard across the face. "You know what, Bettie? I've been way too nice. Maybe I have to start shooting your precious boys to make you understand the severity of the situation."

I didn't know if that was just an empty threat, but I had no choice but to take it seriously. "You touch one hair on one of my boys' heads and your world and every member of the Council's world will come crumbling down. I've made arrangements."

She shot me a skeptical look.

"You can doubt me if you want," I said, "but one thing is for sure: you know I'm not a liar, and I keep my word."

"Maybe," she said coldly. Neither one of us was going to back down from our threats. "By the way, we tracked down Dwayne McCarty. What do you think he's going to tell me when we have a chat?"

My stomach felt sicker than it had after we ate the old-ass soup we'd found in the shack. And I was certain the bitter expression on my face matched the way I felt.

Big Shirley

39

"Mmm," I moaned as Eric sucked on my tongue while his hands roamed all over my body. If I didn't know any better, I'd swear I was about to come. Fully dressed and with just a kiss and a passionate touch, I was as moist as I don't know what. I'd never experienced this much passion with Levi—with any man, for that matter. Most of the men I'd been intimate with over the years didn't want foreplay or any type of caressing. They wanted one thing and one thing only: some pussy. And, yes, that went for Levi too. No one ever wanted intimacy, or romance even.

Until now. Until Eric.

Perhaps making out in the front seat of his convertible wasn't the most ideal situation, but for me, it was pure romance at its best, which was something Levi knew nothing about. Besides, it kind of made me feel like one of those school girls in love with the most popular boy at school, and out of all the other girls he could have chosen, he chose me.

A sudden jolt in my belly reminded me that I'd also been chosen by the less popular boy at school, and I was carrying his baby.

"I can't," I said, pulling away from Eric in a quick movement. "I gotta stop this," I more or less commanded myself. I was in a trance with Eric. He was a dream come true. The bad part about it all, though, was that he wasn't my reality. Levi and this baby were. *Fuck!* A cheat I may have been—hell I'd been a whore my entire adult life—but this loyalty thing was a gift and a curse. Levi needed me, and it was time I woke up from this fantasy and accepted my life for what it was . . . nothing. And apparently that's all it ever would be.

"Why? What's wrong? Why are you stopping?" Eric seemed to be in as much of a sensual trance as I was. He looked dazed and confused, as if he'd just awoken from a dream.

"Levi," I said.

Eric's look went from dreamy to looking as if he had found himself in the middle of a nightmare. His eyes darted around nervously. "Where? Levi's where?"

"Levi is the reason why I gotta stop." I got myself situated in the seat as I pulled down my blouse that Eric had raised during all his fondling and whatnot.

"Forget about Levi." He turned my head to face him. "This is about us. This is about me and you. The last thing you should be thinking about is Levi." He sat back against his seat with a stiffened back and began to straighten his own clothing. "Know what it's like to be all hugged up with a woman and she's thinking about another man?"

It was clear his ego was bruised, but that hadn't been my intention. "I wasn't thinking about him. It was the kick from the ba—" I halted my words. In my attempt to explain myself to Eric, I'd almost told on myself. It was bad enough that Eric knew I was Levi's woman, but for him to know that I was carrying Levi's baby sure would have sent him riding off. As if I wasn't fixing to send him on his way anyhow. Oh, hell. It was time to come clean.

"Eric, I'm pregnant with Levi's baby."

"I had a feeling about that," he said without a trace of emotion in his voice. "Let me ask you one question. If it wasn't for the baby, would you be with me?"

"Yeah." I nodded. "Without hesitation."

"Well, fuck it," he replied, now sounding stronger, more determined. "That cat can't take care of no baby." His ego had seemingly been healed as he turned to me, taking my hands into his. "Just pack your things up and come with me. As a matter of fact, don't pack. Leave it all. Let's start a new life together with all new everything, including a nice wardrobe for you. We'll go down to my peoples' place on Saint Simons Island."

My belly began flipping. I was not sure if it was the baby kicking, nervousness, excitement, or what. All I knew was that the good life was being offered up to me on a silver platter for the taking, yet I was torn. No sooner than I pictured the wonderful life Eric was offering me, an image of Levi would pop into my head and spoil the whole thing.

I shook my head. "I can't. He needs me. Levi needs me. Me running around town with you is bad enough. I swear every time I look at that man I feel like I'm going to fall apart. I'm doing so wrong, and he's done nothing but right by me." I hated to be dumping all of this on Eric, but it wasn't like I had Chippy or Nee Nee to talk with anymore. "To just up and leave him . . ."

"I don't understand what the dilemma is," Eric said. "Like you just said, he needs you, but you don't need him. Do you want some simpleton who you do more for than he does for you raising your baby?" Eric poked his chest out. "Or do you want a real man like me?"

I looked up from the dark parking lot we were sitting in to the sign that read Big Shirley's. "But he doesn't have anybody but me and this baby."

"What about his brothers?"

I let out a harrumph. "You mean the brothers who done ran off, chasing big dreams in the city, and left him behind?" I rolled my eyes, getting all heated about how so-called family had just up and left us behind like we weren't worthy. Sure, I had made my feelings known about how moving to Atlanta wasn't really something I desired, but still, Levi would have floated any which way the wind blew. All his brothers had to do was say jump and he wouldn't even ask how high. He would simply jump as high as he could. Anything to appease them.

"Levi's brothers left him here for me to take care of." My heart began to hurt more so for Levi than for myself as the words I'd just spoken sank in.

It wasn't even a question of whether Levi's brothers loved him. The Duncans had an unbreakable bond. Everyone who knew them knew that. But I didn't see them bending over backward or forward to try to convince him to move to Atlanta. And trust me, like I said, it wouldn't have even taken that much convincing. Then again, maybe it would have.

Maybe they had tried, but Levi, knowing I wanted to stay put, refused to make the move. It was possible that maybe Levi did want more than pussy from me. Maybe he did want love. Maybe he wanted . . . to love me.

"I'm sorry, Eric. You are a good man, but—"

He placed his index finger over my lips, prohibiting me from finishing what I was about to say.

"I love you enough to let you go." His words surprised me. "I can see what this is doing to you. You are a good woman, and I don't want to be the one responsible for making you anything other than that."

I appreciated Eric making this easy on me. "My feelings really were into this."

"Mine too," he replied, "but I can't sit here and play this game."

I completely understood. I'd played the role of Cinderella long enough. My coach was about to turn back into a pumpkin. "I'm sorry."

"No, I'm the one who's sorry," he said.

I had to hurry out of that car before that look in Eric's eyes made me climb back on top of the fence I'd been straddling ever since I started cheating on Levi.

I made my way inside and headed straight for the bar. The look on my face must have revealed the fact that I needed to drown my sorrows in alcohol. Before my ass even hit the bar stool, Moe slid me a shot of bourbon that he must have poured the moment he saw me walk in the door.

"Thank you," I said, picking up the drink.

"Don't mention it. It's on the house." Moe winked, but I couldn't even fix my face to laugh at his humor.

With drink in hand, I turned to scan the place. From the looks of the cars I'd seen in the parking lot, business was pretty decent. I spotted Li'l Momma as I placed the glass to my lips. She cut her eyes at me like I'd stolen her money . . . or her man. I threw my shot back and then turned around, placing my empty glass on the bar. "What the hell is wrong with her?"

Moe shrugged. "I don't know. Probably starting to realize this is her last night."

"Well, I'll tell you what I do know, and that's that I'm getting good and sick of these bitches around here. They complain all the time and are so damn needy." I held up my glass. "One more."

"Is Levi upstairs? Probably about time I gave him some pussy," I said as Moe took my glass.

"I can tell you that Levi is *definitely* not upstairs." He let out a snort under his breath.

"What is that supposed to mean?"

"Hell, Levi left with Chippy about three–four hours ago. Thought you knew."

"What? With Chippy? What the hell would Levi be doing with her?"

"Dunno, but he ain't the only one who went with Chippy. He took his dogs with him."

My heart just about jumped from my chest to the ground. When a man takes his dogs with him, that only means one of two things. Either he took them for a walk and he'll be home soon, or he took them and he ain't never coming home. Something told me in this case, it would be the latter.

"You might want to talk to Li'l Momma. I'm sure she knows. Hell, her and Chippy spent about an hour talking before Levi tore out of here.

That drink was the last thing on my mind as I hopped up off that barstool, landing practically right in front of Li'l Momma.

"What did you say to her?" I snatched Li'l Momma up by the arm. "What did you say to Chippy? And don't you dare lie to me, you little bitch."

Li'l Momma stood there looking me in the face, torn between the truth and a lie. She must have had a shot or two herself, because a little bit of liquid courage rose up, and she spoke to me like a defiant child finally standing up to her mother.

"The truth," she said. "That you been running around with some clown in a suit while Levi's been sitting here miserable."

Slap!

If that bitch hadn't had any liquor, I bet she wished she had, to numb the pain of me knocking her dead in her big-ass mouth! "Get the fuck outta my club!" I hollered, watching her try to peel herself up off the ground. It was difficult, due to the fact that she was somewhat dazed from the blow.

I stormed off to my room to avoid the urge to stomp her. I didn't know what was in the water these bitches were drinking that made them forget that they were no better than me—that they were and always would be whores.

Slamming the bedroom door behind me, I began pacing, then suddenly stopped in my tracks when something caught my eye.

"Well, I'll be damned," I said, staring into the half-empty closet. I walked over to get a closer look. Not a single thing of Levi's remained. I turned my attention to the partially opened drawers, which were also emptied of anything that belonged to Levi.

My heart began to palpitate so fast I felt like I was going to collapse. You know what they say about how you never know what you've got 'til it's gone? Well, this moment was a perfect example of that. The first person who had ever truly made me feel needed and wanted was gone, and I was devastated. Who would need me now? The johns sure didn't. That ship had long sailed.

I raced over to the window. I don't know why I thought there was a chance in hell I'd see Levi, and I don't know what I would have done had I seen him. But I didn't have to cross that bridge, because he wasn't out there. But someone else was.

Eric was still sitting outside. I couldn't believe he was still there. Maybe a life with him truly was my destiny. Without another thought, I started grabbing my things and packing them as quickly as I could. Then I remembered what Eric had said about starting over again with all new things, and I said to hell with it. I left behind whatever I hadn't already packed and raced out to the parking lot.

The moment I hit the door, I could see the tail lights of Eric's car, heading for the exit.

"Eric, wait! Eric!" I called out, toting my belongings and this baby as best I could. "God, don't let this one get away," I prayed out loud.

The next thing I knew, Eric slammed on his brakes, which gave me a sudden burst of energy. I picked up my pace again as the car slowly rolled back toward me.

"What's going on? What's wrong?" Eric asked, looking concerned.

"Nothing's wrong. Everything is right." And in my mind, everything was right. Sure, I hated the fact that Li'l Momma had snitched on me, causing Levi to leave me, but maybe this was how things were supposed to be. No, I decided, there was no maybe. This was exactly how things were supposed to be, and it was time I realized that I deserved a good life just like the next ho. Perhaps I should have thanked Li'l Momma instead of decking her. If it hadn't been for her, I could only imagine what the rest of my life would have looked like. Now I didn't have to imagine.

"The hell with Levi," I said to Eric, and our faces formed the biggest identical grins ever. "The hell with the Duncans period. It's me and you. I'll follow you through and back if I have to." I threw my belongings into the back seat of Eric's convertible, and we rode off into the night. My fairytale had come true.

40

It was ridiculously late when I finally pulled into the driveway of our house. It had been another long day, starting with me getting up at five thirty to feed and spend time with my infant son. Although he was only a couple months old, Vegas was already showing signs of being an early riser, just like me. I would change him and give him a bottle while reading the morning paper aloud to him. I don't know if it was the sound of my voice, but I swear, he was alert and seemed to comprehend what I was reading. I could tell that he was going to be smart.

The hour or so that I spent with my son in the mornings was just the beginning of my day, The majority of my time was spent taking care of business at the dealership, and most importantly, selling cars. Business had picked up tremendously since our grand opening. Folks from all over Georgia would come not only to check out our inventory, but to see if there really was a black-owned dealership that sold luxury cars. I felt like some kind of a celebrity.

After the dealership closed and the doors were locked, my day still wasn't over. I would come home for a quick meal with my family and then head over to meet with the Council. For hours, we would discuss business at hand and strategize over moves that would benefit all of us. Not only was I learning a lot about the business world, legal and illegal, but they listened to what I had to say and appreciated my input. It made me feel valuable, and I was beginning to understand why Mr. Mahogany had invited me to take the seat he offered. I only wished that I could have shared everything with my brothers. The only saving grace I had was the ability to talk to Chippy about the moves the Council was making.

My only regret was that ever since the vote on the Young Bloods, Mr. Mahogany had been keeping his distance.

I turned off the car ignition and mustered up enough energy to get out and drag myself to the side door where I entered nightly. Just as I put the key into the lock, I heard something behind me in the darkness. I quickly turned around, reaching for the small piece I carried in the front pocket of my jacket.

"Man, it's about time you showed your ass up. Where you been?"

"What the fuck are you doing here?" I said, both relieved to hear the familiar voice and angry at the same time. "Man, get the hell away from my house."

I stared at Lou as he came out of the shadows. I hadn't seen him since the cookout, and I was still pissed at him for what he'd done. He had tried calling the dealership a few times, but I refused his calls, and every time he called the house, Chippy hung up the phone as soon as she heard his voice. She had vowed to stab him when she laid eyes on him, and I believed her.

"Come on, LC. Don't be like that."

"Motherfucker, do you know the severity of what you did? How you disrespected my wife? She's still pissed at me for what you did, and she swears she's gonna get you, man," I warned him.

"I'm sorry. If you'd just let me explain—"

"Ain't shit for you to explain. You ain't no dummy, Lou. That's why you sneakin' around here instead of coming here in the day. There's no explanation for that." I tried not to yell, fearing that Chippy would hear us and come to see what was going on.

"LC, if you would just listen for one minute—"

A set of headlights pulled into the driveway behind my car, and again, I reached for my pistol. "Who the fuck is that?"

"It's probably Larry. He had to put on some clothes and take care of something before he came over here."

Sure enough, the car door opened, and Larry stepped out, yelling, "What the fuck y'all standing around for? I told you to be ready when I got here. Let's go."

"Go where? I ain't going nowhere. I just got home."

"He ain't buying what I'm selling, bro." Lou walked away, and Larry stepped to me.

"Then let me make it simple for you, LC. Lou ain't crazy, and Momma's alive. Now, get in the fucking car," Larry said, making it clear it was an order, not a request.

"What the fuck are y'all talking about?"

"Lou found the cat that has something to do with taking Momma. The dude confirmed that Momma is alive. He knew where she was, but he wouldn't tell us, so I tried to choked it out of him." He hesitated for a minute then added, "I didn't mean to kill him."

My heart began pounding at the thought of my mother possibly being alive. As much as I wanted it to be true, I didn't know if I would be able to handle the disappointment if it wasn't. "How do you know this man wasn't lying? How do y'all know she's alive?"

"Because the motherfucker had this." Lou held something up in the air. I took a step forward to see if it really was what I thought.

"Is that—?" I whispered.

"It is. It's Momma's." Lou put the pearl-handled .45 in my hand. I looked at it carefully. It was my mother's gun, the one that had gone missing the same night she had.

"Now we just gotta find her. Let's go," Larry said again.

"If you killed the guy who had it, how are we gonna find her?" I asked, still staring at the gun.

"We gotta go talk to Donna. She—"

"Fuck Donna." I stopped Lou before he could go any further. "Now I'm starting to understand what went down, but I still don't wanna have shit to do with her."

"LC, you don't understand," Larry told me. "She's the only one who can help us at this point. Eddie might have said something to give her a clue to where they got Momma."

"I'm trying to catch her before she goes to work at the Waffle House, and we gotta drive all the way to Brunswick," Lou added.

"I ain't going," I said. "Y'all know she don't mean me and mine no good. She ain't the only one who can help. I'll go see Mr. Mahogany."

"Hell no. We can handle this ourselves. This is a family matter, and that motherfucker ain't family!" Lou shook his head. "Donna's the one who's been helping Lou this whole time, LC. We don't have time to deal with Mahogany right now." Larry touched my shoulder. "I get it, he's your business partner and you think he has all the connections, but this is a problem he ain't gonna be able to help fix."

"He can and he will. Trust—" I started, but Lou stopped me.

"Fuck Mahogany and fuck you too, LC. Come on, Larry. Let's go find Momma." He headed toward Larry's car.

"LC, man, you really not gonna roll out with us?" Larry frowned.

"No, you guys go. Where'd you put the body? I'll get rid of it."

"A'ight, man, have it your way. I put him in the freezer in the garage. Go over there and handle it, but don't make too much noise. You know Curtis is a light sleeper," Larry said, sounding disappointed that I wasn't going with them.

He walked toward his car, and I headed in the house. I knew my brothers were pissed because I wasn't with them, but there was no way I was going to ask Donna to help me with anything, not even finding my momma.

I had to call Mr. Mahogany and tell him what was going on. Walking over to the phone on a small table in the corner of the living room, I noticed a small piece of paper with my wife's handwriting: *Went to Waycross. Will be back before late. Kids are at Nee Nee's. Love, Chippy.*

"What the hell?" I said aloud to no one. This entire time I had been wondering why Chippy hadn't come out complaining about my loud-ass brothers, and come to find out she wasn't even home.

The ringing of the phone caused me to jump.

"Hello?"

"Hey, baby."

"Hey, where the hell are you?" I asked my wife.

"I'm about halfway home."

"Okay, I'll try to wait up for you. Lou and Larry just left."

"What? Why the fuck was Lou at my fucking house, LC?" Chippy yelled so loud that I held the receiver away from my ear.

"Calm down, babe. You're not going to believe this. . . ." I told her everything that had transpired since my brothers showed up.

"Oh my God. Where are they now?" she asked.

"They went to find Donna at some Waffle House in Brunswick," I told her then pulled the phone away again because I expected her to start yelling when she heard Donna's name.

Donna

41

I waited until the very last minute to leave for work. I had been up most of the night, waiting for either Lou or Eddie to call, but neither did, and I was worried—about Lou, at least. It was slightly after five in the morning, and my shift started at five thirty. I dialed Lou's number one last time and got no answer, so I relented and headed out.

The streets of Brunswick were pretty much empty, and so was the parking lot when I got there. We didn't really get busy until around eight on Saturdays, so I wasn't surprised. After I parked and got out of my car, I scanned the lot, hoping to see a car that belonged to one of the men I was waiting to hear from.

"I thought we had a deal." The voice came out of nowhere, startling me. I stopped in my tracks, squinting in the pre-dawn darkness toward the direction it had come from.

"Chippy," I whispered, recognizing the shadow of a woman walking toward me. "What the fuck are you doing here?"

"What the fuck were you doing at my house?"

I prepared myself for the fight that I knew was coming. It had been a week since the last time we stood face to face in the front yard of her home, and I could see from the anger in her eyes that she had been thinking about me as much as I had been thinking about her.

"Don't play stupid. You know exactly why I was there," I hissed.

She rushed toward me and snatched the collar of my uniform. I stumbled backward, reaching my arms out to steady myself and to block her.

"We had a deal. You swore to me!" she yelled in my face.

"You had a deal with a junkie. I'm not that woman anymore." We stood head to head, eyes locked.

"Do you think you can just take him from me?" She reached for me again, and I moved just in time.

"He's mine. He's always been mine." I snickered, determined not to be intimidated by her although my heart was pounding. Any other time, I would have been frightened. Everyone knew that Chippy had a crazy side. She was the one responsible for the scars on that woman Shirley's face, and there was also talk about her killing her own mother. But I knew that this confrontation was a long time coming, and I wasn't going to back down. I had too much at stake and was ready to fight for what was mine.

"Never gonna happen, bitch," she growled.

"Why don't we ask LC about that?"

"Keep my husband's name out your mouth."

Smack!

This time, the palm of her hand connected with my cheek. I reached up to rub the stinging on my face then instinctively, my fingers balled into a fist, and I punched her in the stomach.

"Yeah, I ain't a weak junkie like I was in the past. I'm stronger than you think," I told her. She flinched, but it didn't stop her from coming at me again, this time with so much force that I did fall backward. Within seconds, she was on top of me, and she grabbed two handfuls of hair. I don't know why this bitch was always going for my hair. My legs flailed under her body, and we both grunted and groaned in between blows.

"What the hell is going on here?" My manager came around the corner.

I don't think Chippy even realized he was there until he pulled her off me. I scurried to get away and grabbed onto the side of my car to pull myself up off the ground. I felt a hand on my body, lifting me, and I looked up to see Larry, scowling. I snatched away from him and turned my attention back to Chippy. We were both panting and looked like ragged messes: hair tousled, clothes torn, and faces covered in dirt and sweat.

"Shit! Chippy, Donna!" I heard Lou's voice before I saw him.

"Donna, are you all right? Should I call the cops?" my manager asked.

"It's okay, Jerry," I said, trying to regain my composure despite my ripped uniform.

"You know I don't have that kinda stuff going on here at my place. I won't stand for it."

Shit, the last thing I needed was to get fired. That job was damn near the only thing I had left in life.

"I'm sor—"

"Hey, no damage done, Jerry," Lou said, releasing Chippy, who still looked at me as if she wanted to kill me. "Lemme just have a few moments with Donna, please."

"A few minutes? Her shift started damn near ten minutes ago," Jerry replied.

Lou reached into his pocket, took out a couple of folded bills, and passed them to him. "This should cover any time she missed."

Jerry looked at the money then said to me, "You hurry up and get yourself together before coming in here."

"I will." I nodded.

"This ain't over, bitch!" Chippy tried to lunge for me again, but Lou held her tightly. "Stay away from my family."

"I just wanted to see him, that's all," I said.

"Why? He's mine, he's happy, he's fine." She spat at me. "I'm warning you to stay the fuck away from him."

"You don't tell me what the fuck to do. If I wanna see my son, I'll see him. And he's not yours. He's mine!"

Again, she lunged at me. "Well, I got papers that say he's not. I'm his mother, Donna, and there's nothing you can do about it!"

LC

42

I showed up at Mr. Mahogany's house unannounced a little after six a.m., because I knew he played tennis with his driver at that time. I didn't call ahead because I didn't want to disturb Belinda, who had made it very clear she did not like when people called before seven in the morning. That was funny, considering when I stepped out of my car, she was rushing out of the house, dressed and made up like it was three in the afternoon, with two brothers carrying suitcases behind her. She had to do a double-take to notice me, otherwise she would have breezed right past without saying a word.

"Oh, LC, how you doing, honey?" She gave me that fake-kiss shit on each cheek. "He's around back with James."

"Thanks," I said. "You look like you're in a hurry."

"I am." She smiled. "Going down to Saint Simons Island and the beach for the weekend."

"I won't keep you then. I need to speak with Mr. Mahogany about my mother."

"Your mother? What about Bettie? Did they find those bastards that killed her?"

I now had Belinda's full attention. That's the thing about women: they have this sensitive and nurturing thing about them. Not five seconds ago she looked as though she was headed out to conquer the world, but just the mention of my mother and she put the world on hold. That's just one of the reasons why I respected her and Mr. Mahogany the way I did. If you were a part of their circle, you were like family. That's a concept my brothers hadn't adapted to.

"Not yet." I told her. "But my brother has found proof that she's alive."

Belinda turned her back to me and took a few steps toward the gentlemen. She whispered something to them, probably telling them her trip was being postponed, and then walked back to me.

"Come on. I'll take you around back." She looped her arm through mine as she led me to their front door. We walked through the living room and then to the den and out a sliding glass door into their perfectly manicured backyard with a pool, pond, and tennis court.

"Honey, you have company." She waved at her husband, who was wearing an all-white short set.

"LC!" Mr. Mahogany shouted, sounding surprised to see me. "Was I supposed to meet with you today?" He looked across the tennis court at James, who shook his head at the same time I gave my answer.

"No, I just needed to talk to you."

"It's about his mother," Belinda chimed in. "Like I said before, we always have time for a friend in need."

A look of concern crossed Mr. Mahogany's face as he walked over. I had to admit, other than my brothers and Chippy, no one else had expressed such deep concern or protectiveness for me. It made me feel all the more confident about my decision to talk with Mr. Mahogany.

"What's going on, son?" Mr. Mahogany asked. "Something we can help you with?"

Belinda walked over to her husband's side, evidence that they were a joined force. That was me and Chippy. That would be us in the future as well: a strong black couple. They looked like a force to be reckoned with. That's what I aspired to be.

"His brother convinced him his mother's alive," Belinda said on my behalf.

"Bettie alive?" Mr. Mahogany said, extending his hand to the bench. "That sounds a little far-fetched, doesn't it?"

"It did until early this morning." I took a seat, and Mr. Mahogany sat next to me. Belinda stood by his side. "My brother Lou showed me proof that she may be alive."

Silence fell over our group. For the first time since I'd known him, Mr. Mahogany was at a loss for words. I wasn't sure if it was because he was shocked that my mother was alive, or if he thought I was crazy for believing that my mother, for whom we'd had a funeral, could be alive.

Mr. Mahogany finally spoke up. "Proof? He showed you definitive proof?"

I nodded my head. "There's this guy Larry killed. He had my mother's gun," I said. "How would he have gotten his hands on—"

"Whoa, hold up." Mr. Mahogany raised his hands. "Slow down and tell me everything you know."

"Well, I don't know much," I said. "The man who had her gun is dead. But I know she's alive."

"LC, I know it must be hard," Belinda said. "No one wants to accept the fact that someone they loved so dearly is gone, but understand that just because the man had your mother's gun doesn't mean she's alive."

"Under ordinary circumstances, I'd agree with you," I said, "but this isn't ordinary circumstances. My brother knew all along. We just wanted to accept the fact that our mother was gone and move on. He was right. We were wrong."

Mr. Mahogany took a moment to process my words.

"I just need your help with this," I said.

"We can get EJ right on this," Belinda willingly offered. "See what he can find out."

"That's not a bad idea," Mr. Mahogany said. "He knows people in the area."

"And he knows people who know people in the area," Belinda said, immediately convincing me that EJ's help may be just what was needed to get to the bottom of the situation with Momma. "We can call Walter Matthews, the U.S. Attorney, and have him look into the cops who supposedly found her body."

"Yeah, between all of them, someone is bound to know something. And whatever they find out and let us know, you'll know," Mr. Mahogany added.

"You two don't know how much I appreciate this," I said, more grateful than words could express.

"It's nothing," Mr. Mahogany said.

"Thank you again."

Belinda kissed her husband then hugged me before heading back in the house. I waited until she was out of sight before I said, "I hate to ask you this, but I need another favor."

Chippy

43

"Chippy, I need for you to calm the fuck down." Lou pulled me a few yards away from Donna. I was so angry that I wanted to scream. I hadn't had this much hate in me since the day I realized my mother knew my stepfather was raping me and just stood by and let it happen.

"Get the fuck off me, Lou. This is all your damn fault anyway. If it wasn't for you, she wouldn't be in our lives right now." I tried to escape his grasp.

"I know you're mad, and you got a right to be. This is all my fault. But, Chippy, this ain't about you or me. This is about Momma."

I frowned at him, wondering why he was still believing that his mother was alive. "And they say Larry is the crazy one. You're a fucking lunatic, Lou. You think that heifer is really trying to help you find whoever killed your momma? She's lying. She's just saying that to get to—"

Larry cut in. "Chippy, he ain't lying. Momma is alive."

"What?" This was the first time I'd heard one of the brothers agree with Lou on this subject, and it made me pause.

"Yes, she's alive," Larry said. "Listen, I know how much you love that boy. Everyone does. Ain't nobody gonna take him away from you and LC. I wouldn't ever allow that to happen. But you can't change the fact that Junior is Donna's son and you took him from her."

"I didn't take him. I saved him," I replied defiantly.

Tears filled my eyes as I thought about Junior. There was no way to describe the amount of love I had for that little boy. From the day he was born, he brought so much joy into my life. I couldn't imagine how I would handle it if anything ever happened to him. I was ready and willing to do anything for him, including laying down my life. Despite what anyone else thought or said, he was my son. Hell, had it not been for me, he probably wouldn't have been born. I closed my eyes and thought back to that day, almost five years ago, when I discovered his existence.

"Hey, Chippy!"

I turned around in the parking lot of the Piggly Wiggly and saw Paula, one of the girls I knew from Big Sam's, walking toward me. Last I'd heard, she stopped working and was living with one of her old johns, but based on the gold hot pants and halter top she wore, it looked like she was still turning tricks. I wasn't one to judge, though, and Paula was a nice girl, so I stopped to talk with her.

"Hey, girl. How's things going?"

"Same ol' same ol'. I heard you got married," she said.

"I sure did." I held up my left hand and proudly displayed the bridal set on my ring finger. "I heard you got a man of your own."

Her eyes widened as she stared at my ring. Then she looked back at me. "No, not anymore. I'm back working at Big Sam's, or Shirley's, or whatever they calling it now."

"What happened?"

"He got hooked on that stuff and lost his damn mind. Stopped going to work. He even stopped coming home at night."

I shook my head in disappointment. "That's terrible."

"Hell yeah. You know I will put up with a lot of things, but when a nigga start stealing from me, I draw the line. I work too damn hard for my money." Paula patted the small gold purse hanging from her shoulder.

"I understand," I told her.

"It's like he turned into a whole different person. I would have to drive down to G Street all times of the night looking for him in those abandoned houses. It's terrible down there. I couldn't take it anymore, so I left him." Paula said with a sigh.

"I don't blame you. At least you're back working and you're somewhere safe."

"You're right about that. But I'm happy for you and LC. Lord knows he dodged a bullet with that girl Donna. It's sad the way she's all strung out, especially being pregnant and all."

I frowned at Paula, wondering what the hell she was talking about. "Donna?"

"Yeah. LC's ex, she is in a bad way. I ran into her a couple of times down on G Street while I was down there looking for Calvin's dope-fiend ass."

I didn't know what was more shocking: the fact that Donna was a dope addict, or that she was pregnant. Pregnant. Having a baby. It had been months since I had seen her. I tried to think about exactly how long it had been. Then my heart began racing as I started to wonder exactly how pregnant she was. LC and I had been married almost four months. There was no way the baby could be his. Or could it?

There was only one way to find out.

"Well, Paula, it was good talking to you. I gotta go," I said, turning to leave.

"You ain't going in the store?" Paula called after me.

I didn't answer her as I raced back to my car and pulled out of the parking lot. Donna was pregnant. I wondered if LC knew. I couldn't remember the last time he had even mentioned Donna's name. He had been consumed with running the station, and he had been talking about expanding it to include a used car lot. Hell, we hadn't even been talking about me having a baby.

I drove around for hours, wondering what to do. Before I knew it, the entire day was gone. I called LC at the station and told him I was going to be home late, deciding not to explain that the reason was because I had to go and find his ex-fiancée, who was now possibly carrying his baby.

After the sun had set and darkness filled the sky, I set off on my mission. G Street was located in a part of town people avoided. The street was lined with dilapidated shotgun houses, most of which were boarded up and abandoned. It was scary to see during the day, and now, as I drove down the street at night, it was even scarier.

As I searched for Donna, I paused in front of one particular house. A couple of men and a woman were standing around and then disappeared inside. I noticed another man heading in the same direction, so I decided to take a chance. I knew better than to leave my car parked out front. Instead, I parked farther down the street, making sure to lock the door when I got out.

Chippy, this has got to be the craziest shit you've ever done, and you've done some crazy shit, *I thought as I pulled my coat tighter around me. The fear of being brutally raped and murdered was overshadowed by my determination to see if what Paula had told me was true.*

"Uuuuuhhh, hey!" A man called out to me as I got closer to the house.

I stepped away from him, wishing I had thought to bring a knife, a gun, or at least something heavy in case I needed a weapon. I didn't even have my purse. I placed my fingers around my car key and positioned it in a way that I could easily stab someone if need be. It was pitch black, but I could make out the shadow of a woman staggering toward the side of the house. I walked a little closer, and although she looked familiar, I wasn't sure.

There was an opening where a door should have been located. The woman went inside, and I went in right behind her. Inside, it looked like something from a horror movie. Men and women were cowering in corners, looking like zombies. Suddenly, the woman turned around, and I stared in disbelief.

"You leave me be!" she hissed at me. "Get away from me."

"Donna?" I whispered.

"Get the fuck away from me, bitch!"

I couldn't move. Her skin was ashen, and her eyes were dark and sunken. Her hair, once long and full, was now matted and covered in what looked like mud. Gone was the once-pretty young woman, and instead I saw a walking skeleton, dressed in a tattered dress and ragged flip-flops. My eyes traveled down her body and landed on her swollen belly, which was clearly protruding. She must've noticed what I was looking at, because she quickly covered her stomach.

"Shit, you are pregnant," I said.

"No shit, Sherlock." Her words were slurred.

"Is . . . is it LC's?" I demanded.

She began laughing like a mad woman. "Fuck LC . . . and his baby."

My heart sank as her words confirmed my worst fears. "Does he—did you tell him?"

"Fuck you." She rolled her eyes and stumbled away.

"Donna, you've gotta get out of here. You're sick," I told her, stepping closer and putting a hand on her arm.

"Leave me the fuck alone."

"No, you're coming with me. I can't leave you. Not like this. Not while you're having LC's—"

"Fuck LC." She stared right into my eyes with a look of pure hatred.

"Donna, please," I said. "Come on."

"What do you want?" She leaned against the filthy wall, and I put my hands on either side of her face to get her to focus.

"I want you to come with me. If you stay here and keep doing this, you're gonna die, and so is the baby."

"I don't care. And it ain't your baby, so you shouldn't either. You hate me anyway. Get the fuck out and leave me alone."

"I'm not leaving you here, so shut the fuck up and come on." I pulled her toward me and started dragging her out of the house. I didn't know where the hell I was taking her.

She tried to pull away, but it was pointless. She was too weak, and I was way stronger. I put her into the backseat of my car, and she went to sleep. I drove to the only place I knew she would be safe and no one would find out.

I turned onto the tiny dirt road that led to Ms. Emma's house, and by the time I pulled up, she was already standing on the porch, shotgun in hand. Ms. Emma was an older woman who lived in the back woods with her seven children. She was the closest thing to a doctor for those folks who couldn't afford one, or those who just didn't trust hospitals. When Big Sam's henchmen beat Levi damn near to death, she nursed him back to health.

I got out, and when she recognized me, she rushed over. She saw Donna in the back seat and didn't say a word as we helped her out of the car and took her inside. The two of us bathed her and gave her what was probably the first hot meal she'd had in months, based on the way she gobbled it up. Then, Ms. Emma made her drink some concoction mixed with hot tea.

Donna had just climbed into a cot Ms. Emma had prepared in a back room when I pulled up a chair beside her.

"What the fuck do you want now? You kidnapped my ass and got me God knows where in some back woods farm. I'm not staying here after tonight," she told me.

"You can't leave. You have to stay here—at least until you have the baby. I'll stay here with you," I offered.

"I'm not staying here. You've lost your damn mind. Especially not with your ass. You're probably trying to kill me anyway . . . and my baby."

"I'm not trying to kill you. Shit, if I wanted to kill you, I would've left your ass in that shit hole where you were staying. I'm trying to save you and LC's—I mean, your baby."

She turned her head slowly and looked at me with sadness in her eyes. "Does he know?"

"No," I answered. "Not yet."

"Good. Even more reason for you not to care." Her angry attitude was back. "Now, leave me be."

"I do care. I'll be back to check on you tomorrow."

"I won't be here," she mumbled.

I got up and walked to the front of the house. I thanked Ms. Emma and handed her all the money I had in my purse, promising that I would pay her more to make sure Donna was okay. She agreed not to say anything to anyone about her being there.

I went back the following day, and the day after that. For nearly a month, we nursed Donna back to health and got her clean. Then, late one afternoon, her water broke, and she went into labor. Donna moaned and groaned, screamed and hollered for hours, until finally, she pushed the baby out.

"It's a boy!" I screamed when she finally delivered.

"He's tiny, but he's healthy." Ms. Emma took the slimy, squealing newborn and wrapped him in a blanket.

I could see that Donna was exhausted, physically and emotionally. As Ms. Emma made sure her afterbirth needs were handled, Donna finally drifted off into a deep slumber. For hours, I held that beautiful baby boy in my arms. I gave him his first bath, his first bottle, and did as any new mother would—counted his fingers and toes. He was perfect, looking like a tiny version of LC. I knew that, had he been there, LC would have been beaming with pride at his first-born son. I also knew that this baby being born would change our lives, especially with Donna being the mother. I couldn't take any chances.

Donna began to stir on the cot, and her eyes opened.

"You wanna hold him?" I asked, holding the baby out to her.

She shook her head then closed her eyes again. "No, I want to get outta here."

"What are you going to name him?"

"I don't know. I don't even care. I don't even want that damn baby."

"Donna—"

"Chippy, why won't you just leave me alone? What the fuck do you want?" She turned her body away from me.

Then I got an idea.

"Let me have him. I'll take him."

She whipped her head around and looked at me like I was the crazy one. "I ain't giving you shit. I'll put his ass in an orphanage first, bitch."

"But he's LC's son. He should be with his father." I was sure she could hear the pleading in my voice, but I didn't care. I already loved that little baby, and I wouldn't ever let her give him to anyone else.

"Fuck you and LC. That baby's going to an orphanage."

My first thought was to kill her. It wouldn't have been that difficult. I'd just go over to my purse, pull out the little .22 I carried, and shoot her in the head. Ms. Emma wouldn't be too happy about it, but that wasn't anything $10,000 *wouldn't solve. Then I thought about Ms. Emma's kids running around outside and put that idea to rest, only to come up with what I felt was a much better one.*

"I'll pay you."

She stared at me, I suppose trying to figure out if I was serious. "What do you mean, you'll pay me?"

I could tell she was contemplating my offer, and I felt hopeful it would work. "I'll give you a thousand dollars and a one-way bus ticket to New York. But you must sign papers giving me and LC full custody. You also have to promise not to contact me, LC, and our family ever again."

"A thousand dollars?" she repeated.

"And this." I held up a small, clear bag that held the thing she had been asking for the past month. It had been in my bag for quite a while. Ms. Emma had told me to get a few grams because it might be needed to help ease her off the drugs. This was all that was left of the original, but it might be just what I needed.

She reached for it, but I took a step back. "Do we have a deal?"

As I stood before her with her son cradled in one arm and the plastic bag in the other, I wondered which one she was truly reaching for. The room stood silent, until she finally announced, "Deal." I felt slightly bad about giving her the drugs, but I was desperate, and she was going to find some sooner or later anyway.

"Do you understand, Chippy? Chippy?" Lou's voice woke me from my trance.

I turned and stared at him. "What?"

"I need for you to just get in your car and leave so we can handle this."

I was still mad, but I knew there was nothing more I could do right now. "Fine."

"Where did you park?" Lou asked.

"Around back."

We walked past the front of the building. I looked inside and saw Larry talking to Donna near the front door. Lou must have noticed my body tense up, because he put a hand on my shoulder and said, "Keep walking."

We made our way around to the back, where things only got worse.

"Fuck," I muttered under my breath.

Lou asked, "Where's your car?"

"Fuck the car. Where the hell is Levi and those damn dogs?"

Big Shirley

44

"Saint Simons Island is beautiful, isn't it?" Eric asked. He was lying beside me on a beach chair, holding my hand as we stared up at the sky with dark shades covering our eyes.

"Beautiful doesn't even begin to describe it," he said.

This right here was the life—the life I deserved. I'd finally convinced myself that I was worthy to be at this beach house vacation home, lying out and catching the sun's rays without a care in the world.

Eric squeezed my hand and turned to look at me. "Funny, I was just thinking the same thing about you."

The sunglasses may have hidden his eyes, but they didn't hide the expression of admiration etched on his face. Imagine that, me, ex-ho Big Shirley, now not only knew what love felt like—a gentle and caressing squeeze of the hand—but also knew what it looked like.

"Thank you," I said. "And thank you even more for actually meaning it."

Guys had said a lot of things to me in my years. It wasn't anything out of the ordinary for a man to say all kinds of bullshit to get the pussy, or even when he was already in the pussy. But that wasn't the case with Eric. He meant what he said. I could feel it. I could see it.

I looked out toward the water. "I could stay here forever."

"I used to say that same thing," Eric said. "The good thing about it is that you can, if you want to." Eric nodded to his left toward the beach house. "My parents have owned this home since I can remember. We can come here whenever you want. Other than holidays, nobody is ever here."

I lifted my back from the chair, looking over the rim of my shades. "Are you sure about that?"

"Yeah. Why? You don't believe me?"

I pointed toward the house. "Looks like we've got company."

There seemed to be some sort of commotion going on at the house. We were at least a hundred yards away, so I wasn't quite sure what was happening, but there appeared to be several people—four or five, maybe—up at the house.

Eric stood up from his chair and began waving his arms toward the house. There was no movement for a few seconds, and then someone up at the house began walking toward us while the others went inside.

"What's going on? Who are those people?" I asked.

"Can't see well enough to be sure, but it's probably some people my parents sent down."

I removed my dark sunglasses to get a better look, and I couldn't believe what I was seeing. "Oh, shit," I mumbled under my breath. "Can't be."

"What's wrong?" Eric asked.

"I know that woman," I said, feeling defeated. Why on earth would she be at Eric's family's vacation home, interrupting my fairytale? "I know her."

Eric chuckled. "Well, that makes two of us."

I wasn't surprised that Eric knew her. "Yeah, I suppose everyone knows Belinda Mahogany."

"Yeah, that's true." He was still chuckling, but whatever was so funny, he was the only one of us in on the joke.

"What's she doing here?" I asked.

"She owns the place. Well, her and my old man."

"No, that can't be right, because that would mean . . ." I snapped my neck toward Eric. "You're a Mahogany?"

His face contorted with confusion. "Of course I am. You mean to tell me you didn't know my last name?"

"Hey, EJ." Belinda embraced him lovingly when she reached us. "Fancy meeting you here," she said to me flatly, nowhere near as thrilled to see me as she was her son.

"Mom." He pulled away from her. "Mom, this is Shirley, the woman I told you about, and Shirley, this is my mother, Belinda Ma—."

"We've met," Belinda said in a nice-nasty snarl.

"So I hear. At least that takes the tension out of introducing Mom to my new girl," Eric said with a laugh.

"New girl. I see." Belinda nodded, but it was definitely not a nod of approval.

Eric must have picked up on her tone, because he changed the subject in a hurry. "So, uh, Mom, you didn't tell me what you're doing here." He looked back up toward the house. "Is Dad here too?"

"No. Your father isn't here," she replied. "EJ, I had a slight problem in Jonesboro. We had to bring the package here before transporting it to Atlanta. I need you to go help the boys." She shifted her eyes to me. "Meanwhile, I'll stay here and get to know Shirley a little better."

"No problem." Eric turned to me. "You gonna be okay? I'll be right back. And just remember, her bark is worse than her bite."

"Easy for you to say," I said, deciding it was time I return Belinda's glare. If I started letting her push me around in the beginning, she'd push me around until the end. I'd never disrespect Eric's mother under normal circumstances, but I was nobody's punk. Never would be.

Eric headed for the beach house, leaving me alone with his mother. I watched him walk away, not knowing what to do or to say to Belinda at this point.

"Levi, right?" Belinda said. "That's the Duncan brother you belong to."

"I don't *belong* to a Duncan," I said. "I don't belong to anyone. Yes, Levi and I used to be a couple, but that's over."

She nodded while turning her lips up into an arrogant grin. "I don't know whether that's true or not. But I've never been a controlling mother. Eric is my son, not my man. I don't oversee who he dates. I can either approve or disapprove, but I make no demands when it comes to who he wants to be with."

Surprisingly, her words were somewhat reassuring.

Then she added, "So, if you are with Eric, then you are with us."

This conversation was going better than I imagined. It almost sounded like she was welcoming me into the family.

Then she laid out what I would have to accept to be part of this family.

"We plan on moving to the southern region of Georgia and taking over the Duncans' business. You got a problem with that?" she asked.

"No, ma'am," I answered without hesitation. If that's what it would take to hang on to this new life with Eric, then so be it. It's not like the Duncans had treated me as much more than a second-class whore anyway. Still, in the back of my mind, I did wonder why Eric hadn't ever mentioned his family connection or their plans to me.

"Good. I'm sure Eric will talk to you about it once things are engraved in stone. I think you'll like it."

"I'm sure I will," I said. She was including me in the move. That was more than I could say for the Duncans.

"It's good to know where you stand. I just hope you are a woman of your word, Shirley. These days, all a man, or a woman for that matter, has is their word."

"I'm exactly who I say I am," I replied. "And who I say I'm not. I'm not a Duncan." I figured it was worth repeating, since Belinda didn't seem totally convinced yet.

She looked me up and down before her tight lips formed a smile. "Perfect. If you make my son happy, then I'm happy. And from the looks of things, my EJ is happy."

"I can assure you Eric makes me happy. I believe I can speak for him when I say we plan on making each other happy . . . for a long time." I was in love with Eric, and nothing was going to come between us. Not even his iron-fisted mother.

She looked down at my midsection. "Chippy told me about you being pregnant. I guess all we have to do now is get rid of that Duncan baby you're toting around, huh?"

And just that quickly, she reminded me of the one thing that actually could come between Eric and me.

45

"Thanks again. I don't know what I'd do without your help." I glanced over at Mr. Mahogany, who was still dressed in his tennis outfit, sitting in the passenger's seat of my car. We'd just left his house, and his man James was following behind me in his car.

"I told you it was nothing."

"I know, but I also know you weren't exactly pleased with me for speaking out at the Council about the Young Bloods meeting last week." I searched his face for a reaction, but of course I didn't get any.

"That, young man, is where you are wrong."

"Am I?"

"The teacher never wants the student to show him up in the classroom. That's just human nature. Call it ego if you like." Mahogany rolled down his window and took out a cigarette.

"I wasn't trying to show you up," I said.

"I know that, son, but when you get to be my age, one of the hardest things to do is admit when you're wrong. Especially for a man like myself, whose life and the lives of the people around him depend on him being right."

I nodded my understanding.

"But Catt and Major Homes told me how you handled those boys, gathering all their leaders up and explaining the benefits of using your product. Catt said you reminded her of a young me." He paused to take a drag from his cigarette. "I also think giving them each a brand-new *Smokey and the Bandit* Trans Am was a great touch."

"So you're not upset?" I asked.

"No, I'm not upset. Who could be mad when the projection of our cut of their sales is a million dollar this year?" He chuckled as we pulled into Larry's driveway, James not far behind. "It seems the student is a quick study and will soon surpass his teacher."

I took that as a compliment as we climbed out of the car. "He's in the garage," I said. He raised a hand to James, signaling for him to stay put.

I pulled open the garage door and turned on the light, praying that Nee Nee and the kids were still asleep, or at least that she would have the sense to keep the kids inside. Mr. Mahogany entered the garage behind me, and then I closed the door.

I walked over to the freezer and opened it up. "He's in here."

Mr. Mahogany approached, peered inside the freezer, then quickly stepped back. It confused me that Mr. Mahogany was acting as if he'd never seen a dead body before. I knew damn well that wasn't the case.

"Everything okay?" I asked.

Mr. Mahogany took a moment to regain his composure then leaned in to examine the body again. "Everything's fine. He looks familiar, but it's not the man I thought it might be."

Mr. Mahogany had told me a lot of things in the past few months, but that was the first blatant lie.

Shirley

46

"Stop dragging your feet. You're getting out of here whether you like it or not!"

I woke up to the sound of Eric yelling. At first I thought I was dreaming, because after his mother left, we'd made love and fallen asleep in each other's arms. I rolled over in the bed to search for him, only to find that he wasn't there. Sitting up, I rubbed my eyes and stared out the window. The sky was bright, although, looking at the clock, I realized the sun was about half an hour from setting.

"Well, I don't like it. I don't like any of this shit!" I heard a woman shout.

"Calm down and be quiet!" Eric demanded.

My first thought was that he must be arguing with his mother, but then I remembered that, to my relief, she'd left a couple hours after she arrived.

"I told y'all not to take off her gag," Eric said.

"This old broad is stronger than she looks." It was another male this time.

What the hell is going on? I tossed a dress over my head and went to the balcony to find out where the voices were coming from. In the driveway, Eric was pulling on a young girl whose hands were tied behind her back, while two other guys were pulling on an older woman, who was also tied, but she was giving them hell. Both women were barely dressed, and neither one wore shoes. Three other men were waiting outside by a van.

"Eric, what's going on out here?" I yelled. Everyone froze for a moment, and then Eric looked up at me.

"God dammit! Get back in the room. I'll be up there in a minute," he shouted.

"Help us, please!" the old woman whined and twisted as she tried to escape the men's grasp. One of them backhanded her, and she fell to the ground. Another man from the van came over and pulled her off the ground. I felt sorry for her, but I didn't move. I'd learned my lesson about meddling in things that weren't my concern, and I had the scars to prove it.

"Get back upstairs, Shirley." This time Eric's voice was a bit softer, but his glare was more threatening. I decided that it might be wise to go inside and mind my business, until . . .

"Shirley! Is that you, honey?" the old woman called out my name as if she knew me. I stopped dead in my tracks as I realized who she was.

"Miss Bettie!" I shouted her name. It sounded like her and looked like her, but I couldn't wrap my brain around whatever the hell was going on. Miss Bettie was supposed to be dead—only this woman was far from dead. She looked as shocked to see me as I was to see her. My God, had Lou been right all along?

The other men continued wrestling Miss Bettie toward the door, but seeing me had made her fight even harder. I stood where I was, still unable to move.

"Call my boys, Shirley!" Miss Bettie called out to me as they dragged her to the van. "Tell them I'm alive!"

"Shut that bitch up!" Eric demanded.

Whack! One of the men hit Miss Bettie upside the head with a gun, and she crumpled at his feet. He then turned the gun on me and said, "You want me to handle her, E?"

My eyes went from the barrel of the gun to Eric, my heart pounding in anticipation of his answer. I silently pleaded with him, praying that he would let me live.

"Naw, she ain't gonna say nothing. Me and her got big plans. We gonna take over south Georgia and eventually the entire South. Isn't that right, Shirley?" he asked.

One more glance at that gun and I decided to tell him everything he wanted to hear. "Eric, I made my decision when I got in that car with you last night and came here with you this morning. I left everything to be with you."

"That's my girl. Now, do what I said. Go back inside."

"I'm gonna take a walk on the beach." I needed to get away from that house to think. "This is a lot to take in at one time."

"You do that. I'll be down there as soon as I finish."

I turned and quickly went back inside. A few minutes later, I was on the narrow path through the dunes. I sat down in the sand and stared into the waves crashing near my feet. I could not believe Miss Bettie was alive, and even worse, that Eric and his family were her abductors. What kind of a family had I gotten myself involved with? I had no doubt in my mind now that if I didn't get rid of my baby, Belinda would have me killed. Shit, these people were starting to make the Duncans look like boy scouts.

My life was so fucked up. I began to cry.

"Sh–Sh–Shirley, d–d–don't cry."

I felt his hand on my shoulder, and I held my breath as I turned around.

"Levi? How did you find me?" I jumped up and threw my arms around his neck. Despite everything that had happened, I'd never been so happy to see anyone in my entire life.

"I–I f–f–followed you." He looked proud of himself.

I looked past him, expecting to see LC, Larry, and Lou, or maybe even Chippy. "But how? Who brought you here, Levi? How did you find me?" I asked, still looking behind for someone who wasn't there.

"I–I s–saw you, Sh–Sh–Shirley. I was i–i–in the car, a–a–and y–you was wi–wi–with th–that m–m–m–man at the g–gas sta–sta–station."

I'll be dammed, I thought. Eric and I had stopped at a gas station in Brunswick on our way there that morning.

"You were in Brunswick?" I asked, trying to piece together the scene.

"Y–y–y–yeah. M–me and Ch–Ch–Chippy was at the W–W–Waffle House."

This was crazy. Thinking back, I remembered that there was a Waffle House restaurant across the street from the gas station we went to. Why he would have been there with Chippy was a mystery to me, but just then, I felt a fluttering in my stomach, and I realized that maybe it wasn't my place to try to figure it out. Maybe Levi, the father of my baby, was put there at that moment to save me from making the biggest mistake of my life. Maybe God was trying to send me a message.

"You drove by yourself, Levi?"

"N–no."

"Who's with you?"

"M–m–my d–d–dogs." He smiled proudly.

I stood in awe of him. Wow, Levi could drive. No one had ever told me he could, and I doubted that they even knew. This man was more intelligent than we had been giving him credit for.

"So, where are the dogs?" I asked.

He turned to point at the dunes. "L–l–laying down."

"What the fuck? Where did this nigga come from?" Just then, Eric and two of his goons came walking toward us.

"Eric, I—he—" I began to panic. Things were about to go from bad to worse.

Levi moved in front of me, prepared to protect me. I don't know what made Eric think he would be able to physically assault Levi, who was taller and bigger, but he took a swing at him. Levi caught his fist midair and then charged at him, knocking him to the sand.

"Levi, no!" I cried out.

As the two men wrestled, Levi's stature worked against him. Unlike Eric, he had a harder time regaining his balance in the sand. The two other guys joined in, kicking and stomping Levi. Eric ended up on top of him, punching Levi in the chest and face.

Levi was moaning in pain as he tried to fight back, but the gentle giant was no match against three attackers. I stood by and watched helplessly as they landed blow after blow, until suddenly, four huge Rottweilers jumped over the dune and charged the men. All hell broke loose. I couldn't stop scream-ing as I watched the dogs ripping at their clothes and limbs, blood spewing from their wounds. One of the men managed to break free long enough to pull out his gun. Shots rang out, and amidst the commotion, two dogs fell to the ground, dead.

"Nooooooooooo!" Levi pushed Eric off of him with superhuman strength then charged at the shooter, knocking the gun from his hand.

Instinctively, I scrambled to pick it up. Meanwhile, Levi had the man by the throat. I heard a snap, and then Levi dropped the lifeless body next to the dead dogs. Chaos continued as the two remaining dogs tore the other man to shreds.

From the corner of my eye, I saw Eric. He was bleeding and his clothes were torn, but he had managed to scramble away from the dog attack. Now he was holding a gun and aiming it at Levi.

"Eric, don't!" I shouted.

He turned toward me for a brief second but kept his gun raised.

"Please," I said.

Eric sneered at me and turned back to Levi.

Standing before me were two men I loved, and I had to make a choice.

I squeezed the trigger. The bullet hit Eric in his neck, and he dropped to the ground. "Sorry, Eric, but how could I ever tell my baby I let his father be killed?"

"Sh–Sh–Shirley?" Levi looked over at me.

"Come on, Levi. We gotta get the hell outta here. Now."

Donna

47

"What the fuck do you mean, 'Where's Levi'?" Lou's voice was so loud that I heard him through the front door of the Waffle House, where Larry and I were talking. I was still wiping the angry tears from my eyes and trying to get myself together before clocking into work.

"Did he say Levi?" Larry looked at me.

"That's what it sounded like."

Without another word, we both headed back outside.

"You're never gonna believe this shit," Lou said, rushing over. Chippy followed close behind him.

"What now?" Larry looked like he'd about had it.

"Chippy's car is gone, and Levi took it."

"What? Why was Levi with you?" Larry asked Chippy, who was now distraught for a whole other reason that wasn't caused by me.

"I got him from Big Shirley's. Li'l Momma told me that Shirley's been cheating on him with some dude, and she's planning on opening her own place. I couldn't just leave him there," Chippy told them. "He was sitting right in my car with his dogs. I don't know what happened."

"Wait until I see Shirley," Larry growled. "I'm gonna kill that cheating bitch."

"This don't make no kinda sense," Lou said. "Couldn't nobody have jumped in the car and stole it with Levi's big ass and them dogs in it."

"Well, maybe he took the car himself," I suggested.

They all turned and looked at me as if I had lost my damn mind. The thought of Levi taking off in Chippy's car was kind of far-fetched, but it was possible.

"Shut the fuck up, Donna. You know Levi can't drive. Someone must've taken him." Lou began pacing back and forth.

"I'm sorry," Chippy said. "I told him to wait right there."

"I don't believe this shit. How the hell are we gonna look for both Momma and Levi?" Larry asked.

"We ain't looking for Levi," Lou answered.

"Huh?" we all asked at the same time.

Larry pointed at me and Chippy. "They are."

"Who the fuck is *they*?" I folded my arms. "I have to work. I'm surprised Jerry ain't came out here and fired my ass anyway."

"Fuck that job. This is both y'all's fault, so y'all both go find him."

"How is this my fault? I ain't have shit to do with this." I glared over at Chippy and rolled my eyes. "She's the one who brought her ass to my job and left him in the car, not me."

"She wasn't rolling on the fucking ground by her damn self. Larry and I gotta go find Momma." He turned to Chippy and said, "Look, you lost his ass; you better find him."

"I don't even have a fucking car," Chippy reminded him.

"Donna does. Now, both of y'all go find my fucking brother. I mean that shit. Let's go, Larry." Lou was so damn forceful it was almost sexy.

Before Chippy and I could protest again, the brothers had taken off across the parking lot and jumped into Larry's car, burning rubber as they pulled out. I couldn't believe what he expected us to do. First, trying to find Levi's ass was gonna be like finding a damn needle in a haystack. We didn't even know what direction he had gone in. Second, as much as I wanted to help Lou, there was no way I wanted to be around Chippy's ass. Third, if I left, I was definitely going to be fired.

"What the hell are you waiting on?" Chippy interrupted my thoughts. "Let's go."

I didn't respond.

"Fine. If you don't wanna leave, then give me your damn keys and I'll go find Levi by myself." She held out her hand.

"Listen, I know you're used to bossing folks around and having them do what the fuck you tell them, but I ain't one of them, okay?" I glared at her.

"Donna, we got customers in here waiting." Jerry came out the door and called for me. "You're late!"

"I'm coming," I yelled back. "Give me five minutes."

Chippy was still holding out her hand. "I need your keys before you go in."

"I'm not giving you shit. Are you crazy?" I snapped.

"Look, Donna, either you give me the keys or I will fucking take them. Lou has been going on and on about how you're being so fucking helpful and don't have an agenda, now here you are being the bitch that I know you truly are. I was right about you all along."

"You don't know shit about me, Chippy, or everything I've done over the past few weeks to help. I was the only person who believed Lou when he said Miss Bettie was alive. All of y'all said he was crazy and didn't wanna listen, but I did. And yeah, I do have an agenda, because like it or not, the Duncans are family. My family. The only family I have left." I didn't want to let her see the tears that were threatening to fall, but it was no use. A single tear slipped out and traveled down my cheek.

Chippy stared at me for a second then finally said, "If you're so worried about family, then get in the fucking car and let's go find Levi. What the fuck are you waiting on?"

I glanced at Jerry, still watching us from the doorway, then back at Chippy. I could only pray I was making the right decision as I reached into the pocket of my uniform and took out my keys.

"Let's ride," I said to Chippy.

For hours, we rode through the streets of Brunswick, hoping to spot Chippy's car. At first, there was an awkward silence and we didn't say anything. After a while, I couldn't stand it anymore, so I broke the ice.

"Chippy, I wasn't going to take him from you. I promise. I just wanted to see him. I always think about how he looks now, how big he's gotten . . . you know, shit like that. I was curious. I'm his mother; I'm not a threat."

She considered my words for a minute, but when she answered, she didn't sound mad. "I guess that's understandable, but you have to realize why I was upset. We had a deal."

"I wasn't in my right mind when we made that deal and you know it, Chippy. One thing I've always respected about you is that you're a smart woman, which is probably why you made me the offer that you did. You knew that I was a dope fiend, and you dangled a fix in front of my face during one of the hardest days of my life. You knew I would make the choice that I did." Admitting that I chose heroin over my son was not something I was proud of, but I had waited a long time to have this conversation, and now it was time.

"I . . . I did what was best for Junior." Her voice cracked slightly.

We approached a stop light that turned red, and I turned to look her in the eye. I could feel some sort of understanding between us, a kind of truce, you might say.

"You did what you thought needed to be done to keep your husband," I said. "You knew that if I kept the baby and LC found out, he would be spending time with his son, and that would mean time away from you. And although you knew he loved you, in the back of your mind, you knew that there was a slight chance that his love for his child might reignite his love for me. So, you decided to get rid of me."

Chippy just stared at me. She didn't deny what I said, because we both knew I was right, but she did try to spin the story in her favor. "LC would've never let you have Junior strung out the way you were. He would have killed you. I honestly believe that."

"I don't believe he could kill me," I said. Deep down, I felt that LC still loved me. At least that was what I wanted to believe.

"Well, trust me, if he didn't do it, he would have had Larry do it," she said as the light turned green and I continued driving.

I sighed heavily. "Kind of scary thinking about the man you loved doing something like that."

"Don't take this wrong, but love doesn't live there no more, Donna. LC and I are soul mates with an unbreakable bond.

As special as you think you and him were, it doesn't hold a candle to what we have."

"I think I found that out on my wedding day. You don't have to gloat."

"I really wasn't trying to. I was just trying to make a point." She actually sounded sincere.

"Point taken." I decided to change the subject. "I never thanked you for saving us, me and Junior. Truth is, if you hadn't come and kidnapped my ass, we probably both would be dead. So, you're owed that much."

"Donna, I'm sorry—"

"Don't. Please don't patronize me. I still don't like you, and you don't like me. We ain't friends, and we never will be. This ain't no fucking Kumbaya moment, Chippy. It just is what it is. We both made choices that we have to live with. You made yours, and I made mine. I've said my peace, and that's all I ever wanted to do."

"I respect that. And you're right, you'll always be a bitch that I can't stand," Chippy responded.

"Now, where the hell is Levi? We been down every street in Brunswick at least three times. The sooner we find him, the sooner we can get the hell away from each other."

"Let's go to Waycross. Maybe he's at Big Shirley's," Chippy said.

"Yeah. Plus, I could use a drink."

We made it to Big Shirley's, and all eyes were on us when we walked inside. I know folks were shocked not only to see me, but to see me there with Chippy. She spoke and acted like it was no big deal as we walked over to the bar.

"Have you seen Levi?" she asked the bartender.

"No, Miss Chippy. Not today."

"Give us two bourbons. I'm going to Shirley's office to use the phone," she told him.

"Sure thing, Miss Chippy," he said.

"You gonna wait here?" She looked over at me.

"May as well," I said, sitting on one of the stools.

"Lawd, who woulda ever thought there would come a day when prissy-ass Donna would be sitting at Big Shirley's whorehouse having a drink." She chuckled.

I was just about to respond when the front door burst open and Shirley came rushing inside, with Levi right on her heels.

"Shirley! Levi!" I shrieked.

"And in walks the only woman in the world who I hate more than you right now," Chippy said with a scowl.

Larry

48

We pulled into the parking lot of Donna's building and sure enough, there was a blue Continental, which I assumed was Eddie's. We jumped out, and Lou began looking through the glove compartment of Eddie's car, while I fumbled under the front seat until my fingers found what I'd been looking for.

"Bingo," I said, holding up the keys.

"There ain't shit in here but eight tracks and chewing gum," Lou said.

"Let's check out the trunk," I suggested. We walked around to the back and I popped it open.

"What the fuck is this shit?" Lou asked, waving his hand in front of his nose. "Is that garbage?"

"Looks like it." Inside the trunk was a garbage can and several plastic bags full of trash that looked like someone had already rummaged through. Papers were strewn everywhere.

"That Eddie was one strange motherfucker," Lou replied.

We took out the garbage can and began to sift through the papers. It appeared that whoever the trash belonged to was an important person, based on the business envelopes and letters. These weren't just standard bills. They looked like official documents.

"Who the fuck is Dwayne McCarty?" I asked, holding up an envelope and reading the name on the front, "It looks like this is his shit."

"Dwayne McCarty? That's the guy the dude was asking Eddie about right before he smoked him." Lou took the papers from my hand. "Said he had something to do with Momma."

"You ever heard of this cat before?"

"Hell no. But we're about to meet him."

"I guess we're headed back to Atlanta, huh?" I took back the envelope, tearing off the address and putting it into my pocket.

"Yeah." Lou slammed the trunk and we hurried back to the car, heading to Atlanta in search of Dwayne McCarty and hopefully, another clue to finding our mother.

"Hey man, wake up. We're almost there." We'd just hit the Buckhead city limits when Lou tapped me awake. We had grabbed a map when we stopped to gas up and use the bathroom. It had been a long-ass night, and it seemed that the day was going to be even longer. I hadn't had much more than a cat nap here or there over the past twenty-four hours, but I wasn't tired. Driving a tractor trailer had taught me how to condition my body to endure very little sleep.

"Hey, let me ask you a question," Lou said as I sat up and looked around.

"What?" I asked.

"Are you sure that it was a good idea having Chippy and Donna pair up like that to find Levi? We probably shoulda just brought Donna with us." He sounded genuinely concerned, which surprised the hell out of me. He wasn't one to get sentimental.

"They'll be fine. Chippy may be crazy, but she ain't *that* crazy," I assured him.

"Shit, I think Big Shirley would beg to differ. We see just how crazy Chippy is every time we look at Shirley's face."

"Man, fuck Big Shirley. Here I was thinking that she really loved him."

"Me too. But it's her goddamn loss."

Lou was laughing, and I gave him a strange look. I didn't see a damn thing funny about everything that had been happening lately.

"We own a whorehouse," he explained. "Our brother's not gonna have a problem getting laid, but with that cut-up face of hers, she's gonna have one hell of a time finding a job."

"You know, I never thought about it like that." I started to laugh too.

Lou turned to me. "Hey, Larry, you think maybe Levi really can drive?"

"Hell no. Who the hell woulda taught him? Think about it. Do you really think Levi is capable of stealing a car and driving it? Come on, man. That's crazy talk."

"Hell, I ain't think that nigga could make a baby either, but it happened," Lou replied.

"Damn, you got a point there too." I nodded. "Well, we'll deal with that shit later after we find Momma. We gotta figure this out first."

"This is the street, right?" Lou asked.

"Yeah, we're close to this cat's house." I pulled the address out of my pocket and double checked. "Yep."

Lou let out a low whistle as we turned down the street. "This is a rich-ass neighborhood." I sat up and looked out the window at the huge houses we passed.

"There it is." I pointed at a huge brick house with a perfectly manicured lawn.

Lou slowed down a bit then parked about a block from the house. We'd learned from our old loan sharking days you never park in front of someone's house. I prepared myself to jump out of the car, but he stopped me while my hand was still on the door.

"Wait a second," he said.

"What's wrong?"

"Something's going on over there. Look." There was a bunch of guys near a van parked outside his house.

"Maybe they're his security. I told you those papers looked important, and look at these houses. It's obvious he's rich."

"Naw, these ain't no security-type dudes. Let's just wait this out a second," he said.

We watched as two guys opened the back of a blue van. They both were armed and waiting on something or someone. A few seconds later, three men came out of the house. One was white, and his hands were tied behind his back and his mouth was gagged. The men tossed him into the back of the van, then they all climbed in.

"You think that was the guy we're looking for? Dwayne McCarty?" I turned and asked Lou.

"I'm thinking it is. Come on. Wherever they're going is the same place we are."

The van took off, and we followed.

49

"Chippy!" I rushed over to the bar where she was standing. I had no idea why she happened to be there, but seeing her was a sight for sore eyes. Then, in my peripheral vision, I caught a glimpse of the woman seated on one of the stools, and I stopped walking so suddenly that Levi bumped into me. "Why the hell are you here?"

"I'm here with her," Donna pointed at Chippy.

"That's a damn lie and we both know it. You need to get the hell out of my place before we throw your ass outa here." I walked over and stood in front of her, "Now get the fuck out."

"She ain't going nowhere." Chippy walked over and stood in front of me, "As a matter of fact, I should be asking you why the hell you're here. You think we don't know about you cheating on Levi? When Larry and Lou get here, you're the one who's gonna get thrown out."

Chippy was so close to me that I could feel her breath on my face. I took a step back. There weren't many woman I'd back down to in a fight, but she was one of them. The last time the two of us had a confrontation, she caused permanent damage, and I wasn't about to take the chance of her doing it again. Besides, I was more concerned with finding the Duncan brothers and telling them what happened.

"Looks like you're the one who needs to be leaving, Shirley," Donna said with a smirk. Then that bitch had the nerve to look past me and say, "Levi, are you okay? We've been looking all over for you."

"Yeah, where the hell have you been, and where the hell is my car?" Chippy walked over to him.

"I–I–I g–got Sh–Sh–Shirley." He smiled at her.

"What the hell you mean, Levi? Who took you to get Shirley?"

"He did. He drove himself. He said he saw me, and he followed me," I explained.

"Followed you where? Where the hell were you?"

I lowered my eyes and quietly said, "Saint Simons Island."

"Saint Simons Island?" Chippy repeated.

"Chippy, I know you're pissed, and I'll explain everything, but we gotta go find Lou and them quick," I told her.

"I'm beyond pissed," she replied. "You better tell me what the fuck Levi is talking about, because the last thing you should be asking about is finding his brothers. They are not gonna want to see your cheating ass."

"Miss Bettie is alive!" I blurted out. "I saw her. I know where she is, or at least where she was, and you're never gonna believe who's involved."

Chippy screwed up her face like I was talking gibberish. She didn't believe a word I was saying.

"Belinda Mahogany. She took Miss Bettie," I said, but that only made Chippy more skeptical.

"What? This makes no sense." She shook her head. "Even if I believe she's alive, why would Belinda have Miss Bettie?"

"I don't know, but the Mahogany family has some plan to take over south Georgia. They sent their son Eric to seduce me into working for them." It hurt to say it out loud, but I had to admit to myself that Eric had probably never really cared about me. I was a pawn who could give them information in their campaign to get rid of the Duncans.

"Yeah, and it worked," Donna laughed derisively. I was gonna have to fuck her up in a minute.

"Where the fuck are they now? We have to go find them and make him tell us where Miss Bettie is," Chippy said. I wanted to jump for joy that at least now she believed Miss Bettie was alive.

"Belinda's back in Atlanta, and Eric is—"

"H–h–he's dead. Sh–Sh–Shirley shot h–h–him," Levi volunteered.

"What?" Chippy looked to me for an explanation.

"He was going to kill Levi, so I had to shoot him. I couldn't let anybody hurt my baby's daddy."

If I was thinking I might earn some praise for protecting Levi, I was wrong. Chippy moved right on without commenting on it.

"If the Mahoganys are involved, then . . . oh my God! LC!" Chippy ran toward my office, and we all followed behind her. She grabbed the phone on my desk and dialed.

After a few rings, she said, "Shit, he's not home. Let me try the dealership." Again, we waited as she dialed.

"I need to speak to my husband *now*," she said frantically when someone answered. "It's an emergency . . . What? When? How long ago? . . . Okay." She hung up the phone, looking scared. "LC is with Mr. Mahogany now. We have to get to Atlanta."

"Wait." I rushed to the closet in the back of my office and unlocked it.

"What the fuck are you doing? We gotta go," Chippy said.

I pulled out a large trunk from the back and popped it open, reaching inside and tossing her a revolver. I took out another small-caliber pistol and held it out.

"Who is that for?" Donna's eyes widened and she stared at it. "I said I would help find Levi, and I did. I ain't say shit about no gun."

Chippy took the gun from my hand and shoved it at her. "You said you were family and would always be, and there wasn't shit I could do to change that. It's time to go handle family business. Take it, and let's get the fuck up the road."

Donna carefully took the gun from her. I reached back into the trunk and picked up a shotgun and another .45. I stood up and said, "We ready."

Minutes later, we were all piled back into Chippy's car: me, Chippy, Donna, Levi, and his dogs, as we hauled ass up the highway to Atlanta.

Bettie

50

"Look, Bettie, I'm not going to argue with you anymore, and I don't want to fight with you. Things are getting down to the nitty gritty here. It's time to stop playing around."

I sat tied to the chair, completely unmoved by Belinda's words as she stood in front of me, attempting to be threatening but unable to lose the uppity tone that instilled anything but fear into me.

"What part of *I'm not telling you shit* don't you understand?" I replied. Belinda might as well have hit record and replayed my words in order to save me the breath and time. By now she had to know that my words were bond. I hadn't told her shit thus far, and I wasn't gonna.

"So, you're not telling me anything?" she huffed.

I leaned forward and raised my voice. "Not. Telling. You. A. Damn. Thing." I rested back against the chair.

I could see her anger rising, and it amused me. She took a step closer and grabbed a handful of my hair. Not wanting to give her the satisfaction, I didn't even flinch.

"Where the fuck is it?" she demanded. When I still didn't respond, she smacked me across the face with the back of her hand. My head jerked from the blow, but I refused to cry out in pain.

"You know, Bettie, I thought you were a wise woman, but apparently not. After being away from your family all those years, you would think that you would be ready to see them again," she said, trying a new approach.

"I am, and I will."

"They already think you're dead. There's no reason for me to let you live at this point."

My mind flashed back to the sight of Shirley up on the balcony at that house by the beach where they'd held me for a while. What was she doing there? I'd only seen her for a second before one of those bastards hit me on the head, but she didn't look particularly stressed or disheveled like she was a captive. In fact, she'd yelled out to Belinda's son like they were familiar. I hoped that she had done what I'd asked her and called my sons, but I couldn't be sure. Even if she had, they'd moved me from that house, so it would take some work for the boys to find me. Until then, I had to do what I could to stay alive.

"You can't kill me. If I die, you'll never find what you're looking for, and you know that. If you were gonna kill me, you woulda done it a long time ago," I said more confidently than I honestly felt.

"What's to stop me from killing your sons one by one until you tell me?"

My stomach churned at the thought of losing one of my boys at the hands of this bitch, but I couldn't let her see my fear. "Like I told you, if anything happens to my boys, there will be hell to pay, and all over the South will never be the same. I made sure my family and everyone I love is well covered and protected. Even you said it: I'm a wise woman, Belinda."

"Is that so?" She gave me a devious smile and then walked out of the room, returning a few minutes later with the monster, who held Lisa by her hair. "So, everyone you love is protected?" Belinda asked. "What about her? You seem to care about her a hell of a lot." She raised her arm and pressed a gun against Lisa's temple.

"Oh God, please don't kill me." Lisa began to cry.

"Well, then you better convince your friend Bettie over there to give me what I want."

I stared at Belinda, whose hands were trembling slightly as she held the gun. She and Lisa made eye contact for a quick second, and I noticed that for all of her howling, Lisa's face was not wet with tears. All of a sudden, the truth became crystal clear to me.

"Please, Miss Bettie. She's gonna kill me." Lisa's crying became louder. "I don't want to die."

"Lisa, I need you to be strong. She is not going to kill you."

"You willing to bet her life on it?" Belinda yelled.

"You're not going to kill her," I said.

"I will. I'll kill her if you don't tell me." Belinda's hands started shaking even more obviously as she pressed the barrel of the gun harder against Lisa's head.

"Please, Miss Bettie. Please!"

"Fine. You wanna know what I know?" I asked.

"Yes!" Belinda said.

"I know that bitch has been working with you this whole time. That's what I know," I spat.

Belinda gasped.

"What?" I saw the reaction in Lisa's face, whose tears had dried up pretty damn fast.

Belinda was looking at the monster with an expression that asked, *What do I do now?* His dumb ass stared back at her with a blank face.

"Let's just stop this little charade, because it's gone on long enough," I said.

"You think you're so smart, don't you, bitch?" Belinda lowered the gun and released Lisa's hair. Lisa stepped away from her to go stand next to the monster.

"How did you know?" Belinda asked.

I had to laugh at my answer. "I didn't until just now."

Belinda's face turned crimson, and I suspected at that moment it wouldn't have taken much to provoke her into really killing me. "Shut up, bitch!"

I watched Lisa lean against the monster, and he wrapped a protective arm around her shoulder. What the hell were they, some type of weird satanic couple?

"She told me that what she's hiding was worth ten million back then and considerably more now," Lisa announced.

I was totally confused. It looked like somehow I had been conversing with the enemy, giving her secrets she could feed back to Belinda and her goons. Thank God I hadn't told her where I had hidden anything.

The door opened, and a guy walked in, announcing, "We got him."

My heart began pounding. I prayed that he wasn't talking about one of my sons. I had made sure that things would be handled if anything happened to one of them, but it would still mean they were dead. That was a pain I never wanted to experience.

"Well, what are you waiting for? Bring him in." Belinda exhaled loudly then turned back to me. "I think this may make you change your mind."

I sat and waited with terrified anticipation for the men to return. Finally, they shoved someone inside. His body slammed up against the wall, and he crumpled to the floor, groaning in pain. A flood of relief washed over me as I realized the man was white. It wasn't one of my sons.

When the monster went over and pulled the man off the floor, I got a good look at his face and realized I knew him.

Dwayne McCarty looked like he'd been through hell. His clothes were disheveled, and his face was bruised and swollen. He looked a mess now, but I'd always thought Dwayne was a good-looking white boy, much like his father, who had died a few years back. I had always admired and trusted both of them, but he looked scared.

"Do you know who I am?" Belinda asked him.

"No." His voice cracked.

"Do you know her?" She pointed at me.

He looked at me, and when we made eye contact, I nodded that it was okay for him to tell the truth.

"Yes."

"How?"

"I'm her lawyer," he said.

"Then you should know why we're here," Belinda said.

"No, I don't." He shook his head.

"How long have you been her attorney?"

"A few years." Dwayne was still doubled over in pain as he answered her questions.

"And who was her attorney before you?"

"My father," he replied.

"And your father gave her something that belongs to me." Belinda stepped closer to him.

"I don't know what you're talking about," he said. The monster took out his gun and pointed it at Dwayne's head.

"Tell me what you do know. Bettie here claims that her family is well protected, and we know that you're a key player in whatever it is that she's talking about. Now, explain it."

Again, Dwayne looked over at me, and I gave him a small smile meant to comfort him—as much as that would be possible in a situation as fucked up as this. Poor guy had had no idea what he was in for when he took over his father's clients. He'd been an innocent kid back then; now he was in way over his head.

"Go ahead. Tell her, Dwayne. Explain to her what happens if anyone harms anyone in my family."

Dwayne was quiet for a few seconds. Finally he said, "There is a contract in place with certain outfit out of New York."

"What kind of contract?" Belinda snapped.

"Well, if anything happens to a member of the Duncan family, a series of hits will take place."

"A series of hits? On who?"

"On a group known as the Council. And their families. Everything is in place," he said slowly.

"What the hell do you mean everything's in place? I can kill you right now and that will stop the whole fucking thing." She pointed her gun toward him.

"If anything happens to me, the contract is set up to be executed as well. We are all protected. My father and Miss Bettie have paid and put things in such a way that no one can stop it."

"Fuck that! You can't stand there and tell me that bull. There's no way . . ." Belinda began ranting in frustration while waving her gun around. Lisa stood in the corner, and the monster took a step back out of Belinda's way.

Belinda got up in Dwayne's face. "This bitch just got out of jail. How the fuck can she afford to put a contract hit out on the whole fucking Council?"

"From the gold," Dwayne answered.

I closed my eyes. That was the one thing I hadn't wanted him to tell. Belinda was now one step closer to finding out everything she wanted to know.

Her eyes widened. "Gold. What gold?"

"Her gold. It originally belonged to the KKK, and somehow ended up in the hands of her husband. When he died, she hired my father, and they set up the contract. That's all I know."

"That's my father's gold, isn't it?" Belinda glared at me. I smirked back. "Where is the gold now?"

I looked up and saw the monster and Lisa were both waiting for his answer with as much anxiousness as Belinda. "I don't know," Dwayne said. "She only gave my father a million of it."

LC

51

What was Mr. Mahogany up to? My mind was still back at Larry's garage, frozen on the moment I had opened the trunk and showed Mr. Mahogany that body. His mouth may have said he had no idea who the dead man was, but the expression on his face said otherwise. He knew that man, which meant he knew something about my mother, and I wasn't going to rest until I figured out what the hell was going on. I knew one way of finding out was to follow his ass, but I'd have to hurry up and change vehicles. Him and James would have the body loaded out of Larry's garage into theirs and be heading off in no time, which meant I basically had no time to get changed, hop in a different car, and tail them, but I was still going to try my damnedest to do just that.

I knew Mr. Mahogany and James would spot a tail from my cherry red Corvette Roadster from a mile away, so I'd given him some BS excuse about a meeting with the fire marshal that I couldn't miss. I was sure he and James wanted to discuss our mystery guest in the freezer, so he told me he'd handle it. Everything in me wanted to believe that I was wrong in my interpretation, but I would have been lying to myself. And I wasn't no liar.

I was out the door, in my car, and speeding down the road in a matter of seconds.

"Yes!" I exclaimed when I passed Larry's place and saw that they were just now heading up the driveway. I put the pedal to the metal, getting a nice distance ahead of them before pulling over.

Slumping down in the car, I waited. As soon as they passed, I eased back onto the road and followed them. I had no idea where they were heading, but supposedly Mr. Mahogany knew a place where he could dispose of the body and it wouldn't be traced back to us. But right about now, I didn't trust a damn thing the man said.

I followed them for about fifteen minutes, and they ended up at a warehouse, which didn't seem out of the ordinary. Plenty of bodies had probably been disposed of in warehouses, dismembered, destroyed by chemicals and what have you. So nothing put up a red flag yet. What did seem peculiar was that when Mr. Mahogany and James returned to the car, it was not to get the body and take it inside, but to get in and drive away.

I followed them at a safe distance, and they ended up stopping at a house where, once again, they went inside, then exited and drove off without unloading the body. Now I was alarmed. I suspected they weren't really looking for some-place to get rid of the body; they were looking for someone.

As badly as I wanted to just whip my car in front of theirs, stopping them in their tracks, and demand to know what the hell was going on—what they knew about that dead man in the trunk and his connection to my mother—my chances were better if I kept following to whatever their final destination was. So, I continued to follow them from building to building for almost three hours, until they finally, believe it or not, dropped the body off at funeral parlor.

I was frustrated, confused, and pissed off. I'd trusted this man. I looked up to him. He was my mentor, for God's sake, and now it looked like he might be wrapped up somehow in my mother's kidnapping. I wracked my brain, trying to understand his motives. What could he possibly have to gain? Part of me still wanted to give Mr. Mahogany the benefit of the doubt, thinking perhaps he didn't have anything to do with my mother, but I was certain he knew the person who did—and clearly, his ties to them were stronger than his ties to me.

Once they left the body, they went back to the same routine of driving from place to place.

"Why the hell are they here?" I asked myself as I watched them pull up to a five-story building that was still under construction. It was Saturday, and no construction was going on, yet there were several expensive cars in the lot. I watched as Mr. Mahogany got out of the car and went inside, alone this time, and James drove off.

I pulled a little farther down the block, where I planned to park as I plotted my next move. Then, as if things couldn't get any weirder, I spotted another familiar car already parked there.

"What the hell are they doing here?" I mumbled under my breath.

I eased up behind them and parked, then got out and rapped on the passenger's side window.

"LC, what the hell are you doing here?" Larry asked when he rolled down his window.

"I could ask you the same."

"Hurry up and climb in the back before they see you. Every time you look up, somebody news is popping up around this place."

I hopped into the back seat. "Now, do you both mind telling me why you're sitting out in front of a warehouse that Mr. Mahogany just happens to be inside of?"

"We've been following these cats that kidnapped this white dude named Dwayne McCarty," Larry said.

"When Mahogany showed up, we almost lost our minds. Why the fuck are you here?" Lou asked. "We left you to take care of the body."

"That's been taken care of, but save that story for another time. I been following Mr. Mahogany all day. I'm pretty sure he's got something to do with Momma," I said, fuming. "And if he does, I'm gonna kill him."

"I knew that motherfucker was shady!" Lou said. "I ain't never trusted that cat from day one."

Larry looked over the seat at me. "You really think he's involved?"

I hated to even say it. I simply nodded my head.

"Well, we're gonna find out for sure." Lou turned back around, and we all kept our eyes glued on the building.

"Momma's in this building," I said after a couple minutes.

"Why you say that?" Larry asked.

"I been following this guy all day, and everywhere he went, he's gone in and come right back out." I stared at the building. "It doesn't look like he's coming out."

"Then you know what that means," Lou said, opening his door. "We're going in."

On that note, Larry popped the trunk. One by one, we got out of the car, each retrieving a gun, then headed to the warehouse to get answers.

Bettie

52

"Where is it?" Belinda slapped me so hard blood flew from my mouth. "Where the fuck is the gold?"

No sooner than I had sat back, the door flew open, and I snapped forward again. I was somewhat shocked, but at the same time, I knew it was only a matter of time before a guest appearance would be made by the person behind it all. The circus surely couldn't continue without the ringmaster.

"Humph. I was wondering when you were going to show up," I said.

Unlike me, Belinda looked somewhat surprised to see her husband standing there.

It had been almost twelve years, but he was still a handsome specimen of a man whose presence demanded respect from everyone. He was dressed to play tennis, not to go knock some old lady around.

"Honey, what are you doing here?" Belinda ran to his side, but her body language was no longer dominant. She was being submissive as hell, especially when Mahogany seemed to ignore her as he looked over at Dwayne, then at me.

"What the fuck is going on here?"

He eased into the room, his companion closing the door behind him. They all parted, giving him space as he approached me. The words that came out of his mouth stunned me.

"I'm sorry," he said with sincerity in his eyes. I'd never heard of someone apologizing to a person prior to killing them, but I supposed there was a first time for everything.

"You're sorry?" Belinda screeched.

Mr. Mahogany's face fell, like he was totally disappointed by his wife's outburst. He turned to her and asked, "What have you done?"

"I've done what you and your so-called Council couldn't do." There wasn't an ounce of submissiveness in Belinda's acid tone now as she seethed with anger at her husband. She walked up on Mahogany, leaving very little space between them. "You promised me that woman was going away forever, but you let her out. My son works his ass off, and you give Sam's seat to this bitch's son." She pointed a finger at me while she glared at her husband. "What kind of father are you?"

"Better than the one who raised you," I said with a laugh.

"You know just as well as I do that EJ wasn't ready for that seat," Mahogany shot back at his wife. "Which makes me a damn good father by not placing my son in a situation that he couldn't handle."

"He was just as ready as LC," she said. "We both know the real reason EJ isn't sitting on that Council is because he was that man's lover."

I didn't understand all the details of what they were talking about, but that woman had just aired her son's sexual preferences in front of everyone in the room. I couldn't believe the husband and wife were discussing their family business publicly like that.

"So what if he and Sam were lovers?" Mr. Mahogany answered her. "I didn't approve of it, but that has nothing to do with him being immature. Too immature to sit on the Council."

"He's only immature because you made him that way."

"I made him that way? You stood over him, watching everything he did, every move he made, like he was a baby. Look at the mess he made with the Young Bloods." Mr. Mahogany was shouting, and Belinda took a step back. "You didn't think I knew about that, did you?"

"Guess who bailed our asses out of that one?" He asked and then answered his own question. "That's right, LC."

I smiled proudly. I didn't know how I felt about LC being wrapped up with the Council yet, but I knew that anything my college boy got involved in, he was going to do it right.

"LC this and LC that!" Belinda yelled. "I'm sick of this motherfucker LC! What about your son?"

"What about him? Is he so important that you've got this woman locked up and tied to a chair?" he asked.

Belinda looked at me as if she was imagining the most violent way she could kill me. Then she turned back to her husband and asked, "How did you know anyway? How did you find us?"

I was interested in that answer myself, since he didn't seem to have a part in this.

"I knew you were involved the minute I saw Leroy's body. James was driving me around all day searching for you before I found your car parked over here." He looked at me and shook his head. "I still can't believe this. I still can't believe you went this far over EJ."

"This wasn't just about EJ. This was for you, too. We both know she has those records. We don't want them to get in the wrong hands."

"She doesn't have those records," he said.

"What?" Belinda said, her tone low and menacing. "How do you know that to be true?"

Mr. Mahogany answered matter-of-factly. "Because I have the records. That was part of the deal of letting her out of jail."

"Why didn't you tell me?"

"You were too hot-headed for me to share anything about it. That's how you are whenever it comes to your father."

Her face turned red with rage. "What does my father have to do with this?"

"Those records don't show the Council complicit in anything. They show this was all your father's doing. His business was the one that would have been affected the most by the end of Jim Crow, not ours. He talked the Council into stealing the gold so he could steal it from us. That's why he killed Duncan. He just never expected Bettie to seek revenge."

Belinda was quiet for a moment, as if she was trying to find a reason for all of her efforts to not have been in vain. "What about the gold?"

"That gold has nothing to do with this."

"The hell it doesn't!" she protested. "That's my father's gold. It's his legacy."

"That gold belongs to Bettie and her family. The Council made that decision"

"My father got killed over that gold. That gold belongs to me." Belinda was screaming at this point.

"Your father got killed because he was an ass, plain and simple."

Belinda slapped Mr. Mahogany across his face so hard that I think my head snapped.

"How dare you say that about my father? How dare you!" Belinda cried, her voice cracking. "That man loved you."

Mr. Mahogany looked at his wife in total disbelief. "This was a mistake, Belinda. The Duncans are on to you. The same way I figured this all out, they are going to. You're only but a step ahead of them—a small step, at that. You don't know the depth of what you've done, and now I have to clean this up." He turned away from his wife and walked over to me. "Again, Bettie, I'm so sorry." He walked behind me and began untying me just as gunfire rang out.

53

I went to the side of the building where I had seen Mr. Mahogany enter. Lou and Larry went on the other side. The second I turned the corner, I recognized one of Mahogany's guys standing near the door, smoking a cigarette. I gripped my piece tightly, hiding it behind my back.

"Mr. Duncan. What are you doing here?" he asked when he saw me approaching.

"Meeting with Mr. Mahogany," I answered, trying to act as natural and as calm as I could. Maybe, just maybe, I could bluff my way in.

He gave me a strange look then, after a few seconds, shook his head. "Naw, he ain't here."

"You sure?" I asked. "I seen his car in the parking lot."

"Uh, yeah." He looked nervous. He lifted his arm to reach inside his jacket, and I pulled out my pistol before he could get his weapon.

He raised his hands, and I walked over, reached in his inside pocket, and retrieved his gun. I turned him around and pressed the gun to his back.

"I'm telling you he ain't here," he said.

"Bitch, I saw him come in the side door. And if he ain't here, then why the fuck are you here?" I whispered. Lou and Larry came from the other side, giving me a thumbs up. "Now, I'm gonna ask you one more time: Is Mahogany in there?"

Dude finally gave up. "Yeah, he's here."

"What about my momma? Is she here?" He turned to look at me over his shoulder, slowly nodding his head.

I struck him upside the head with the butt of my gun, and he fell to the ground. Without hesitating, I stepped over him and hurried inside with my brothers.

As soon as we entered the building, Larry and Lou took out two dudes. There was no trying to stop it, because they were about to do to us what Larry and Lou had done to them. Larry pointed at a door, and we burst in. I'm sure there were other people in the room, but the only people I could see were Mr. Mahogany, standing next to Momma. She was sitting in a chair, untying the ropes around her ankles. My heart leaped with joy seeing her alive, but I had to take care of Mr. Mahogany before I could get her out of there.

"You motherfucker," I said, pointing my gun right at him. "You've had my mother this entire time. You son of a bitch."

Some big black dude rushed toward me, but before he could take two steps, Larry blasted him in the stomach with his shotgun.

"Nooooooo!" a young girl, who had been standing in a corner, rushed over and fell to the big man's side. Some scared-looking white guy I could only assume was Dwayne McCarty ducked and ran to the other side of the room. I kept my gun on Mr. Mahogany, preparing to murder his ass without a second thought. Tension filled the room.

"LC," Mr. Mahogany said. His voice was eerily calm as he raised his hands.

"Don't," I told him. "The only words out of your fucking mouth should be you telling your fucking wife good-bye. They're going to be your final words."

"Son, I need for you to understand that I had nothing to do with this. I didn't know anything about this, I swear."

"I'm not your fucking son," I told him, cocking the gun. "Now, this is your last chance to say good-bye to your wife."

"LC, if you don't shoot that motherfucker, I will," Larry said.

"No! Ain't none of y'all gonna shoot him. Do you hear me?" Momma said.

Those were the first words I had heard my mother speak since she disappeared. It was beautiful to hear her voice, but she confused the hell out of me.

"LC, put the gun down."

"But, Ma—"

"I said put it down!" She was as stern as I remembered.

"Yes, ma'am." I felt like a little boy, but I followed her orders and lowered the gun.

"I know y'all think he had something to do with this, but he didn't. Believe it or not, he was untying me before y'all busted in," she explained.

"But if he didn't do it, who did?"

My mother pointed at Belinda. "This bitch over here."

All eyes turned to Belinda, who was looking disheveled and angry. She held a gun by her side as her eyes darted around the room like she couldn't decide who to aim it at.

"So, you mean to tell me she orchestrated all this behind Mr. Mahogany's back?" Larry asked, sounding dumbfounded.

"Yes," Momma and Mr. Mahogany said in unison. You could see the embarrassment all over his face.

"Well, I'll be damned. You can't trust nobody these days," Lou added.

"Mr. Mahogany!" James came rushing into the room with guns in each hand. He froze when he saw what was going on. It was a miracle he didn't get shot or shoot one of us.

"Put the gun down, James," Mahogany ordered.

"I . . . I need to talk to you, Mr. Mahogany. It's important," James said.

"Now's not the time, James. In case you can't tell, we're a little busy figuring things out," he replied to his man. In spite of everything, I was pretty damn impressed with how calm Mr. Mahogany remained.

"I'm sorry, but I think you need to hear this right now." Ignoring all the guns, James walked over to his boss. He lowered his head and sighed. "I don't know how to tell you this, boss, but . . ." He hesitated before finally saying, "EJ is dead."

Belinda screamed.

"What! How?" Mr. Mahogany looked heartbroken.

I locked eyes with my mother, who shook her head at me.

"They found his body on the beach, not far from the house, sir."

"See what you've done, Belinda? You caused this." Tears filled Mr. Mahogany's eyes.

"You're right," she said. Then, she took a step back, and before anyone could react, she raised her gun and pulled the trigger.

Mr. Mahogany's eyes widened as he fell backward. The bullet had struck him in the head. James reached out in an effort to catch him before he hit the floor. At that moment, everything seemed to move at breakneck speed.

"Belinda!" Momma gasped.

"He was right. It was all my fault," Belinda said, sobbing. She pulled the trigger again; this time, the bullet entered her own head.

Chippy

54

It was late in the afternoon when we finally arrived in Atlanta. Between pregnant Shirley constantly having to pee and Levi's dogs, we had to stop quite a few times. And then there was Donna and her constant sighing and eye-rolling at the two of them in the back seat. I wasn't too thrilled to be on the road trip either, and her attitude was just making it worse.

"Where are we going now?" she asked when I turned into the neighborhood where we lived. "I thought we were going to find LC."

"Why you so worried about LC?" Shirley asked. "He ain't none of your concern."

"Well, that's not what I was told when y'all gave me this." Donna held up the pistol she had been holding for the entire trip.

"I have to check on my children and see if Nee Nee's heard from anyone," I told her.

"And I have to pee anyway," Shirley added.

"M—m—my p—p—puppies are th—thirsty," Levi said.

Donna exhaled loudly and shook her head. "None of that surprises me."

"Keep talking shit and you're gonna get knocked upside the head with that gun you're holding," Shirley threatened.

I ignored the posted speed limit and hauled ass, pulling into Nee Nee's driveway so fast that I hit the curb, causing everyone in the car to bounce. Before anyone could complain about anything else, I was out of the car and headed up the walkway.

"About time you got back. I was worried," Nee Nee said when she opened the door. "Did you find—"

She stopped mid-sentence and looked past me at the passengers getting out of my car. I brushed past her and went inside, leaving her confused as hell.

"Where are the kids?" I asked, then called out for my son. "Junior?"

"Chippy, what the hell?"

"Mommyyyyyyyyyy!" Junior came running and leaped into my arms. I hugged him tight and kissed him on the top of his head. I was so glad to see him.

"Hey, baby," I said.

"I'm not a baby. Vegas is!"

"You're always gonna be my baby," I said with a laugh. "But where is your baby brother?"

"He's in the kitchen," Curtis announced.

"The kitchen?"

"He's in the swing," Nee Nee explained. "I was shelling peas for dinner, and the boys were helping. Well, they were really making a mess."

I walked into the kitchen with Junior and Curtis on my heels, and sure enough, there was Vegas, looking content in his swing. I picked him up and cradled him in my arms as I returned to the living room. Nee Nee was still looking confused as Donna, Shirley, and Levi came in the house.

"Can I use your restroom?" Donna asked.

"You need to wait. I know your ass heard me say I had to pee when we first got here. Move," Shirley said as she brushed past her.

"J–J–Junior! C-C-Curtis! I have a p-p-puppy f-for you," Levi announced, holding out one of the small dogs.

The two boys squealed and ran over to their uncle, who began crawling on the floor, playing with the dog. As big as he was, Levi still looked like a kid.

"Thanks, Uncle Levi!" both boys exclaimed.

Shirley came walking in from the hallway and announced, "I need a drink. Where the hell is the liquor?"

"Is it okay if I go to the restroom now?" Donna asked sarcastically.

"Who are you?" Junior asked her. It was a moment I had hoped would never come, but here he was, standing face-to-face with the woman who had birthed him.

She glanced over at me, and I gave her a nod.

Donna knelt down in front of Junior and smiled kindly at him. Her voice was soft as she said, "I'm Aunt Donna."

"Aunt Donna?"

"Yes, Aunt Donna." Her eyes sparkled with tears, but thankfully the boys didn't notice.

Not to be outdone by his cousin, Curtis ran over and said, "Are you my Aunt Donna too?"

Donna shrugged at him and said, "Sure, I'm your Aunt Donna too."

"Nee Nee, I know you got something strong in here to drink. Now, tell me where it is," Shirley snapped impatiently.

"Restroom, please, Nee Nee." Donna ignored Shirley and asked as she stood up.

"Down the hallway and to the right, Donna. Top cabinet over the refrigerator, Shirley," Nee Nee replied. When both Donna and Shirley were out of earshot, she asked, "Will someone please tell me what the hell is going on?"

"I will, but first, have you heard from Larry or Lou?" I asked. Now that I'd seen my boys and knew they were safe, it was time to pull everyone together and find Miss Bettie.

"They called a few hours ago from a gas station. He said they were on their way to Atlanta," Nee Nee said. "Wait, you haven't talked to LC since you've been gone?"

"Not since late last night. I've been calling, but I haven't talked to him." I sighed. I had to find my husband. There was no telling what Mr. Mahogany was capable of, or LC, for that matter, when it came to his mother.

"Nee Nee, you ain't gonna believe this." Shirley came out of the kitchen holding a glass of what looked like bourbon. "Miss Bettie is alive. I saw her with my own two eyes."

"What! Where?" Nee Nee's eyes bugged out.

"At Shirley's boyfriend's house at the beach," I said, cutting my eyes at Shirley. I was still pissed about her recent antics, and I didn't want her to think that it was all water under the bridge. She still had a lot of explaining to do.

"Levi, come on and take that puppy outside before it pees on Nee Nee's nice carpet," Shirley quickly said. "Come on, boys. Let's go outside and—"

The front door opened, and Larry walked in. Lou was right behind him.

"Daddyyyyyyyyy!" Curtis ran over and jumped into his father's arms.

"Hey, boy." Larry lifted him off the floor. Although his face was fatigued, he still lit up when he saw his son.

"About time y'all got home," Nee Nee said. He walked over and gave her a long kiss.

"I see y'all found him." Lou pointed to Levi; then, when he noticed Shirley, he added, "I told you to find Levi. Y'all could've left her cheating ass wherever the fuck she was. And where's Donna?"

"I'm right here." Donna entered the living room. If I didn't know any better, I'd swear she and Lou seemed happy to see one another.

"Lou, have y'all heard from LC? I've been calling everywhere, but I can't reach him. I'm worried, because Shirley said Belinda—"

"I'm right here, sweetie." LC's voice came from behind me, and my heart skipped a beat. I turned around and ran to my husband. He looked as if he had been through hell, but he was still the most handsome man I had ever laid eyes on.

"Dammit, LC. I was so scared. Where the hell were you? I thought the Mahoganys had done something to you. They're the ones who have your mother."

"Those motherfuckers ain't got me. I'm right here."

We all turned and stared at the front door, where Miss Bettie was now standing. I couldn't believe it. She was alive, and now she was home.

"M–M–Momma!" Levi ran over and picked Miss Bettie up, swinging her around the same way Larry had done to Curtis. Then, in true Levi fashion, he began covering her face in kisses. "Y-you're h-home again!"

"Boy, if you don't put me down . . . I keep telling you when you do that I have to pee!"

Levi put her down, and she spoke to all of us. "Yes, I'm home again with my family, and this time, I ain't going nowhere."